"WHAT'S WRONG, MOM?" Troy asked.

"Well . . ." She took a sip of coffee. "I just wish the Jets were winning as much as Summit."

Troy frowned at her for raining on his parade. "They've won a couple of games . . . and I'm *trying*, Mom. I am. I said I was, and I *am*."

"Oh, I'm proud of you, Troy." Her smile lost its baggage for a moment. "All those touchdowns. Don't think I'm not. But I worry about the Jets. Mr. Cole had such big plans for the team, and all that money."

Troy nodded because he guessed he understood. It wasn't going to dampen his enthusiasm, though.

"Do you know if we win our next three games it'll be a perfect season?" Troy's voice bubbled. "That's never been done before in Summit High School football history. After that, it'll be on to the playoffs. Think about it, Mom. Seth said Mr. Biondi told him that if we do that, he *knows* we'll get the support for a new stadium. When that happens—with the record we'll have—St. Stephen's isn't going to be the place to be anymore . . . Summit is!"

HARPER

An Imprint of HarperCollinsPublishers

FECT
SON

A **FOOTBALL GENIUS** NOVEL

New York Times Bestselling Author

TIM GREEN

*For the coaches and players of the Skaneateles
2011 football team and their 9–0 perfect season!*

Library of Congress Cataloging-in-Publication Data

Green, Tim, date

    Perfect season : a Football genius novel / Tim Green. —
First edition.

            pages   cm

    Summary: "A friendship is tested and a new one formed
as Troy White, the football genius, gets to play varsity football for the first time, on a team that has to end its losing
streak"— Provided by publisher.

    ISBN 978-0-06-220870-5 (pbk.)

    [1. Football—Fiction. 2. Friendship—Fiction.] I. Title.

PZ7.G826357Pe   2013   2013032159

[Fic]—dc23   CIP

                                                    AC

Typography by Joel Tippie

14 15 16 17 18   OPM   10 9 8 7 6 5 4 3 2 1

❖

First paperback edition, 2014

ALSO BY TIM GREEN

CHAPTER ONE

TROY'S MIND SPUN THE entire car ride to the school. He dug deep for an idea—any idea—that would give them a way out. The junior high and the high school stood side by side, two brick buildings that might have been prison cell blocks. Rusty chain-link fences surrounded them. The only things missing were barbed wire and some guard towers.

"That's disgusting."

"Troy." His mom had her hands planted on the wheel of the VW Bug. "Don't judge a book by its cover."

"Why do we have to *do* this?" The question exploded from his chest.

She scowled at him. "Do I have to go through it again?"

1

"I just don't see how we can *owe* money when we don't *have* any money." Troy banged his head softly against the window.

"The IRS doesn't care that your . . . *father*"—she could barely say the word because, to her, the man was a snake—"put five million dollars into a criminal enterprise. They don't care that the FBI seized every penny, and they don't care about you going to a private school to play football. They care about *us* paying taxes on the money we had. They're the I-R-S. They don't have feelings."

They pulled around to the side of the school where the football field sat wedged between the parking lot and another chain-link fence holding back nothing but an empty lot grown over with crabgrass and old tires. Slung between two bleached telephone poles, the scoreboard read "VIS T RS" on one side and "OME" on the other.

"See?" His mom pointed to the worn Astroturf covering the field. "It can't be all bad? Artificial turf is good for a passing offense."

"That looks like a plastic rug from a crummy putt-putt golf place." Troy frowned at the faded green field.

"Hey, you get to play football," his mom said.

"Four wins in seven years?" Troy shook his head. "The *other* teams are playing football. These guys are playing hopscotch or something."

His mom parked the car and got out. "Look."

Troy spotted two men wearing construction vests and hard hats and a third—the tallest, skinniest man Troy could imagine—in a dark business suit in the far corner of the field. The man—who was tall enough to be an NBA player, maybe six foot nine—stood with his arms folded across his chest as he watched. One of the workers held a ten-foot stick in the corner of the end zone. The other—along with the tall man in the suit—walked across the field to a surveyor's tripod mounted with a little yellow telescope.

"What are they doing?" Troy asked.

"Getting ready for an upgrade? Hey, maybe new bleachers. Maybe a whole new field. Look at the bright side, Troy. It's easy to be grumpy."

In the guidance counselor's office, Mr. Bryant could hardly say hello before he started asking football questions. "Can you really predict NFL plays? I mean, I know you signed a contract with the Jets and all. I just . . . I see you're a very good math student. Is that part of how you do it? You know, I'm sorry. Really. You're not here to talk about football."

"I'd rather talk about football than math," Troy said.

His mom rolled her eyes. "Troy's a little disappointed at Summit's football program, but he knows the purpose of school is education, not sports, Mr. Bryant."

Mr. Bryant blinked at her. "Well, honestly, I agree in part, but I'd still like to see our football program improve."

"I know the high school team really su—" Troy glanced at his mom's frown. ". . . is bad. But what about the junior high team?"

Mr. Bryant's face grew even longer. "Closest game last year was fifty-four to six against Union. Our starters scored against their fourth string. I hate to say it, but the program is like a fish on the beach, rotten from head to tail. You can smell it a mile away. People are starting to talk about dropping it because the stadium is falling apart and the school is going to have to spend some serious money to fix it."

"We saw someone out there with survey equipment." Troy's mom nodded her head in the direction of the field.

Mr. Bryant gave her a puzzled look and scratched his neck. "I don't know about that. Nothing's been approved, I can tell you that."

"How can this guy who coaches even keep his job?" Troy asked.

Mr. Bryant's eyes darted at the office door and he lowered his voice. "It's just his job. Every summer— they just did it two days ago—they post the position, and every year no one else applies, so it goes to Mr. Biondi. He's the athletic director, so he feels like he *has* to do it. He doesn't want it. He doesn't even call himself 'Coach.' Honestly, the program is in bad shape. We barely have enough kids to field a team."

Mr. Bryant lowered his voice even more. "There's

some talk—you know, with budget crunches—about just dropping the program. The district business manager has been pushing for it, especially because of the cost for a new stadium, and people just don't seem to be interested."

"No football?" Panic jolted Troy.

CHAPTER TWO

MR. BRYANT HELD UP a hand. "Well, it's in the budget this year, but . . ."

"There's no such thing as a school without football." Troy knew it couldn't be possible.

"Not in Georgia," Mr. Bryant said, "but this is New Jersey. It actually happens."

"There's no one in the entire district who can coach football and get things turned around?" Troy's mom asked.

Mr. Bryant put his fingers together and made a tee-pee in front of his chin. "Honestly, when I knew you were coming in, I couldn't help thinking that maybe, just maybe, with your connections you might know someone who'd come here and coach the team. I mean, players are constantly retiring from the NFL. Sometimes they coach." Mr. Bryant laughed. "A pipe dream, I know, but can you imagine if we got someone like that to turn things around?"

Troy looked at his mom to see if she thought the counselor was for real.

Mr. Bryant leaned forward. "Right, why do I care?"

He pointed to a photo of a kid in a football uniform. "I think my son, Chance, might have some ability. He plays left tackle. I know you might not think it looking at me, but he's a huge kid—takes after his mom's side—and I'd like to see him in a better program than what we've got at Summit. But . . . this is where we live. There is a football powerhouse not too far from here—St. Stephen's? But . . . well, you can't imagine what it costs."

The mention of St. Stephen's left Troy's stomach flopping in his gut like a fresh-caught catfish. *He* was supposed to go to St. Stephen's! That was before his father ruined everything. Now he was stuck in a run-down rental house at the end of a run-down street ready to attend a run-down public school with a rotten football team—or maybe no football team.

Troy glanced at his mom. She tightened her lips.

"Mom," Troy said, "we know someone who could coach the team and do an awesome job, right?"

"Seriously?" Mr. Bryant's eyes widened.

CHAPTER THREE

"WHAT?" TROY'S MOM WRINKLED her face in confusion.

"Mr. Bryant, do you know who Seth Halloway is?"

"From the Falcons? The linebacker? I'm a Giants fan, but of course I know who Seth Halloway is." Mr. Bryant grinned and nodded.

"Oh, no." Troy's mom held up her hands.

"Mom, he *wants* to coach. Look what he did with our junior league team." Troy turned to Mr. Bryant. "We won a state championship with Seth."

"He wants to coach in the NFL, or college," Troy's mom said. She turned to Mr. Bryant. "No offense."

"Right, but it's not happening for him," Troy said. "I know. He's been on about twenty interviews and the only thing he got is Furman saying he can 'help out.' They won't even pay him. Those jobs are, like, impossible to get. But if he got some experience?"

"In high school?" Troy's mom asked.

"Why not? It happens, doesn't it?" Troy said.

His mom turned to the counselor. "It's too compli-cated, Mr. Bryant. I'm sorry. Let's talk about classes. Taking Spanish is a good idea."

"Mom, can we at least—"

His mom held up her hand. "Spanish."

Troy knew anything after the hand would be a waste of breath.

They made Troy's schedule. Mr. Bryant printed it out and handed it to him with a shrug. "It was just a thought."

They left and Troy's mom offered to stop at Dairy Queen for ice cream sandwiches. Troy thought about saying no so that she would understand just how upset he was about everything, but he couldn't hold out. The summer sun baked the blacktop outside the restaurant, but when they entered a blast of cool air greeted them. They got two DQ sandwiches and sat in a booth by the window, eating them, when a black Escalade pulled into the lot.

"Oh, boy." Troy could see that his mom saw who was in the vehicle, too. "What do we do now?"

CHAPTER FOUR

"IT'S TY AND THANE," Troy said as he watched his cousins get out of the Escalade. "I thought we were going to see them later."

"What do you mean, 'What do we do now?'? We ask them to sit with us. Don't be silly," Troy's mom said.

"They know we moved in, but they don't know *where*, Mom," Troy said. "And they don't know I'm going to Summit."

"Ty will be fine," Troy's mom said. "He's a sweet boy."

Troy was flooded with dread as his cousins entered the diner.

First came Ty, thirteen and a football player, like Troy. Troy never knew Ty existed until they met at the Super Bowl in Miami, and he learned that Ty's mom was his dad's older sister. Troy really liked Ty. Even though his cousin was on the quiet side, he gave Troy a good feeling. Tate McGreer, Troy's best friend back in Atlanta—who was a girl—also said she got a good feeling from Ty, and that meant something since Tate was really good at reading people.

Troy actually suspected that Ty had a thing for Tate. Troy could only suspect because Ty never talked about Tate; he could barely talk *to* her when they'd been together. Troy knew from Tate, though, that Ty texted her pretty regularly.

People were recognizing Thane, Ty's brother. He was an all-pro wide receiver for the Jets. Most people called him Tiger. He was six foot two and 230 pounds, ran like the wind, and had hands sticky as a frog's tongue.

"Hey, it's Tiger Lewis!" one man shouted from the counter before his wife shushed him with a rolled-up newspaper.

A dad and a little kid on their way out asked Thane to sign the kid's Jets hat. Thane borrowed the wide-eyed waitress's pen and signed the bill of the cap with a smile.

Troy felt his mind whirling. He had no idea how to break the news about having to attend Summit after he and Ty had made elaborate plans with texts and on Facebook to become St. Stephen's next dynamic duo on the football field. Troy was going to be QB with Ty as his top receiver. Even as they moved their things into the house on Cedar Street, Troy kept thinking things would somehow work out.

"Ty is gonna kill me," Troy said.

But before he could come up with a plan, Thane and Ty started coming over to their booth.

"Hey, you're here!" Thane removed his sunglasses and smiled. "We're looking forward to getting together tomorrow night. But, hey, welcome to New Jersey. Not as hot as Atlanta, right?"

"Pretty close," Troy's mom said.

Troy and his mom stood up and they all exchanged hugs before Troy and Ty bumped fists.

"Join us," Troy's mom said.

"I'll order," Thane said. "Ty, you want a milk shake?"

Ty nodded to his brother and turned to Troy. "You guys all unpacked?"

"Pretty much. I just got my school schedule."

Ty frowned. "Schedule? Registration isn't until next Friday. How'd you get your schedule?"

Troy glanced at his mom. She licked some ice cream from her fingers and pretended to look out at the cars passing on the street.

"Uh, at Summit."

Ty's face wrinkled. "What are you talking about?"

"Well . . . man, this stinks, but I can't go to St. Stephen's."

Ty's mouth hung open before he scoffed. "Stop goofing."

"I wish I was." Troy sighed. "It stinks. We just can't swing it."

Ty laughed and looked from Troy to his mom. "You're kidding."

They should have been kidding. Troy had signed a fifteen-million-dollar contract with the Jets. Five million dollars had been paid to Troy when he signed it. The plan had been for them to rent a huge home on the better side of town near Thane and Ty. That was before Troy's father lost every cent of the money in a crooked deal, then vanished.

It was Troy's mom's turn to dive in. "If everything goes well, though, Troy can play with you next year. You'll both be in high school then, anyway. It's just temporary, until we get things straightened out financially."

Ty's face lit up. "Ms. White, you don't have to worry about that. My brother, he can—"

The dark look on Troy's mom's face silenced him.

"I mean . . . isn't there any way at all?"

Troy's mom shook her head.

Thane appeared with two milk shakes and sat down next to her. "Any way for what?"

"Troy's going to have to go to Summit for a year until we get some financial things worked out." Troy's mom fired her words like a machine gun. "St. Stephen's will have to wait."

13

Thane tilted his head with a puzzled expression. "But I can—"

Troy's mom held up a hand. "Don't. Please. I know if we *really* needed it that you'd be there for us, but that's not how we operate. It's not a bad lesson for Troy to learn. Things don't always work out the way you plan them, right?"

Thane got a sad, faraway look in his eyes. "That's right. They don't."

Troy bet to himself that Thane was thinking of the parents he and Ty had lost in a car crash two years ago, and he wished his mom had used different words. They all sat in an awkward silence. Ty sucked down some of his shake before he brightened again.

"Hey," he said, "I got an idea! I know how we can fix this."

Troy stared at him, wanting to believe there was a way. "How?"

CHAPTER FIVE

TY GRINNED. "WE'RE IN the Summit district. I can go there with you. We can play together this year, and then, when things get straightened out, we both go to St. Stephen's *next* year."

Troy felt a surge of excitement. It was something he hadn't considered. He'd seen the buildings and campus at St. Stephen's on their website, redbrick buildings with white columns, noble old trees offering shade to wrought-iron benches on rolling grass lawns. The school had a football stadium to rival those in most small colleges. He never imagined Ty would trade all that for the broken-down Summit football program.

"Really?"

Ty looked at his older brother. Thane pulled his lips back from his clenched teeth and tilted his head.

He cleared his throat.

"What?" Ty asked him.

Thane gave Troy's mom an embarrassed look. "I . . . uh, we sure can talk about it."

"Okay," Ty said, "let's talk."

Thane flashed his little brother an annoyed look. "Later."

"I think your brother is right, Ty." Troy's mom finished her DQ sandwich and wiped her fingers on a napkin. "You can't just change where you're going to school to play football."

Thane's face flushed. "Seriously, I'd really be happy to work something out with you, Tessa, so Troy could go to St. Stephen's, too. I know these guys have big plans."

Up went the hand again. "It's nice, trust me, I appreciate the thought, but no. I can't. Absolutely not. So are you two still ready to have dinner with us tomorrow night? I make a mean plate of spaghetti and meatballs. Right, Troy?"

"She does." Troy tried to sound enthusiastic.

"Our mom used to be this great cook," Thane said, "and she'd get mad at me because spaghetti and meatballs was all I ever wanted to eat."

"I love it, too," Ty said. "Hey, can Troy go with us to the Jets tomorrow? He and I can throw the ball on the practice field."

They finished their ice cream and milk shakes, making plans for Ty and Troy to get together the next day, and said good-bye. On the car ride home, Troy couldn't help himself.

"Mom, he *wants* to help us. I'm going to make a ton of money in the next three years."

She sighed. "And when you do, and we have money to spend, we'll change schools. Troy, it's not easy being a single mom. I'm not complaining, but part of how I've done it is sticking to certain principles, and this is one of them. Now, if you want to spend time with Ty and Thane this summer, you've got to promise me this will be the end of begging to go to St. Stephen's. It's not going to happen. I worry about you. I know a lot of exciting things have happened, but you're still young.

"You have to stop trying to manipulate everyone and everything around you. Some things are just meant to be, and you playing for Summit this year is just one of them. Do you get it? Are we done now?" She ended with a low growl.

"Yes. We're done."

That's what Troy said, but in his mind, he already had a plan of how he just might fix things *without* changing schools.

When they got home, he did some chores that his mom asked him to do, then took his iPhone and set off on a walk down the street. When he got away from the house, he dialed and waited for an answer.

"Hello?" said a man's voice.

"Hey. It's me, Troy."

"Hey, what's up?"

"Well, you know how you said if I ever really needed you, all I have to do is call?"

"Yeah."

"Well, I need you."

CHAPTER SIX

TROY'S EXPERIENCE TOLD HIM that adults could be relied upon only up to a certain point. After that, they were as unpredictable as a fumble. You never knew which way they were going to bounce. He tried to push the phone call out of his mind and focus on his trip to the Jets facility. It was no small thing, being hired as a twelve—now thirteen—year-old kid by an NFL team. The Jets' owner hadn't done it without thoroughly testing Troy, and, at the time, Troy had been pretty puffed up about his talent and the way he was using it to help his favorite team in the entire world—the Atlanta Falcons—become world champions. So when he had to prove his worth, he'd done it with great pride. Predicting play after play while watching an old Jets game on tape, he'd passed the owner's test with flying colors.

Some people in the media said Troy was simply at the right place at the right time. They openly doubted his "football genius," and claimed that the Falcons would have won the big game with or without him. The only opinion that mattered on that front, though, was the Jets' owner's, and he'd signed a contract with Troy and his parents making Troy a "consultant" for the team in the upcoming season.

Thanks to his mom's insistence, he had to work during the season only on game days. That meant traveling with the team when they were away. During the week—and throughout the team's four-week training camp—Troy would go to school, attend football practice, and do chores around the house just like any other kid.

The next morning, Troy's mom was already up and dressed in a business suit with breakfast on the table. She was excited because she had been called back for a final job interview. Troy sat down, bleary-eyed and scratching his head.

"Troy," she said as she cleaned the frying pan, "I called Mr. Cole, just as a courtesy, to let him know you'll be at the facility later on with Thane and Ty, and he said he'd appreciate it if you stopped by his office for a couple of minutes so he could have a chance to talk with you."

"Talk about what?" Troy couldn't explain exactly why, but the owner made him a bit uncomfortable.

"Whatever he wants. You're a big investment."

His mom gave him a list of things she wanted him to do around the house before he went with Thane and Ty. "Lunch is in the fridge. If you finish everything, you can read until Thane comes to get you, but no Xbox. Now I've got to go try to nail down that job. Wish me luck."

"Luck," Troy said.

He watched her go and listened to the VW Bug crawl down the gravel driveway and whine up the street. He sighed and cleaned his plate before attacking the list of jobs. He finished with time enough to read, and that's what he did, out under the tree in back while he ate his ham and cheese in a folding lounge chair. He liked their backyard, and the way that beyond the fence a dense wood whispered to him. It reminded him of home in Atlanta, only the wood behind his house there was a pine wood. This one was oak, maple, and ash, and he knew that when winter came, there would be no cover, only a web of branches between them, some power lines, and the back of a shopping mall.

Troy got lost in *Seconds Away*, thinking the main

character, Mickey Bolitar, was pretty cool. When someone kicked his foot, Troy jumped. The book tumbled to the grass.

"What!" He looked up into a face so familiar, and yet so different it sent a shiver right through him.

CHAPTER SEVEN

TROY'S FATHER SMILED AND showed a new gold tooth. His spiked hair was reddish-orange instead of brown, and he had a beard. With a gold loop hung from one ear he looked like a cheesy pirate. "How's my boy?"

"Dad? What are you doing here?"

"Where else should I be?" His father scooped up the football from the grass and tossed it into the air before catching it.

Troy shrugged, his mind going from point to point on the globe. "Cuba. New Zealand. India? I don't know. Don't they want to kill you?"

"They want to kill Drew Edinger, not Sam Christian. That's me now. Funny you mention New Zealand." His father caught the football again and chuckled. "That's where my passport is from. How are you?"

Everything that had happened and everything that was happening boiled up inside Troy in an instant. He held his breath and felt his face turn color, then let it out with a hiss that ended in a bark of disbelieving laughter.

"How am I?" Troy sang the words with "I" ending on a low note and shook his head.

His father stared. "People say a boy starts to get sassy when his father's away."

Troy stared right back. "You mean for the first twelve years, or just these past months when the FBI and the Mafia have been after you?"

"Remember scuba diving in the Georgia Aquarium? How many kids get to do that? The whale shark? That manta ray? Riding around in a Porsche Carrera? You weren't complaining then."

Troy's mouth hung open.

"See?" His father stood a bit taller.

"No, I don't see," Troy said. "I can't even go to St. Stephen's, and the public school I have to go to has a dog poop football team. That's *if* they have football at all."

"Problems are just obstacles." His father smiled. "You can go over them, under them, around them, or through them."

Troy didn't return the smile and his father's face got more serious. "Look, Troy, I know I've had my issues, but I know how to stay out in front of things. Trouble is something I'm good with, so . . . what do you think? Can I help?"

"Sure. Got a spare five million dollars?" Troy watched his father wince as the arrow hit home, but it didn't make him feel any better. In fact he felt worse, and his voice grew tired. "Why are you here?"

"I know things have gotten tangled up, but I care, Troy. I care about you."

Despite everything, Troy felt his heart swell with hope and . . . he guessed it was *love*, and that made him mad. "And you have a plan, don't you?"

His father laughed. "What are you talking about?"

The words gushed out of Troy's mouth. "If you know what's going on with me and the Jets, you can bet on the games, win some money."

His father huffed. He dipped his face down and touched his own chest. "Me? I . . . How did you know?"

"It's like football." Troy didn't try to keep the disgust out of his voice. "Sometimes the pieces just come together and I know exactly what's going on. At least you didn't try to deny it."

"Well." His father found his smile again. "I can't see how a little inside information would hurt anyone."

Troy suddenly wanted his father to leave. "Do you know what Mom would do if she knew you were here?"

"Call the police?" His father put the football under one arm and held out the other hand for Troy to shake. "Got it. I'm going anyway. No need to worry about me.

Good luck, son. You don't have to love me back, but I love *you*."

Part of Troy wanted to shake his father's hand, but he couldn't. Not after what the man had done and what he wanted to do now. When his father took his hand back, Troy wanted to cry out, but his father had already turned and was halfway across the lawn before Troy's thoughts were anything but a jumble.

When the man reached the corner of the house, he turned to look at Troy and flashed his grin.

"Catch!" He fired the football at Troy.

Troy's hands snatched the whistling ball from the air. He caught it, but it stung.

"You know what?" His father's voice carried across the lawn as confident as ever. "One day you're going to need me, Troy. And one day I'm going to be there for you when no one else will."

The words stunned Troy. They were so similar to what Seth Halloway had once said to him. Troy gripped the ball, bit into his lower lip, and blinked.

In that same instant, his father was gone.

CHAPTER EIGHT

WHEN THANE AND TY pulled up in the big black Escalade, Troy was over the little scene with his father, having stuffed it into the same back closet where he kept the fleeting memory of the Georgia Aquarium. What made him more uncomfortable now was the shabby house he and his mom were living in. So he jumped into the SUV and slammed the door shut behind him.

"Okay, let's get out of here." Troy clapped his hands. "I'm ready."

"Sure." Thane put the truck into gear and Troy's stomach crawled until they reached the better part of the neighborhood where the homes were more in line with where Ty and Thane lived.

"We'll be moving into one of these as soon as we get all this junk worked out." Troy pointed at a large brick mansion on the corner.

Ty and Thane looked at each other and shrugged. Troy huffed to himself. They might not care, but he did. At least when they came to dinner that night, the sun wouldn't be shining on the peeling paint.

Once they were away from Cedar Street, Troy found he was glad for Ty and Thane's company. It was exciting to have a cousin who was an NFL star, and someone like Ty who shared so many of the same dreams. Soon they were talking about pro football and how long it would be before the NFL took over the world.

When the conversation turned to how Thane would be leaving in a couple of weeks for training camp and Ty would be staying with their housekeeper, Troy got an idea.

"If your brother lets you play in Summit, maybe you could stay with us. We could get in lots of practice throwing together."

Troy looked for a positive reaction from Thane. His older cousin said nothing, but Troy took that as a good sign.

When they got to the facility, Thane took Ty to the field before he went inside to work out with the team.

"Meet you out back." Troy tossed his football to Ty, then went in to find the owner.

The Jets had a new facility that looked like something from the future, all white and glass and chrome with a big, barnlike structure in the middle of everything that housed the indoor field. On the second floor, he found Mr. Cole in a huge office overlooking the four grass practice fields out back. The Jets' owner sat behind his desk talking on the phone. Troy glanced out to see Ty in his Jets T-shirt, then back to Mr. Cole, who was all business. He wore a crisp dark suit and a blue shirt with a deep blue tie. There were flecks of gray in his dark hair Troy hadn't noticed before, and his black eyes soaked in Troy. He held up a finger and then pointed to a leather couch.

Troy sat down and tried not to listen in on the phone conversation. Outside he saw a boy in a purple jersey approach Ty. Judging by his size, he looked a year or two older. As Ty and the other kid began to throw a football back and forth, Troy wished he were down there with them.

"Troy White." The owner's voice startled him. Mr. Cole came around his desk and shook Troy's hand before he sat down in a leather chair opposite the couch. He crossed his legs and let one foot dangle in the open space between them. "Nice to see you."

"It's good to be here." Troy tried to sound confident.

There was something so powerful about the NFL owner, something almost magical, that Troy found it difficult to speak. Also he couldn't free his mind from the idea that all he had to do was ask and if the owner wanted to, he could make all Troy's problems disappear. The owner could advance Troy money on the second year of the contract and—snap—just like that, he'd be at St. Stephen's. The temptation was extraordinary, but something about the intensity of the owner's eyes, and his mother's voice in the back of his head, kept him from asking.

"You all settled in?" the owner asked.

"Yes." Troy tried not to frown at the image he had of the shabby house.

"Good, and set with a school?"

Troy sucked in his breath. There it was, the opening he needed. It was right there, and Troy knew that when opportunity knocked, it usually happened only once.

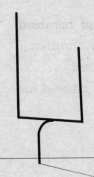

CHAPTER NINE

"**HONESTLY, MR. COLE? I'M** not set." He studied the owner's face to gauge his reaction. The owner gave away nothing, but inclined his head for Troy to go on.

An antique clock ticked beneath a glass dome on the desk.

Troy took a breath and went for it. "You heard about all that stuff with my father and the FBI, right?"

"I read about it."

"So, all the money you paid me is . . . well, it's not *gone*, but the FBI seized it, and it could be years before I can *get* it. But it's still mine—that's what the lawyers say—so the IRS wants the taxes." Troy spoke carefully, wanting to get it right.

"That's the way it works, yes." The owner narrowed his eyes. "So, you're in a pinch . . . financially."

"And I was hoping to go to St. Stephen's to play football," Troy said. "It's a private school and it's pretty steep. They're a powerhouse."

"And that can't happen now." The owner frowned. "But if I advance you even more than the five million I already gave you, your problems will be solved . . ."

Troy stuck his hands under his legs and crossed his fingers.

He gave a nod.

CHAPTER TEN

THE OWNER SMILED, BUT then the smile melted like a snowflake on a stove. "I'm sorry. I don't expect you to understand, but this is business, Troy. I like you. I like your mom. That's not what this is about. I've paid you a lot of money and I need to see a return on that before I start giving out more money."

The owner stared until Troy shifted in his seat and uncrossed his fingers.

"Sometimes a dark place brings us to a light brighter than we ever imagined." Mr. Cole shifted his gaze outside the window. The emerald grass down on the fields seemed to glow.

And then it was over. The opportunity, Troy knew, had passed him by.

Mr. Cole perked up suddenly, as if coming out of a

trance. "Great. Well, you make yourself at home here. You can come and go whenever you want. The team will be gone in a couple of weeks—we go to upstate New York for training camp, Cortland College—but I'll still be around here with the rest of the front office. Nice fields, right?"

"Beautiful." Troy wondered if he had only imagined asking the owner for help, or if he hadn't been clear.

"Good, well . . ." The owner stood up and Troy knew the meeting was over, just like that. "Here, I thought you might like these."

He handed Troy an envelope.

"Backstage passes and front-row seats." The owner grinned at him and nodded at the picture on the wall behind his desk. "Helena. She's playing at Yankee Stadium in two weeks."

Troy's mouth dropped. Helena was the owner's wife and an international superstar. Her concert was being billed as the hottest ticket since Katy Perry had done her worldwide tour.

Troy didn't know what to say, and real appreciation overwhelmed him. "Wow, are you sure?"

"Just promise you won't sell them. I hate when people do that." The owner kept smiling, but something dark passed across his face. "They're for you to enjoy."

"No, of course I won't. Thank you again."

"Well, I've got connections on the inside. There are four, so you can bring a couple of friends." The owner winked, shook hands, and showed Troy to the door.

Troy walked down the stairs and outside into the bright sunlight. The door swung open behind him and he turned to see a large black man with graying hair. The man had the build of an NFL linebacker and he wore Jets shorts and a T-shirt. On either side of him were two other men Troy was pretty sure were scouts for the team. They looked at him curiously. Then their eyes brightened with recognition and they smiled and said hello before continuing out onto the field.

Troy headed across the grass to the far field where he saw Ty and the boy in the purple jersey throwing the football back and forth. Troy glanced over his shoulder and saw the two scouts pull out their stopwatches while the big guy got down in a stance in front of some cones. Troy kept going and stuck the tickets Mr. Cole gave him into the band of his shorts.

"Hey," he said to Ty. "How's it going?"

"Troy, this is Chuku. Chuku Moore."

Troy tilted his head. "What?"

Chuku offered his hand. "Means 'child of God,' but you don't have to pray to me or anything."

Troy extended his hand to the boy with skin the color of coffee mixed with cream. Chuku had close-cut hair, a brilliant smile, and a mischievous but friendly gleam in his dark eyes. Troy noticed now that the jersey— a Ravens Ray Lewis jersey—had a signature running down the straight edge of the white number five.

"Ravens fan?" Troy said.

"Used to be." Chuku nodded toward the man who was now sprinting through the cones in a blur. "Till they let my dad go."

"That's your *dad*?" Troy watched the man take off out of his stance and move quickly around and through the cones.

"He tore up his knee two seasons ago. Took him this long to rehab. He played twelve years for the Ravens."

"And he's trying out *here*?" Troy knew twelve years was about the maximum anyone played in the NFL, especially a linebacker with a hurt knee.

"He long-snaps, too." Chuku stuck out his chin.

Troy wasn't that impressed. Every NFL team had a long snapper who usually played another position only in an emergency. It meant Chuku's dad was just about finished, but his special skill as a long snapper on the punt team might give his career a few last dying gasps.

As if Chuku sensed Troy's lack of respect, he said, "He ran a 4.4 before he got hurt. Fast, huh?"

"Pretty fast." Troy put some enthusiasm into his voice to be nice. "You play, too?"

Chuku snorted and chuckled. "Like Victor Cruz, only faster."

A doubtful grin stretched Troy's cheeks. "Well, with your dad and you, we may have the *three* fastest people in New Jersey on this field right now."

Chuku's eyes traveled up and down Troy's frame.

Half his mouth curled into a smile and he raised an eyebrow. *"You?"*

Hot annoyance flushed Troy's face. "Not me. Ty."

Chuku turned. "Chicken legs?"

Ty laughed and blushed and pulled his shorts up to his mid thighs to examine what did look like chicken legs. It bothered Troy even more that Ty was going along with the insult, unfazed. At the Super Bowl, when Ty's team won the 7-on-7 championship trophy, Ty had outrun the very fastest kids from all four corners of the country, and Chuku's lack of respect just didn't float with Troy.

"He's faster than *you*, I can tell you that." Troy stuck out his chin.

Chuku burst out into wild laughter. "You for *real*?"

"Are you?" Troy asked.

"How old are you, Chicken Little?" Somehow Chuku's tone came out like a friendly joke, and that made Troy even madder.

Ty said, "Thirteen."

"Well, I'm the same age even though people think I already drive, so I guess it won't be illegal." Chuku turned to Troy. "I bet you anything you got I beat my dawg here in a race."

"Forty-yard dash?" Troy asked.

"Come on, guys. What's the difference?" Ty said. "Let's play catch."

"No, no, no." Troy held up a hand. "You don't just say

you're faster than everyone else and get away with it. You're *not* faster than my man."

"How about you put your money where your mouth is?" Chuku's smile, like his voice, remained friendly as he peeled off the signed Ray Lewis jersey and dropped it in a heap on the grass. The tank top he wore was skintight. Troy and Ty could see that Chuku's muscles were like steel cables.

"You want my Jets T-shirt?" Troy asked.

"That's no bet. You think I'm a chump?" Chuku laughed. "Bet something that matters. This thing is *game-worn*. This goes for three grand if you want to *buy* it. You *got* anything worth that much?"

Troy wanted to scream that he made five million dollars, but he didn't *have* the money and he sure didn't want to have to explain to this kid why not. Then he had an idea.

"I got *these*." Troy whipped the tickets and backstage passes out of his shorts without even thinking. "And even a pencil neck from Baltimore knows they're worth two of those Ray Lewis jerseys."

Chuku studied the backstage passes and the tickets, unable to hide his surprise. "Helena? Where'd you get these?"

"Nothing for you to worry about." Troy dropped the passes and tickets down on top of the purple jersey. "You just worry about how you're gonna get another Ray Lewis jersey so you don't have to tell your kids one day about the one you *used* to have. Let's go." Troy pointed to the goal line. "You two get on the line."

"Troy," Ty said, "I don't think—"

Troy cut him off. "Just line up and run this big mouth's butt into the ground. I always wanted a Ray Lewis game-worn jersey."

"That's right, line up, Chicken Little." Chuku flicked his legs out into the air, stretching them before he got into a sprinter's stance on the goal line. "The sky is *fallin'*."

Ty shook his head, sighed, and got into his stance.

Troy marched to the forty-yard line and turned around. He raised a hand. "On your mark . . . get set . . . go!"

Ty and Chuku burst out of their stances and ran toward Troy like rockets riding the wind.

CHAPTER ELEVEN

IT WAS CLOSE, THAT'S all Troy could say.

"I tried." Ty was breathing heavily. "He's fast."

"Told you." Chuku was relaxed and casual. "Backstage. Dang. You guys want to throw the ball? My hands are as good as my feet, maybe better. Nah, maybe nothing's better than my feet. Ha ha."

"Yeah, let's. Come on already." Ty grabbed the football and tossed it to Troy.

On the other field, the scouts were running Chuku's dad through another drill and timing him with their watches.

Troy's head still spun from losing, but he set up in the middle of the field so he could call out routes for the two of them to run, as if everything were fine. He certainly wasn't going to act as if the whole thing bothered him. He sent Ty on a post route and connected with a bullet. From the corner of his eye, he watched for a reaction from Chuku, but the new kid either didn't see or wasn't impressed. Troy burned inside.

"Run a ten-yard comeback," Troy said to Chuku, then barked out a cadence and pretended to take a snap.

Troy took a three-step drop and rifled the ball at Chuku's head before he even got out of his break. The laces whistled and for an instant, Troy almost felt bad. Chuku planted a foot at ten yards and broke back. The ball was on him, but Chuku's arms popped up like toast. The ball didn't even make a sound, so soft were his hands. Chuku tucked the ball and broke back up field, running all the way to the end zone.

"Touchdown." Chuku laughed to himself.

Troy ground his teeth.

From the other side of the field, Chuku's father shouted through cupped hands, "Chuku! I'll be out in a while! You good?"

"I'm good!" Chuku returned the shout and the three men disappeared back inside.

Troy wondered how long Chuku would be weighing them down, but as time wore on, two things happened. First, Troy's respect for Chuku Moore grew like Jack's beanstalk. Second, try as he might, Troy couldn't help liking the kid and his friendly, nonchalant manner. To Troy life seemed like a fight against the tide, while Chuku seemed to be going with the current, carefree and easy, just enjoying it all.

Finally Chuku's dad emerged from the facility alone. "Chuku! Come on, boy!"

Chuku ran over to Troy, smiling. "Nice to meet you guys."

"You're a pretty good receiver," Troy said.

"Pretty good?" Chuku's smile widened. "I was just fooling around out here. A. J. Green's got nothing on Chuku Moore."

Chuku shook Troy's hand, then Ty's, before grabbing his jersey and the tickets and scooting off toward his dad, who had already turned and was trudging toward the gate.

Father and son disappeared before Ty asked, "You think his dad is gonna get signed by the team?"

"I have no idea." Troy tossed the ball in the air and caught it.

"Can you imagine if he did move here?" Ty wiped the sweat from his forehead. "And then, after you get everything worked out, the three of us at St. Stephen's in a couple of years? Man, we could do some damage. Win a couple of state championships. All three of us five-star recruits. We could go visit all the big schools *together*. Maybe make ourselves a package deal?"

Troy winced at the sound of St. Stephen's. "Yeah, well, who knows. It's no big deal. We got each other. We don't need that kid."

"Yeah, but you know better than anyone that teams

can double-cover one guy with deep speed, but not *two*. It doesn't take a genius to know that." Ty paused. "Sorry about your tickets."

"I'm sorry for you." Troy patted Ty's back. "Who do you think I was bringing with me to that concert?"

"Really? Man. Well, I ran as fast as I could and he beat me by a full stride. I've never seen anyone that fast."

Thane appeared at the doorway to the facility and shouted much the same as Chuku's dad had done. "Let's go, guys!"

They joined Thane and walked through the offices toward the front. When they left the lobby, a Mercedes SUV pulled up in the circle. The window rolled down and Mr. Cole leaned toward them.

"Troy, you bringing these guys with you to the concert?"

CHAPTER TWELVE

TROY DIDN'T MISS A beat. "Sure."

"Great, I'm off to Europe for a few days, but I'll be back in time to see you all there." Mr. Cole waved and the Mercedes sped off.

Troy swallowed. He wouldn't be bringing anyone to the concert, but the lie came off his tongue slick as spit. He couldn't even help it. It bothered him no end that he was like that. It reminded him of his father, smooth and slippery and sliding through the cracks in life. That was no way to be. Now he had an even bigger problem.

"That was as friendly as I've ever seen him." Thane stared at the SUV. "What concert?"

"Mr. Cole gave me some tickets and backstage passes

44

for the Helena concert at Yankee Stadium," Troy said.

"But he lost them on a bet." Ty acted as if Thane were one of them.

Troy winced. "I'll get them back."

"Oh. Wow. Well, okay." That was all Thane said about it, but Troy could see the concern on his face.

They got into Thane's Escalade and headed to Troy's place for dinner. On the way, Thane treated them to more Dairy Queen, then picked up two loaves of fresh Italian bread and a cheesecake at a local bakery.

"Don't want to show up empty-handed," Thane said.

Even in the evening light, Troy's rental house seemed shabby, and when they pulled up behind the VW Bug in the gleaming new Escalade, Troy thought of the new Mustang he told Ty about wanting to get for his mom. The little bug of a car and his big talk made Troy feel ashamed.

Troy forced a chuckle and shook his head. "I know you guys aren't used to digs like this, but it's only temporary."

Ty smiled. "You don't have to use a broken Porta-Potty for a bathroom, do you?"

Troy's mouth fell open.

Thane laughed. "Our uncle Gus had Ty shacked up in a place that makes this house look like the Ritz."

That raised Troy's spirits a bit, but it was still a dump.

Inside, the smell of tomato sauce and sound of sausage snapping in a sea of onions led them right to the kitchen.

Thane sniffed. "Smells good."

Troy's mom turned to face them, smiling. "And you all are looking at the new PR manager for McArdle & Swain."

"Huh?" Thane looked confused.

"It's a law firm. I got the job!"

"That's great, Mom," Troy said.

"Congratulations! Let's celebrate." Thane showed her the cheesecake.

"Very nice. Thank you. Sit right down, boys. There's a pitcher of iced tea on the table." Troy's mom pointed with a wooden spoon.

Troy and Ty sat down, but Thane stayed by the stove and asked if he could help.

Ty leaned toward Troy and whispered, "'Get back the Helena tickets?' How are you gonna do that?"

Troy pointed at his mom and shook his head not to discuss it. Under his breath he said, "Later."

He had a forkful of spaghetti halfway to his mouth when they heard the purr of an engine and the crackle of gravel and tires in the driveway. Footsteps on the front porch were followed by a knock on the screen door. Whoever it was didn't bother waiting for an answer. The door squeaked open and the footsteps continued into the house and through the front hall. Before Troy could turn his head around, his mom's mouth went slack. Her eyes widened in shock and she covered her mouth as she struggled to rise from her chair.

"Oh, my gosh."

CHAPTER THIRTEEN

TROY'S HEAD SWUNG AROUND, even as his mom dashed from her place to meet Seth Halloway halfway across the kitchen floor. She hugged him and he picked her up and swung her in a big circle.

"Seth!" Troy beamed and stood up, too.

Seth grabbed him and pulled him and his mom into a hug. "Thought I'd surprise you both!"

"Oh, my gosh." Troy's mom glowed and she brushed some fallen hair from her face. "Seth, you remember Troy's cousins—our cousins—Thane and Ty."

Seth shook hands with the two brothers he'd met in Miami the previous winter during Super Bowl week. "Hey, guys."

"Sit down. Eat." Troy's mom was already reaching for the cupboard.

"I didn't mean to barge in on you, but I figured the surprise was worth the risk," Seth said.

"So, what happened?" Troy's mom gave Seth a plate and sat back down. "I thought you were fly-fishing in Montana before you went back to help out at Furman."

Seth cut a meatball in half, stuck a piece in his mouth, and chewed. "Well, I *was* fishing, then I got a call about another job."

"Another job?" Troy's mom raised a single eyebrow.

Seth swallowed and took a drink. "You know the thing at Furman was only as a volunteer anyway?"

"I think you mentioned it," Troy's mom said, "but you have to start someplace."

"Yeah, but then I heard about this other thing. It's not that I need the money. I'm set, you know that, but it is nice to get paid. Makes you feel like you're worth something, even if it's a couple of thousand dollars."

"What 'other thing'? Stop with the suspense already, will you?" Troy's mom nudged Seth's shoulder.

Seth glanced at Troy. "Word is, there may be a job right here, in Summit."

CHAPTER FOURTEEN

TROY'S MOM LAUGHED OUT loud. "What? What job?"

"At . . . Troy's school." Seth spoke carefully. "Well, the high school."

Troy looked down at his hands. He hadn't been certain Seth was even listening to him when he called him up the other night.

"He's in junior high," Troy's mom said.

"But he could play in high school, right?" Seth said. "We go pretty good together, don't you think? The Georgia Junior League state title?"

"I don't know." Troy's mom began to sputter. "I've never heard of an eighth grader playing in high school."

"I have." Seth twirled a bundle of spaghetti onto his fork. "He has to pass a physical test and you need a doctor to sign off, but a high school coach can bring a kid up to varsity from junior high if he's good enough. Ha. And we all know Troy's good enough."

Seth jammed the spaghetti into his mouth and looked around the table to see if anyone disagreed. A current of excitement pulsed through Troy's body at the mention of playing on varsity.

"How much have you grown the last few months?" Seth asked him after swallowing.

"Four or five inches. I'm five ten." Troy sat up straight.

"Big enough." Seth went back to eating.

Troy's mom looked at Troy and spoke slowly. "Was all this . . . your idea?"

Troy shrugged and forced a smile. "Sort of."

"Sort of?" she asked.

"Well," Troy said, "really it was Mr. Bryant's idea."

She frowned at Troy and said, "A pipe dream, isn't that what he called it? But I thought I made it pretty clear that was the end of it."

"I told you Seth would like the idea." Troy clenched his hands beneath the table. "Mom, what's *wrong* with it? Aren't you glad he's here?"

"Of course I'm glad." His mom blushed and turned to Seth. "But I know what you want to do and where you want to be. I can't believe coaching some terrible high school football team in New Jersey is going to help you get there faster than Furman."

"I think you made it pretty clear after Troy signed

his contract that you weren't twisting my arm to leave everything and come here," Seth said, "but I hope you're not gonna twist it for me to leave, either."

Everyone in the room looked at Troy's mom. The others might not know the importance of her reaction, but Troy did. He knew if his mom didn't want him there, Seth would be back on a plane to Atlanta by midnight.

His mom kept her hands in her lap and looked down at the table. Troy studied her face. He could see she was thinking, but didn't know what. He had stopped a while ago trying to figure out why adults did some of the things they did, especially when it came to love—and he was pretty sure his mom and Seth loved each other.

Finally, she cleared her throat and stood up.

CHAPTER FIFTEEN

TROY'S MOM MOVED OVER to where Seth sat. She put her hands on his cheeks and kissed his forehead.

"I think I needed you to come up here in spite of me, not because of me," Troy's mom said. "Does that make sense?"

"Honestly? Yes."

Troy looked at Ty and rolled his eyes.

"Good." Troy's mom straightened up and then sat back down. "Now all we have to do is figure out how to get you that job."

"Well, I'm already working on it," Seth said. "I landed at one and went right to the school. Mr. Bryant helped me get an application together and he introduced me to the athletic director, Ed Biondi . . . Mr. Biondi to you guys. Great guy. He's going to interview me tomorrow.

You should have seen the look on his face. He was pretty excited not to have to coach this year."

"Is he the one who does the hiring?" Troy's mom asked.

"Biondi said he wants the principal involved, too, so he has some support from her. Then it goes to the school board. If they approve it, I'm in. Should be easy."

"And . . . what about a place?" Troy's mom asked.

Seth looked at his spaghetti. "I got a hotel room in town, and if I get the job, I planned on finding an apartment. This isn't about me invading your life."

"I *feel* like you should be staying with us," Troy's mom said. "Until you're settled in. We've got an extra bedroom."

"I appreciate that," Seth said, "but I snore and it'll look better if I'm on my own. It's not gonna go down well with some people if Troy ends up as our starting quarterback—which I'm sure will be the case. If I'm staying here, it'll only make it harder." Seth's face lit up. His voice bubbled with excitement. "Honestly, I know it sounds crazy, but I think it's my best opportunity to make a name in coaching. With Troy as my quarterback?"

Seth chuckled. "Heh, we'll turn mud into money. If I turn a program around overnight, I'll have all kinds of offers. People respect a guy who starts on the ground floor."

"What about the basement?" Troy couldn't help the

sharp comment, and he wondered if Seth knew how terrible the team really was. "They haven't won a game in two years."

"Oh, it can't be that bad." Seth snorted and shoveled more spaghetti into his mouth.

"I'm serious." Troy wanted Seth to coach the team, but he also wanted him to know how hard it would be. "Right, Ty?"

"They're supposed to be pretty bad," Ty said. "But I haven't seen them play."

Seth wiped his mouth on a napkin. "At the high school level, trust me, it's about coaching. I played in a town with a horrible coach. He got fired my sophomore year and they brought in George O'Leary."

"The coach at UCF?" Thane asked.

Seth nodded. "We won the league championship my junior year and the state title the year after that. That's what good coaching does."

"They had *you*," Ty said.

"Right, and we'll have you two guys." Seth smiled at them all.

Thane cleared his throat. "Uh . . ."

"'Uh,' what?" Seth asked.

Troy dipped his face into one hand and shook his head.

CHAPTER SIXTEEN

"TY IS ALL SET up to go to St. Stephen's." Thane's face grew long. "It's a private school. It's a powerhouse."

"Really?" Seth looked at Troy.

"I . . . I guess I thought maybe he might change his mind?" It was the best Troy could come up with. He never said Ty was going to Summit, but he didn't tell Seth he wasn't, either. They both knew Troy would need a fast receiver, and they both knew there were few people faster than Ty.

"Yeah, I mean, if I'm coaching the team, we could end up as a powerhouse, too," Seth said. "With Troy at QB, you know Ty is going to get a ton of balls thrown to him."

"Will you guys run a spread offense?" Ty asked.

Seth nodded. "For sure. Hey, it might take us a

season or two to turn it around completely, but can you imagine five years of you guys playing together?"

Troy pumped his voice full of excitement. "And if we turn it around, you know other players from Summit are gonna think twice before they go to St. Stephen's."

"That's what happens now," Ty said. "All the best players leave. St. Stephen's recruits them right out of Pop Warner."

"Wait," Troy's mom said. "I thought you can't recruit in high school."

"St. Stephen's is a private school," Thane explained. "They can pretty much do what they want. They say they're recruiting *students*."

"Students who just happen to be the best football players in the state," Ty said.

"When they find out Seth's coaching," Troy said, "I bet not only will kids in Summit stay in Summit, kids will move *into* Summit to play. He'll get coaches just as good as St. Stephen's has, and it's free."

"Maybe," Seth said. "It happened in my town growing up. Kids want to play for a good coach. *Parents* want their kids to play for a good coach."

"Wait a minute." Troy's mom held up both hands and they all turned to her. "That's recruiting, right? You can't recruit high school kids unless you're a private school, can you?"

"It's not recruiting if you don't ask them to come," Seth said. "Anyone can move anywhere. Kids move into school districts for all sorts of reasons—a good band, a science program, special needs. You just can't try to lure them in by giving them something."

"Well," Thane said, "it *would* be good if someone could compete with St. Stephen's. Right now, they slaughter everyone. The only time it's even a contest is when they go play some powerhouse from Florida or Ohio or something. That's how good they are."

"They're *that* good?" Seth asked.

Thane nodded. "Their second string could probably beat the rest of the teams in New Jersey."

"Well, let's see if we can give them some competition. Man, I'm having fun already. So, what about Ty?" Seth gave Thane a serious look. "Are you gonna let him play for me?"

Thane tightened his lips, then spoke. "Honestly? I don't know. Maybe. I want to see how this whole thing shakes out. Come on, don't look at me like that, Seth. You know as much as I do that if a kid isn't in the right situation, it can end his football career before it even starts. Our parents are gone, so I have to fill in. I don't want to mess anything up, so no promises, but I'll think about it."

Troy nudged Ty under the table and gave him a questioning look, hoping for reassurance. All Ty did was force a smile and shrug. Troy looked to his mom for some support, but she wore a frown.

Seth turned to Troy's mom. He saw her look, too, and

gave her a puzzled look in return. "What's the matter?"

"Nothing," she said. "I just think Thane's got a point. Education comes first."

They all sat quiet for a moment, then Troy's mom's cell phone rang.

She answered it.

"Hello, Mrs. McGreer." She smiled.

Troy grinned at the mention of Tate's mom and he caught Ty's eye. Ty faked a look of confusion, as if he didn't know why Troy was looking at him, but Troy winked at his cousin and when Ty looked down at his plate his cheeks reddened. Troy loved Tate like a sister, but his certainty that Ty cared for her a little more than that went up a bit at the sight of his blushing.

"Oh, no." Troy's mom's voice sank, dragging her face, and Troy's stomach, with it.

"I'm so sorry." Tears filled Troy's mom's eyes. Her hand trembled and she sniffed. "Yes, yes, of course. You do that, please. We're here for you. I am so sorry. You will all be in our prayers, Mrs. McGreer."

She hung up.

"Mom?" Troy choked on his words. "What happened?"

CHAPTER SEVENTEEN

TROY'S MOM WIPED HER eyes and sniffed again. "It's Tate's father. He was in San Diego on business and he got into a bad accident. They don't know if he's going to make it."

Troy's mom looked down at her hands. She folded them together and said a silent prayer before she looked up.

"Tate's mom is going out there tonight. She asked if we can take Tate until things work themselves out. They're heading for the airport and there's a flight to Newark leaving soon. Of course, I told her we could."

Troy felt a wave of relief, then a backwash of guilt. The fear that something had happened to Tate made him sick, and that was gone now. He felt bad about her dad, but Troy didn't really *know* her father. He was just a big guy who liked the Chicago Bears. It was the kind of thought, he knew, that came directly from his father's side of the family tree—selfish.

They finished their meal in relative silence. Everyone helped clean up, and Seth decided to stay so he could drive Troy and his mom to the airport to pick up Tate. Troy could tell by the look on Ty's face that he wanted to join them, but Thane insisted they get home.

Thane ended all discussion when he said, "I've got an early morning workout."

Later, on the way out to the airport, Troy's mom played the radio low and no one said anything until his mom shut it off completely. "Puts things into perspective, doesn't it? Here we are all worried about a football program."

"Actually," Seth said, "I was thinking that life's short, and you gotta make the most of it."

Troy's heart soared at the words. Football ran through Seth's veins, and Troy knew from many of their private discussions that attitude was what got Seth into the NFL in the first place. Troy nodded, even though no one could see him in the backseat.

Seth waited in the truck while Troy and his mom went inside. After an airline representative escorted Tate through the security checkpoint, Troy's mom hugged her tight. Tate sniffed, and fought back tears without much success. Troy's mom waved him over and they did a group hug right there in the middle of the terminal with people streaming by.

"I'm okay." Tate nodded and set her jaw. "He's gonna be all right. My mom said God won't want him any sooner than He has to take him."

Tate laughed, and so they all did. Troy's mom called Mrs. McGreer on her cell phone and left a message so she'd know Tate was safe and sound as soon as she landed in San Diego. She and Troy then put their arms around Tate and they all walked down to the baggage claim to get a big suitcase that Troy rolled out to Seth's truck.

"How's the toughest girl I ever met?" Seth leaned into the backseat and kissed Tate's cheek.

Tate blushed. "My mom is trying to get me to become a young lady."

"Doesn't mean you're not tough—look at Tessa." Seth held up a hand and Troy's mom growled and pretended to bite it.

Tate bit her lower lip and her eyes got moist. "I missed you guys."

Troy put his hand on her neck and gave it a squeeze. They kept Tate's mind off her father by telling her everything that had happened and why Seth had joined them in Summit that same night.

When they got home, Seth carried Tate's suitcase upstairs to the extra bedroom across the hall from

Troy's room and said his good-byes once she was settled.

Later, when Seth was gone and the house was dark and quiet, Troy lay awake, staring at a beam of moonlight that streaked across the wall. After a soft knock, the door swung open. Tate came in and sat on the edge of his bed.

"Can't sleep?" Troy patted her shoulder.

Tate shook her head. "Bad things aren't supposed to happen to good people."

"He's gonna be okay, Tate. I know it."

She turned her big brown eyes on him and they glittered in the moonlight. "Is it like when you know what plays a team is going to run?"

Troy's chest tightened. He wanted to say it was like that, but it wasn't true. He didn't know her father would be all right, and for once his ability to lie quick and smooth failed him. "No, I just think so."

She let out a two-ton sigh. "That stinks about what your dad did."

"He should have been in the car accident."

"You don't mean that, Troy."

It got so quiet, Troy could hear the hiss of leaves outside the window.

"No. You're right. That's bad, but he's crazy, Tate."

Troy told her about his father's secret visit and made her swear she wouldn't mention it around his mom. Then he recounted his father's final words about being there when he needed him.

"Well, that's something," Tate said.

"Yeah." Troy stared out the window where a sea of dark leaves flickered and waved. "Something."

CHAPTER EIGHTEEN

THE NEXT DAY, TROY'S mom took Tate with her so the two of them could get their nails done.

"Nails?" Troy twisted his face. His mom, he understood. She was starting a new job, but he had a hard time believing that Tate had slipped so far toward girly things in just one summer. He was glad when they dropped him off at the front door of the Jets facility, where Ty was waiting for him. Ty dashed out to the car. When his head appeared in the window, Troy sat for a minute to see what he would do.

"Umm." Ty stared hard at Troy's mom, but Troy could see his cousin's neck, straining to keep from looking back at Tate. "Hello, Ms. White."

"Ty, you can call me Tessa," Troy's mom said. "Troy calls your brother Thane."

"Okay." Ty clapped his mouth shut, though.

"Ty, aren't you gonna say hi to Tate?" Troy tried not to grin.

"Oh! Hi, Tate." Ty's face went beet red. "What are you up to?"

Tate stuck her face up between the seats, frowned, and tilted her head. "Ty, I just texted you. You *know* that we're going to get our nails done."

Troy choked back a laugh and had to open the door and spill outside to keep from embarrassing Ty. They all said good-bye and Troy's mom drove off.

Troy stood with Ty on the curb. "I think she likes you."

When he looked to see what Ty's reaction would be, he had to hustle to catch up. Ty was marching toward the complex, eyes on the ground, face even redder than before.

Troy stopped torturing his cousin and changed the subject as they went through the building together.

"Where's Thane?"

Ty looked at him suspiciously and spoke with caution. "They're doing patterns inside. We got the field to ourselves."

"Great." Troy clapped him on the back and swung open the outer door. As they reached the edge of the field, Troy was surprised to see Chuku Moore right there out on the grass where they'd been the day before. There was no sign of his dad.

Chuku saw them and made a beeline. "Hey, what's up, Pokey? Genius?"

The Pokey comment made Troy flush with anger, but Ty bumped knuckles with Chuku and didn't seem to mind one bit. Troy looked at Chuku's outstretched hand without doing anything.

"Why are you here?" Troy asked.

"What? You don't like dudes calling you Genius?" Chuku flashed his brilliant smile before buttoning it up. "That some kind of insult to people from Atlanta? In Baltimore, that's hot. People *like* being smart in Baltimore."

"Whatever." Troy shrugged and started to walk past Chuku.

"I'm here because the Jets got themselves a new linebacker," Chuku said. "Thought maybe you dudes might want to hang out. I don't know where we're gonna live, get some apartment or something close by, but now I know . . . you don't like my kind."

Troy froze, then turned around. He scrunched up his face. "Your *kind*?"

"Yeah. The dark kind." Chuku held up his arm and pointed to his skin.

Troy felt embarrassed, even though he didn't think his reaction to Chuku had anything to do with his skin color. He felt trapped and confused and didn't know what to say.

Then he got an idea.

An idea so good, he thought it was genius.

CHAPTER NINETEEN

"YOU ARE SO WRONG." Troy shook his head. "I don't care if you're black, blue, white, red, or green. I don't even think like that. But you're right. I *am* mad, mad because you're faster than Ty and I didn't think that was possible."

"And I got your Helena tickets," Chuku said.

"That, too, but I got an idea that'll prove I don't care what color your skin is," Troy said.

"Yeah? What do you got?" Chuku raised an eyebrow and Ty moved closer to hear.

"Have your dad get a place in Summit. You and me—and hopefully Ty—can play on the same team together."

"How's the team in Summit?" Chuku asked.

"Butt-ugly." Troy folded his arms across his chest.

Chuku laughed. "So why would I move into a place with a butt-ugly team?"

"Because it's not gonna stay that way," Troy said. "You heard of Seth Halloway, the all-pro linebacker from the Falcons? He's gonna be the coach," Troy said.

"For real?" Chuku tilted his head.

"And bring me—and Ty if he's there—and I'm sure you up to the varsity team."

"Dude, I'm faster than any high school kid. I *know* I'll be varsity, but you *look* like an eighth grader. I'm about ready to shave. See this?" Chuku poked his tongue up under his top lip so that it curled out to display a few tufts of fine, dark hair. "They don't put eighth graders on the varsity in *football* unless you're ready to shave. Maybe soccer or wrestling I heard of it, but not football."

"It happens sometimes." Troy rubbed his own empty upper lip. "How would you like to catch the ball for five years in the same system? An NFL system with a spread offense? How'd you like to have colleges from everywhere recruiting you?"

"That's my plan," Chuku said.

"Well," Troy said, "what do you think? Do you want to try to do it?"

Chuku stared at him, frowning. "You know what you are?"

Troy swallowed. "No, what?"

CHAPTER TWENTY

"YOU'RE CRAZY . . ."

Suddenly, Chuku's smile lit up his face like candles on a birthday cake. "But I happen to like crazy people, so why not?"

"Do you think your dad will go for it?" Troy couldn't help himself from grabbing Chuku's hand and shaking it.

"He might," Chuku said. "Talk about crazy . . ."

Chuku nodded toward the building and Troy turned around. Chuku's dad emerged and was heading their way.

"Dad, this is Troy and Ty. Ty is Tiger Lewis's little brother."

"And you're the kid from ESPN." Mr. Moore spoke in a deep, strong voice that vibrated the air like a sports car with no muffler. "The secret weapon that's not so secret."

Troy's hand got lost in the iron grip of Mr. Moore's hand. It was all he could do to keep his bones from snapping like toothpicks.

"You should see him throw. He looks like RG3. Just zips it. I swear, he could throw into double coverage, *triple* coverage, and get the ball there." Chuku spoke with an admiration that belied the conflict between the two of them. "These guys say we should move into Summit so we can all play on the same team. You remember Seth Halloway? He's gonna coach the team."

"Seth Halloway from the *Falcons* Seth Halloway?" Chuku's dad screwed up his face. "He's up here in New Jersey?"

"He's a family friend," Troy said.

"Can we do it?" Chuku asked.

Mr. Moore studied Troy as if to see whether his son was for real. Troy gave an encouraging nod.

Mr. Moore laughed. "Well, we got to live somewhere. We'll see if there's anything decent there. Come on, Chuku. Time to go."

"Can I stay and catch with these guys and you pick me up later? They're gonna throw the rock around."

"Sure," Chuku's dad said. "I've got a couple of things I can do. I'll be back in an hour, though."

The three of them got down to the business of throwing and catching the football, running patterns and making up plays. Troy was in heaven. As good as Ty was, Chuku had an even sharper break out of his patterns, and even when Troy had a grossly errant throw, Chuku twisted and turned like a snake and came down with the ball effortlessly. It was impossible not to be impressed.

After one jumping, spinning, one-handed catch of Chuku's, Troy couldn't contain himself. "Guys, do you know what will happen if I have *both* of you to throw to? I mean, one of you would be awesome, but *both*? Defenses *can't* cover two deep speed guys. One, they can always double-cover with the free safety, but *two*? It'll be impossible! We will slay people!"

Chuku and Ty nodded at each other and exchanged high fives, then they got back to work.

Troy's arm grew sore, but he felt like a kindergartner with his Halloween candy spilled out on the floor. He wanted to have it all. When Ty ran a deep post, Troy's arm flagged and the ball drifted behind him. Ty spun and got a hand on it, but bobbled and ultimately dropped it.

"Come on, Troy. Get that up." Ty kicked the ball.

The criticism burned Troy and his head grew hot. "If you get your hands on it, you're supposed to catch it. Watch Chuku."

"Ha!" Ty marched back toward the fifty-yard line, where Troy was standing. "My brother says when Sanchez underthrows the ball *he* takes the blame for the drop. He might not be a football *genius*, but he's got a *rocket* for an arm. I guess that's the difference . . ."

Troy had ten mean things to say about Ty's brother on the tip of his tongue when a horn beeped from the parking lot. It was Chuku's dad in a big white Mercedes sedan.

"Well, ladies . . ." Chuku gave them fist bumps and a grin that ignored their bickering. "You saw how masterful I was on the football field. Now it's time for me to take my skills to the home front and make sure we wind up in Summit."

"What's the plan?" Ty asked.

Chuku's face went flat. "Guilt."

"Guilt?"

"Dawgs, Denzel Washington's got nothing on Chuku Moore. 'Dad, I left all my friends in Baltimore and now these guys and I got something going and you just got to help me out by getting a place in Summit.'" Chuku let his whimpering words echo in their ears as he nodded with satisfaction. "I can make a grown man cry."

"Your face could make a grown man cry," Troy said.

Chuku leaped at Troy and put him in a playful headlock. Troy slipped out of it and bear-hugged Chuku and they rolled on the ground, wrestling and laughing until Chuku's dad beeped again and Chuku sprang to his feet.

"Gotta go, dawgs." Halfway across the field he shouted over his shoulder, "See you in Summit!"

CHAPTER TWENTY-ONE

THEY WATCHED CHUKU AND his dad pull away.

Troy fought the urge to argue with Ty about who should take the blame on a bad pass. Instead, he did something he knew would make his mom proud. "Hey, man. I'm sorry. You're right about that genius stuff. I want to be a *player*, and that was a bad pass. If I'm gonna be a top quarterback, I need to take the blame. We good?"

Ty grinned and slapped Troy a high five. "You know we're good."

On the way home Ty sat in front with Thane and Troy rode in the back. They were out on the highway before Thane spoke. "I took a peek when we had a break. You guys almost look like you know what you're doing."

74

"Hey," Ty said, "I might not be *Tiger* Lewis, but I'm a Lewis, too."

They all chuckled and rode in silence for a few minutes. Thane's comment had given Troy an idea, but he didn't pursue it until he caught Thane's eyes in the rearview mirror. "So, Thane, you like McElroy *and* Sanchez?"

"Yeah, I seem to connect pretty well with both of them so far. I haven't been able to run my patterns at full speed, though, so it's still up in the air."

"You like him, though, right?" Troy asked. "McElroy."

"Everybody likes Greg. What's not to like?"

"That's good because chemistry is pretty important, right?" Troy met Thane's eyes again.

"You bet," Thane said.

"I mean, people make their careers with the right partners . . ." Troy pretended to be thinking. "Peyton Manning and Marvin Harrison . . . Ben Roethlisberger and Hines Ward . . . you need that chemistry."

They rode in silence some more before Thane looked at Troy in the mirror again. "And you two have *it*."

Troy shrugged. "I like to think so . . ."

"And that's why I should let Ty roll the dice and take a chance on playing at Summit instead of St. Stephen's, where we know the coaching and the program is one of—if not *the*—best in high school football anywhere?" Thane made it seem as if the question was silly.

"And the fact that it looks like me and Ty just ensured he won't be the only thing defenses are gonna have to worry about." Troy spoke confidently.

"Why is that?"

"No one's gonna be able to double-cover Ty all game long." Troy waggled his eyebrows. "We pretty much just guaranteed we're gonna have speed on *both* sides of the offense."

"Oh, really? And how did you do that?" Thane asked.

Troy told him about Chuku Moore.

"Faster than Ty?" Thane looked over at his younger brother. "What say you?"

Ty nodded and shrugged.

Thane sucked in his lower lip before he said, "Well, let's just see if Seth really gets the job, okay? You guys are putting the cart before the horse."

Before anyone could say anything more, Troy's phone buzzed with an incoming text message. He looked down and saw Seth's number.

"Looks like we'll know in about two seconds," Troy said as he hit the button and opened the message.

CHAPTER TWENTY-TWO

TROY CLEARED HIS THROAT and tried to speak casually. "The cart is now behind the horse. He got the job."

"He did? Just like that?" Ty crunched up his forehead.

Troy looked at Seth's text again. "It says the principal told him before the interview even started that Summit was honored to have him even consider it. They interviewed him for half an hour, then offered him the job."

"Hey, that's great. I'm happy for you guys," Thane said. "Look, Troy. I don't want you to get too excited is all."

CHAPTER TWENTY-THREE

THANE SIGHED. "THERE'S NO guarantee about Ty."

Ty looked over at his brother. "Why not?"

Thane shook his head. "There's no question about St. Stephen's being a great football program right now. It's not easy to just come in and turn a team around, even for someone as good as Seth."

Ty frowned and said nothing.

"You want to be with me, though, right, Ty?"

"Yeah. Sure. Of course." Ty nodded.

Troy could see, though, that Thane wasn't completely sold, so he dropped it. They pulled into Troy's driveway and all said good-bye. Troy heaved a sigh as he watched the black Escalade roll away trailing a cloud of dust. Inside, Seth had a mess of papers spread out all over the kitchen table. He was talking on his cell phone but waved for Troy to come in and sit down.

"That's great, Joe," Seth said. "Yeah, I find out for sure tomorrow night, but they said it's in the bag . . . Well, I'm going to get them going with some basic stuff right away, but we'll start officially on August fifteenth. It'll be great. Yeah, he's young, but he can sling it and wait till you see him read a defense. Okay. Bye." Seth hung up and grinned.

"Congratulations!"

"Thanks!" Seth pointed at his papers. "I've been scrambling to fill out my coaching staff, and just wait till you hear who that was on the phone."

CHAPTER TWENTY-FOUR

"WHO?" TROY ASKED.

"Joe Sindoni, our new offensive coordinator," Seth said.

"Joe *who*?" Troy's spirits sank. "Did he play in the NFL?"

"Nope."

"Coach college?"

"Nope, he was the JV coach at a Catholic school called CBA, so being a varsity coach is a nice step up for him. Don't look at me like that. Trust me."

"But . . ." Troy bit his lip. "It's just that Thane was talking to us on the ride home about how great St. Stephen's is. I don't know if Thane's going to let him come."

Seth stood up and put a hand on Troy's shoulder.

"We can't worry about one guy. We need to build this thing from the ground up. It'll be you and me and my staff. Maybe we get Ty, maybe we don't. Don't worry, we'll find an athlete or two and turn them into receivers. The rest of it will be up to us."

Before Troy could tell him about Chuku, his mom and Tate arrived.

"How are your nails?" Troy tried not to sound disgusted.

Tate held up both hands and splayed her fingers, showing off her dark blue polish.

"Yeah. Nice." Troy rolled his eyes.

"Why so sour?" Troy's mom asked.

"He's balled up about Thane maybe keeping Ty at St. Stephen's," Seth said.

"I've been meaning to talk to you about that, Troy." His mom showed Seth her painted nails. "I've told you, you can't manipulate everyone and everything. You've got to leave that alone."

"He hasn't said no." Troy frowned.

"Thane doesn't *want* to say no," his mom said. "But sometimes people *mean* no when they don't say yes. Do you understand?"

Pressure built up inside Troy's head like someone was working a tire pump in his ear. "No."

"Well, trust me. Let it be. If Ty is going to come, they'll tell you. Stop asking." His mom brightened suddenly. "Hey, Mrs. McGreer called while we were having our nails done, and good news . . . Tate's father is stabilized."

"What's that mean?" Troy asked.

"He's not getting any worse." Tate wrinkled her forehead. "But they said it'll be a while before they know how well he'll be able to recover. My mom wants me to get ready to go to school here."

Troy's mom put a hand on Tate's head. "It'll be all right, honey. We're all praying for him. He'll be okay."

"Well, it'd be great if you went here." Troy didn't hide his enthusiasm.

"Your mom even called the soccer coach," Tate said.

"And Tate's going to the last day of her camp, tomorrow. Isn't that great? It'll be a good start if she does have to go to school here," Troy's mom said.

When Tate smiled, Troy relaxed.

During dinner, he explained his new plans to Tate.

"You see, if we have *two* fast wide receivers—Chuku *and* Ty—the defense just doesn't have enough men to cover them both. When someone is that fast, you have to have one guy take the underneath routes and one guy for the deep stuff. It makes everything ten times better if you have two."

"I've never seen you so hyped up, Troy," Tate said.

Troy nodded. "It's just that there's so much at stake here. I mean, when I went to register at school my mom and I saw some people surveying the field. Mr. Bryant—he's the guidance counselor—he said the school had to either upgrade the stadium or end football. So if we can win and turn this thing around, I know the school board and everybody will want a new stadium. It'll be like the beginning of a football dynasty."

Tate glanced at Troy's mom, then leaned close so only he could hear. "Do you think Ty will really come with you?"

"I hope so." Troy lowered his voice, too. "We need him."

"Great food." Seth wiped his mouth and set the napkin down before standing up to help clear the table.

When the kitchen was clean, the four of them went to a movie. On their way home through town, Troy pointed to an apartment building just off the main street. "If Chuku's dad is in, why couldn't they live right there?"

Seth pulled up in front of the redbrick building to take a closer look. A sign said there were places available for rent. "Nice. Perfect. You got his phone number?"

"Yeah," Troy said.

"So text him the number for the rental office. It's there on the sign. Tell him we said they should check it out."

Troy did as Seth said.

"You're really serious about all this, aren't you?" Troy's mom said.

"Of course." Seth started heading back. "Who knows? They have to live somewhere."

"But to move someplace just because you want your

son to be on a football team?" Troy's mom shook her head. "You'd have to be crazy."

"Hey, Chuku's dad plays in the NFL." Seth moved his eyebrows up and down. "You can bet he's crazy."

CHAPTER TWENTY-FIVE

THAT NIGHT TROY'S MOM got a text from Thane asking them all to join him and Ty for a day at their beach house on the Jersey Shore.

"Rats," Tate said. "I've got soccer camp."

"We'll be going plenty," Troy said. "Don't worry about that."

The next morning, Thane's big black Escalade pulled into the driveway just after breakfast. Seth rode up front with Thane while the rest of them spread out in the back. They dropped Tate off at the school on their way. It wasn't until she hopped out that Ty could even pick up his head.

"Bring your football?" Ty asked.

Troy held up his ball before tucking it back under his arm.

They watched a movie on the drive and before Troy knew it, they pulled into the gravel drive of a modern-looking white house full of glass and sharp angles. They piled out and Ty proudly showed them inside.

A huge mobile was suspended above them in the massive entryway. The simple, flat, black-and-white shapes drifting around wires looked like space junk to Troy.

"Thane bought it decorated like this," Ty explained. "The realtor said it was a good deal. People got divorced."

A jealous sigh escaped Troy at the thought that he could have a beach house, if only his father hadn't been such a sketchy character. As he changed into his bathing suit, he gritted his teeth and told himself he could still have a beach house . . . it would just take longer than he'd have liked.

There was a large deck off the back of the house surrounding a rectangular pool that looked like it dropped right off into the ocean. Beyond the dunes, half a dozen lounge chairs rested in the sand beneath two huge white umbrellas. The adults were talking and said they'd meet the kids down on the beach.

"Sunblock!" Troy's mom tossed him a tube.

Troy lathered up and looked around for someone or someones who put out the chairs, kept the pool sparkling clean, and trimmed the dark green shrubs. A brown-skinned man with a dark cap of hair disappeared around one corner of the house.

When they got to the beach, Troy was amazed to see two black-and-red WaveRunners on a kind of trailer with overblown white tires.

"Totally cool." Troy's excitement at the sight of the machines overcame the funk of jealousy. "Can we use them?"

"Thane says that's what they're for." Ty handed him a soda, uncapping his and taking a slug before setting it down on one of the chairs. "Come on, help me."

Ty passed out life vests slung from the handles of the machines. Troy tossed his football under a chair, put his on, then grabbed half of the long T handle of the trailer as Ty raised it out of the sand. Together they wheeled the WaveRunners toward the surf.

Troy couldn't believe how easy it was. The machines were huge, but the design of the cart or trailer, or whatever it was, was so perfect that it took less than two minutes to have the WaveRunners bobbing in the light surf.

"Hop on." Ty pushed the cart back up into the sand, then climbed onto one machine, grabbing the handles before he stepped up and slung his other leg over as if he was mounting a horse.

Troy got on his own machine and did as Ty instructed him, clipping a curly plastic cord to his vest so the key would yank out and stop the motor if he fell off.

With the push of a button, the machine revved to life. One squeeze of his thumb and he was surging ahead, through the light waves, then up and flying, *flying*, behind Ty.

Troy's thumb was sore by the end of the day and his hair was salty and windblown straight back. The football saw no action until Troy scooped it up and tossed it into the air on their way up to the house for dinner. The man Troy had seen before along with a woman who seemed to be his wife served them grilled chicken with rice and curried vegetables out on a linen-covered table on the deck. The sky showed off a rainbow of colors as it wound its way into night.

Troy was full and tired as they rode back toward Summit. Ty alternated between "Angry Birds" on his iPad and texting. Troy smiled because he bet he knew who Ty kept texting—Tate—but Troy kept quiet. He was happy just to bump along and relive the afternoon out on the water. With Ty on the same practice and game schedule, they'd be getting away to the beach house pretty regularly, and Troy couldn't wait. He wondered if Tate would ride with him or Ty on the WaveRunners. That made him grin. He'd almost forgotten about football when Thane guided the Escalade off the highway at the Summit exit and Seth started talking about his spread offense.

Troy listened as the two of them went back and forth, discussing how certain patterns defeated certain defensive coverages. Troy felt the excitement building up inside him because he just knew where Seth was headed with all this football talk. When Thane turned onto Cedar Street, Seth cleared his throat.

"So, Thane," Seth said, "now that I'm locked in as the coach at Summit, I plan on getting the team going right away. That way the kids will know those patterns like their own cell phone numbers."

"Nice," Thane said.

The energy in the truck suddenly amped up. Ty must have sensed it, because he stopped playing to listen. Troy sat up straight, and so did his mom.

"For sure," Seth said. "So . . . do you think you'll be getting Ty enrolled?"

CHAPTER TWENTY-SIX

THANE PULLED INTO THE driveway, put the truck in park, and took a deep breath before he turned to Seth. "Look, I'm really happy for you guys, and I know it's going to turn out great, but Ty and I have been talking . . ."

Troy looked over, straining his eyes to read Ty's face. His stomach sank when Ty looked down.

"We're gonna pass." Thane clasped his hands, laid them into his lap like an unread book, and looked directly at Seth. "I'm sorry."

Troy tried to cap his fury, but the lid had already been sprung. "I'm supposed to help *your* team win? You do this to us and I'm supposed to tell you what the defenses are doing so you can go to the *Super Bowl*, and you won't even let Ty be on our *team*?"

Troy could see two things immediately. First, that

his outburst had shocked his mom so much she didn't know what to say, and second, that everyone else was embarrassed. Troy folded his arms across his chest, ready to stand by his words.

Ty looked up and blinked, as if he was innocent.

Troy tried to keep quiet, but he burned with rage and he got in Ty's face. "Like you didn't know, right? Let's go out on the WaveRunners . . . *buddy . . . cousin.* Let's have a good time. Oh, by the way, you don't mind if I ruin your football season, right?

"Thanks a lot, Ty. Nice friend. Did you text *this* to Tate?"

"Troy, that's *enough!*" Troy's mom gripped his neck in the vise of her fingers and drew him away.

"It's a lot of things." Thane turned around in his seat, keeping his voice calm and quiet. "Let's not get crazy. St. Stephen's was always the plan. Things changed and now they're all mixed up. Ty's had a lot of upheaval. Things aren't always as simple as we'd like them to be."

Thane looked around. "Hey, we're still family. We can still do things like today. We should."

Seth held out a hand for Thane to shake. "I understand completely. Troy will, too. Sometimes he's a hothead."

Everyone looked at Troy. His mind was spinning from all the reasons Ty should be in Summit: their friendship, spending more time around Tate—if that was as important as it seemed—their chemistry on the field, and most of all how if Troy had Chuku *and* Ty to throw deep to, no team could double-cover them. Troy's mom sharpened her already furious eyes and squeezed the blood from her lips, setting her head on a crooked angle toward him and prompting him to say the right thing.

Troy held out a hand to Ty. "Sure. I understand. Maybe next year something will work out."

The look Ty gave him—one of sorrow, pain, and disappointment—flooded Troy with guilt, but only for an instant.

"Traitor," Troy whispered. He couldn't stand to even look at Thane as he slipped out of the truck.

Troy's mom, on the other hand, leaned forward and gave Thane a kiss on the cheek, whispering something Troy couldn't hear before she got out on the other side.

Ty looked up, his face heavy with shame, and gave Troy a fleeting glance before climbing into the front seat. Troy figured he wasn't the only one affected by the news, because they all stood there in the silent darkness watching the enormous truck swim up the street until it glimmered one final time and disappeared in the murk.

"Well." Seth tossed that single word out into the night and let it hang there.

That's when Troy's phone rang.

Troy fished it from his pocket and read the glowing screen. "It's Chuku."

"Hey, maybe we'll get lucky." Seth put a hand on Troy's shoulder. "One out of two wouldn't be bad."

Troy's fingers trembled and he fumbled with the phone before he answered the call.

CHAPTER TWENTY-SEVEN

"HEY, DAWG." TROY COULDN'T read Chuku's voice. He knew that whatever Chuku said next might determine the success or failure of the football season, maybe even have a lasting effect on Troy's entire career.

Troy took a breath, trying to sound casual. "Hey. What's up?"

"Man, you know that apartment you had us go look at?" Chuku paused for a moment that lasted a lifetime. "We *loved* it! Dawg, my dad's registering me at school tomorrow and we're moving in on Thursday! You, me, and chicken legs are gonna kill this New Jersey high school football thing. *Rat-a-tat-tat*, like a machine gun."

Troy laughed. "You jerk. You scared me. But . . ."

"But what? You can't kid a kidder. Don't give me that 'but' stuff."

"Ty's not coming."

Chuku went silent.

"Chuku? You there?"

Chuku clucked his tongue. "That just means more touchdowns for me, dawg. I like little chicken legs, don't get me wrong, but you and me? Never fear, Chuku's here. We gotta think of a *name* for ourselves, like the dynamic duo or something. Killer Kombo, you know, combo with a *k*. I like that. All right, well, all that later. I gotta go."

"You want some help on Thursday? Moving in?"

"Sure. That's great."

"I'll bring Tate."

"Who's he?"

"He's a she. You'll like her. Everybody likes Tate."

"Is she pretty?"

"Yeah, but that's not what I mean. She's like one of the guys."

"*And* she's pretty? You're right. I gotta meet Tate."

"Well, you will on Thursday." Troy hung up and grinned, and they all moved inside, uplifted by a bit of good news.

"Meant to be," his mom said. "And nice that you volunteered to help them get moved in. I'm proud of you, Troy. You're a good kid."

Troy couldn't help blushing, not for being a good kid, but because he had another reason for offering to help Chuku move in. He had a very big problem that he still needed to address, and helping Chuku just might give him the chance to fix it.

CHAPTER TWENTY-EIGHT

WHEN CHUKU MET TATE, he shook her hand and turned to Troy. "She's kind of skinny."

"*She* is standing right here." Tate stamped her foot on the concrete sidewalk. "*She* likes people with manners."

Chuku laughed. "Okay. I get it. You're a firecracker. Skinny, but lots of pop. I like that. No hard feelings. Let's start from the start."

Chuku held out his hand again. They shook, and smiled.

Troy and Tate helped unload the big U-Haul van Chuku and his dad had driven up from Baltimore. When they finished, Chuku's dad dropped them at the Summit Diner and gave them his credit card to get some burgers and milk shakes while he headed out to a doctor's appointment. They watched the big white Mercedes cruise away before going inside and taking seats in a red leather booth next to the window.

Chuku picked up a menu, then looked over the top. "I appreciate you dawgs coming around."

"You got something better you can call me than a 'dawg'?" Tate scowled.

"Well, it means friend," Chuku said.

"Friend is nice." Tate smiled.

Chuku sat up straight and spoke in a British accent. "I appreciate you 'friends' coming around. Cheerio."

Tate nodded as if that was okay with her. "You guys didn't have all that much stuff, anyway. It was easy."

"Yeah . . . we've moved a couple of times before," Chuku said, before dropping his voice. "After my mom left."

Troy could tell by the look on Tate's face that she was thinking of her dad, and that made him think of his own dad, now an orange-haired pirate.

No one said anything until the waitress took their order and swished away.

Troy felt that the time was right. "Hey, Chuku, I was thinking. I got a deal for you."

"Deal?"

"That Helena concert is next Wednesday, right?"

"And I can't *wait*." Chuku grinned.

"You going with your dad?" Troy asked.

"No, I was just gonna drive myself. Didn't you know

you can get a driver's license in New Jersey when you're thirteen?"

"Funny," Troy said, "but I was thinking . . . you've got *four* tickets. Maybe Tate and I could go with you."

Chuku looked suspiciously at Troy, then screwed up his face. "That why you wanted me to come here? That why you helped? Tickets?"

"No." Troy opened his hands and waved them at Chuku. "I want you here to catch touchdown passes. I'm not asking for them for free. They're your tickets. I'm not asking for them back, not even two of them. You won them, fair and square."

"You want to *buy* back two tickets? They're, like, at least a thousand dollars each, maybe two."

"I was thinking more like a trade."

"Trade for what?" Chuku asked.

"Who's your favorite Falcons player?"

"Falcons? Julio Jones. Why?"

"You collect jerseys, right? How about a signed Julio Jones game-worn jersey for those two tickets?"

"How? Seth Halloway?"

Troy nodded. "Coach Halloway, now."

"You like Helena that much?" Chuku asked.

"I like Helena, but it's more about being there. Mr. Cole is not a guy I want to make mad. He gave me the tickets so I could go, and I don't think he'd be too happy about me gambling them away."

Chuku was thinking. "How about Julio Jones *and*

Matt Ryan? Game-worn."

"Deal." Troy barely let the words get out of Chuku's mouth. He knew Seth could get the jerseys for him easily and he reached across the table, shaking Chuku's hand before his new friend could change his mind.

Troy's brain was spinning fast. "Hey, this is all between us, okay? One thing you can't do—either of you guys—is tell Seth. Okay?"

Troy stared at them both, wondering why the color suddenly drained from their faces. Then Troy felt a hand on his shoulder. He spun his head around and Seth sat down next to him in the booth.

"Tell me what?"

CHAPTER TWENTY-NINE

"**SETH, WHAT ARE YOU** doing here?" Troy asked.

"I was driving by and saw you two clowns and this lovely young lady in the window." Seth winked at Tate before he took one of Troy's French fries and dipped it in ketchup. "Tell me what?"

Slick as a snake, Troy cleared his throat and said, "Well, it was supposed to be a surprise, but we came up with a nickname."

"Nickname?" Seth raised his eyebrows and nicked another one of Troy's French fries. "For what?"

"Us." Troy nodded at Chuku, his mind spinning even faster. "'Killer Kombo.' Combo with a k. You know, like the Fab Five, or the Fun Bunch, or the Steel Curtain."

Seth ate another fry. "Hmm, usually people wait until they've done something pretty spectacular before they start giving themselves nicknames."

"We're not short on confidence." Troy grinned, happy to see Chuku nodding in agreement.

"Well," Seth said, chewing, "I guess it was Muhammad Ali who said, 'It ain't bragging if you can back it up,' or was that Deion Sanders? One of them. Maybe both."

"Oh, we'll back it up." Troy's grin broadened, more because he'd successfully diverted Seth's attention than because he loved the nickname.

Seth pointed at Chuku. "You know, your dad used to play on a defense in college they called the Brick Wall."

Chuku nodded. "I heard about that. You knew my dad?"

"Best linebacker Baylor ever had." Seth held out a fist and Chuku bumped it. "How about after lunch, we all head over to the field and get started on some patterns? Tate, you can run a few for us, too, right?"

Troy spoke up quickly before Chuku could make a wisecrack. "Tate was the kicker on our state championship junior league team in Georgia. You should have seen her tackle people on kickoffs."

Tate slurped her milk shake and Chuku tilted his head to consider her.

After they ate lunch and Chuku called his dad to let him know Seth was driving them back, they got into Seth's truck, stopping at a convenience store on their way to grab a few bottles of Gatorade. Troy and Chuku also grabbed a few snacks, even though they'd just eaten, and opened the packages in Seth's backseat.

"No crumbs." Seth glanced at them in the rearview mirror.

Chuku held a cheese Dorito over the seat, offering it to Tate.

"Thank you," she said, crunching it carefully.

"You guys won't be eating like that if you want to make it to the big leagues," Seth said into the mirror.

"I thought potatoes were a vegetable." Troy munched on a Pringles Dill Pickle potato chip.

"I don't even know if potatoes are in those things," Seth said. "They're, like, salted fat."

"You're only young once." Troy took another and shook a few out into the extended hands of his friends. "At least *we* are—young, that is."

Seth pulled into the school parking lot and stopped the truck. "Very funny, wise guy. I hope you're still laughing when you do that mile run tomorrow."

Troy's face fell. "What mile run?"

"I didn't tell you?" Seth pretended to be surprised. "You and Chuku got your physical tests tomorrow to see if you can play varsity."

"Are you serious?" Troy looked at Chuku to see if he was surprised, too.

"I was going to wait until tomorrow so you didn't get all nervous about it." Seth smiled. "But I'm getting so old, I was afraid I'd forget."

"Wow," Tate said, laughing as they got out of the truck. "That hurts. Remind me not to get on your bad side. Do they really have to take a test?"

"Yes," Seth said, "seriously, and it is tomorrow."

"I thought you just picked us," Troy said, feeling stubborn.

"What do we have to do besides run a mile?" Chuku asked.

"A mile in under eight minutes. Push-ups, pull-ups, sit-ups, stuff like that." Seth walked across the hot pavement of the empty parking lot with a football in hand. "It's a fitness test mandated by the state. If you pass, you're all set."

"Even if we can't do whatever it is we have to do, you can just fudge it for us, right?" Troy hurried to catch up.

Seth shook his head. "Nope."

"Seth," Troy said, "stop kidding around. You're not old. I was kidding."

"And I wish I was kidding about fudging it for you," Seth said. "Some guy named Coach Witherspoon gives the test. He's the high school phys ed teacher. Mr. Biondi told me he's fair but tough. He's also the wrestling coach, so he won't be cutting you guys any slack."

CHAPTER THIRTY

"WELL, COME ON." SETH started down the concrete steps toward the field. "I won't wear you guys out too bad, but we can get started on the basics and work on your chemistry."

"Killer Kombo Kemistry." Chuku grinned. "With three *k*'s."

The next day, Troy stared at the locker room door set into the back of the brick junior high school. "At least we got each other."

Bees buzzed around a big green Dumpster, but otherwise nothing moved in the heat. Beyond the parking lot, the school track circled a grass soccer field.

"You make it sound like we're condemned prisoners,"

Chuku said. "We just need to do some push-ups and run a few laps."

"For time," Troy reminded him. "In hundred-degree heat."

"Relax." Seth adjusted the air-conditioning of his shiny new black truck. "It's only ninety-three, and I'll be here watching. He's not gonna do anything crazy. You guys will be fine."

"Plus I'm here," Tate said, snapping her gum from the front seat.

"And you bring what to the table?" Chuku asked.

"Moral support." Tate spoke with the confidence of a guardian angel.

"I just don't see the point in all this," Troy said.

"It's supposed to make sure kids who are too young physically aren't brought up just to create bigger numbers," Seth said. "Every state has it. They don't want kids to get hurt. Anyway, we're here, and there he is. Let's go."

A small, pale blue Chevy Coupe pulled into the empty lot and Troy knew it had to be Coach Witherspoon. He emerged from the small car like a beetle shedding its skin. The man was enormous. He wore a Summit Wrestling cap and dark clip-on lenses over his glasses, but still used a hand to shield his eyes from the sun. Troy got out with Chuku and they went inside with the coach while Seth and Tate waited in the air-conditioned truck.

"Sorry it's so hot today, boys." Witherspoon clapped Troy on the back with a concrete hand when they reached the gym. "Okay, we'll start with pull-ups. All the way up and all the way down. If you don't go all the way up or all the way down, they don't count."

Troy swallowed and wiped the sweat from his brow. "How many?"

"How many? As many as you can?" the coach tittered. His face was like a full moon, with features too small for the vast space. His little mouth curled into a smile.

"How many to pass?" Chuku asked.

"Just ten," Witherspoon said, "so long as they're good ones. Go ahead, hop up."

Troy had no idea if he could do ten pull-ups. He'd never done them before, but he wasn't going to worry about that now. He jumped up and gripped the bar tight, clenching his jaw with determination. Grunting, he pulled himself up, touched his chin to the bar, then let himself down before pulling up again.

"No good," Witherspoon said, looking up from a clipboard. "All the way down. Your arms have to be fully extended. I can't just let you boys play varsity if you don't have the strength and endurance to be competitive."

Troy touched his chin, then let his arms hang all the way straight before starting to pull up again. This time, it was a strain. He grunted and gritted his teeth harder. His chin touched the bar again.

"One," Witherspoon said encouragingly.

Troy let himself down again and couldn't help glancing at Chuku. Chuku's eyes were wide and his mouth was stretched and frozen in horror. Troy pulled himself up again, straining and nearly missing with his chin.

"Two," the coach said. "Make sure you touch your chin. That one was real close. You have to be able to do it right to play."

Troy closed his eyes and let his arms hang straight. He felt a wave of nausea, not because of the strain, but because at this rate he knew he'd never make it.

CHAPTER THIRTY-ONE

SOMEHOW, HE DID.

Troy and Chuku, both of them, barely scraped out the required number of exercises. Coach Witherspoon made them do everything by the exact word of the book. He even *had* some book issued by the state. He showed it to them. Troy bet that if anyone else in the world had given them the test, it would have been ten times easier.

When they stepped out into the blazing-hot parking lot, Troy gave Seth and Tate a thumbs-up. Seth grinned from behind his steering wheel and he nudged Tate, who was probably texting Ty, as usual. The new truck's engine whirred like a jet engine to keep the cool AC pumping despite the heat. Chrome from the grille and rims glittered in the sun. Troy's limbs felt numb as he staggered after Coach Witherspoon across the lot and out onto the track. Troy stopped and Chuku bumped into him, nearly sending them both sprawling on the steaming rubber surface.

"You okay?" Troy asked under his breath.

"I'm ready to fall over," Chuku said.

"Just this mile and we're done."

"Then the pool back at my place," Chuku said.

"That's it, think of the pool. We both will."

"Iced tea," Chuku said. "Sweet. With lemon."

Troy licked his dry lips. "Okay, enough. Focus on the mile. I know you're fast, but don't jump out like a jackrabbit. You gotta pace yourself, so stay with me."

Chuku nodded.

Witherspoon dropped his clipboard in the grass just off the track. Without any ceremony, he held up his stopwatch.

"Four laps. Eight minutes. Ready? Go!"

Neither of them was ready, but Troy could see that Witherspoon had already started the watch. He grabbed Chuku's shoulder, tugging him along. "Come on, let's go!"

Troy made the first bend by forcing himself to put one foot in front of the other. His legs were Jell-O from the fifty squat-thrusts Coach Witherspoon had made them do in under three minutes. No one had said anything about squat-thrusts, but there they were. Chuku stumbled.

"Dig *deep*!" Troy knew the whole thing about playing at Summit meant more to him than Chuku. Even as a long snapper, Chuku's dad made enough to send him to St. Stephen's with Ty if he really wanted. Chuku could tell Witherspoon and the rest of Summit to pound sand.

"Come on." Troy huffed.

"What'd you say?" Chuku huffed and puffed.

"Nothing. Come on. Dig deep."

They were closing in on the first lap. Witherspoon counted out loud.

"One minute forty-seven, one minute forty-eight, one minute forty-nine . . ."

Troy did a quick calculation. They'd have to do almost as good on the next three laps as they had on the first. He also knew the way his legs felt and the way Chuku was staggering that it wasn't likely. Pain burned through the numbness of his legs. By the second lap, they'd eroded much of their cushion.

Sweat glistened on Coach Witherspoon's pasty forehead and he called out, "Three minutes fifty-seven, three fifty-eight, three fifty-nine."

Even if they kept the rate of the second lap, it wouldn't be good enough. A sharp pain attacked Troy's side and he twisted his body, seeking some relief.

"What's wrong?" Chuku huffed out.

"Cramp." Troy winced. He felt hot tears in his eyes. It was so unfair. It had to be a hundred degrees on the hot rubber track, likely more.

The cramp only got worse. It felt like a knife in his gut.

There was no way Troy could make it.

CHAPTER THIRTY-TWO

IT WAS CHUKU'S TURN to pull Troy along. "We can do this."

As they closed out the third lap, Troy realized Seth had gotten out of his truck. He stood on the edge of the grass like a soldier with his hands clasped behind his back, his face unmoving, and his eyes hidden behind sunglasses. Tate stood beside him with her arms folded and when she saw Troy looking, she pumped a fist in the air. The sight of them gave Troy a surge of determination.

"Six minutes ten, six eleven, six twelve . . ."

Troy knew he'd have to run his fastest lap yet, even though his insides burned more than his legs. A grunt escaped him from somewhere deep down inside. He pumped his arms, focusing on them because he knew his legs would follow, and his arms were the only thing on his body not crying out in pain.

"Come. Run." Those were the only words he could grunt out to Chuku as he began to pull away. He didn't want to leave Chuku, but he had to. He couldn't fall short, even if Chuku did. Chuku had options; Troy had none.

It seemed like forever. He could only dream of water and shade, shade and water, oh, how he'd suck them both up like a sponge. Troy took the final turn thinking that he'd never make it. Just then, with the slap of feet on the track and the high-pitched wheezing of a dying man, Chuku surged past him, pumping his head up and down like an idiot doll.

"Come on! Come on!" Chuku urged.

Troy pumped his head, too. Maybe it would work. He could hear Witherspoon's heartless counting.

"Seven forty-nine, seven fifty, seven fifty-one . . ."

Troy pumped and grunted and groaned so loud, he lost track of the numbers. He pulled even with Chuku.

"Yes!" Chuku's choked scream urged him on even more.

Together they stumbled and threw themselves across the line, tripping into two heaps on the track.

Troy rolled over and looked up, sucking in air and twisting in pain. He shielded his eyes from the sun to try to read the coach's face.

"Did we make it?" Troy croaked.

CHAPTER THIRTY-THREE

COACH WITHERSPOON WAS SMILING. He held up his watch to show eight minutes exactly. "You did it, boys!"

Seth's deep belly laugh thundered across the field, cut intermittently by Tate's high-pitched squeals of delight.

"I'll go in and do the paperwork to make it official," Coach Witherspoon said.

"Ha!" Troy burst out, reaching for Chuku. They clasped hands and nodded from where they lay on the ground. As the world stopped its spinning, they watched Coach Witherspoon march off.

"We made it!" Troy hooted and doubled over, lying on his side. Chuku slapped him repeatedly on the back, roaring with laughter himself.

CHAPTER THIRTY-FOUR

SETH HAD THE NAME and phone numbers for last year's players, and he wasn't wasting a minute getting a team together. He sat down with Mr. Biondi as well as Coach Witherspoon to add wrestlers, basketball players, baseball players, and lacrosse players—kids who had the skills but no desire to play on a losing football team—to the mix.

With a list of nearly sixty potential candidates Seth burned up the phone lines talking about how Summit would have a winning season.

A few days later, forty-three players showed up to get their lockers. The roster was nearly double what it had been in the past few years. Eighteen of the recruits hadn't played football in high school before.

Troy and Chuku traded glances as the older kids

marched in, many of them with whiskers or the shadows from shaving. At least ten were enormous, over two hundred and fifty pounds by Troy's guess, and a couple looked as if they'd tilt the scales at three hundred.

Clustered in a rough semicircle around a huge grease-board in the makeshift team room, their faces glowed with admiration at the sight of Seth Halloway, the Falcons' star linebacker. Many couldn't keep themselves from pointing and whispering in giddy undertones.

To a man, they eyed Chuku and Troy with curiosity and suspicion. Troy folded his arms across his chest and sat up as straight as he could, feeling skinny and young. Chuku didn't seem to mind as much, but he wasn't saying anything, either, and that was unusual.

The excitement in the room swelled as Seth introduced some of his new coaches, starting with Coach Sindoni, the offensive coordinator from CBA. Wes Dove, an old friend and college teammate of Seth's who played with the Seahawks, would coach the offensive line. Ron Osinski coached Seth in high school. He'd take the defensive backs and also coach the running backs, while Frank Conover from the Cleveland Browns handled the defensive line.

After handing out a calendar for the summer schedule that included all the voluntary practices, Seth lectured the players about what he expected from them on and off the field. It seemed as if he'd finished when he cleared his throat and motioned Troy and Chuku to come up to stand beside him.

"Now," Seth said. "I'm sure you've seen these two. This is Troy White and Chuku Moore, and they *are* different. They're eighth graders, younger than any of you, younger than any players you're likely to see on a high school varsity team. They're here because they will help us win. That's what this is all about. You guys are gonna work like you never imagined, but it's gonna pay off. The payoff in football is winning, something you haven't experienced. That all changes. These two will go through tryouts just like the rest of you. They both had to pass a pretty vigorous physical test to make it here, and when you see what they bring to our football team, you'll be glad we have them.

"All right, I've got your locks here. Seniors come up first, you get to choose your lockers, then juniors and on down the line."

The room erupted and Troy and Chuku stood aside. No one said anything to either of them until a huge lineman Troy recognized as Mr. Bryant's son held out a meaty hand.

"I'm Chance." His voice was as big as he was and his hand swallowed Troy's whole like a gumdrop.

"Troy."

Chance grinned. "Glad you're here. You, too."

Chance shook Chuku's hand, then disappeared toward the locker room with the other seniors.

"Thanks." Troy blinked at the older player's enormous

back and nudged Chuku. "Nice, right?"

Chuku rolled his eyes at the ceiling. "Man, by the time we get our locks, we'll get stuck in the corners."

"Who cares," Troy said. "We're on the *varsity*."

"Just where we belong, dawg. Just where we belong."

Troy and Chuku finally got their locks from Seth.

"I hope I didn't embarrass you guys," Seth said, "but I figured meet this thing head-on."

"We're not *that* young," Chuku said.

Seth raised an eyebrow and tilted his head. "That apartment you got doesn't have any mirrors?"

Chuku laughed.

"Look." Seth's face turned serious. "I want these guys to treat you with respect, but there's also going to be a little razzing you're gonna have to put up with. Just go with it, okay? Troy? Don't get hotheaded on me. Let the small stuff slide."

"No problem," Troy said. "Really. I got it. Come on, Chuku."

Chuku followed Troy out the side door of the team room, down the hallway, and into the locker room, which was next to the gym. Chatter bounced off the tile walls like rain pounding a tin roof. When Troy and Chuku walked in, it got quiet.

One of the older players who had a brush cut with dark hair and eyes so blue they were closer to purple broke out of the crowd and sauntered over to Chuku and Troy.

He pointed at the corner of the locker room where two empty lockers stood gaping at them. "That'll be our kindergarten corner."

The older player snickered and Troy noticed the barbed-wire tattoo circling the muscles of his upper right arm.

"Tell 'em, Grant!" someone from the crowd shouted, then cackled.

Troy looked to where Chance Bryant was sitting on the bench in front of his locker on the far side of the room, so intent on screwing a cleat into the bottom of his shoe that his tongue poked out of the corner of his mouth. Troy's fist was clenching for a fight, but Chuku grabbed him and propelled him toward the empty lockers.

"Just let us know when nap time is over and we'll meet you guys down on the field," Chuku said.

Several of the players laughed. Seth tooted his whistle from the door and told them to get into their cleats and get down on the field in five, and the normal bustle returned to the room.

Troy leaned close and his voice was hot. "*Nap time? Seriously?* You had to go along with that junk?"

"Come on." Chuku slapped him on the back. "Let's do our talking on the field."

CHAPTER THIRTY-FIVE

OUT ON THE FOOTBALL field, Seth called his new team together and had everyone take a knee. Several of the coaches on Seth's staff had arrived and they stood like giant boulders turned upright. The players had no helmets or pads because practice wasn't "official" yet, but Troy knew every good high school football team worked out together all summer long in shorts and T-shirts. Seth had already started to explain how the practice would run when a couple of kids wandered up. Seth looked at his watch and gave them a deadly stare.

"You're late." Seth's voice sent a shiver through Troy.

One kid shrugged. "The email said this was voluntary, Coach."

"Voluntary?" Seth scrunched up his face. "Voluntary

means mandatory if you want to win. You got that? Do you?"

The boy nodded and took a knee.

"I don't know how things have been around here," Seth said, "but I can guess. I know you haven't been winning. That's going to change, but it's not what I'm going to do that will change it, it's what *you're* going to do. The next time we do anything, anyone who shows up late will run. I should say run extra, because you're all going to be doing more running than you ever knew you could."

There were a few groans.

"Who made that noise?" Seth barked at them, scowling. "You think this is *fun*? I'll tell you what's fun . . . *winning*. That's the only thing that's fun about football. You don't win, it stinks. You win? It's heaven on earth. But you don't win without *work*, so get ready to do a lot of that. You've got coaches like you never had before, coaches who've played at the highest levels and coaches who've won championships. Listen to them. Learn from them."

Seth told everyone to go with the coach for the position they wanted to play when he blew the whistle.

"But don't get cozy," Seth added. "I'll be the one to decide your position, not you. It's a team game, so I'll put you where the team needs you. And if you don't like it, you can go out for Ping-Pong."

At the sound of the whistle Troy and Chuku gave each other a fist bump, then ran to their spots. Two quarterbacks from last year also headed for Coach Sindoni. Grant Reed—the jerk with the Kindergarten Corner joke—was one. The other was a junior—Billy Tomkins, who wore his straight blond hair just past his shoulders. The two older players ignored Troy, throwing the ball between themselves to warm up. Maybe because he was thinking more about showing them up than what he was doing, Troy's first pass to Coach Sindoni went into the turf, where it skittered and bounced away.

The older quarterbacks snickered. Coach Sindoni went to chase down the ball and Grant Reed hissed at Troy, "You stink, you little fruitcake. Go home to your mama before someone pounds your head in."

"What's that, Reed?" Coach Sindoni hollered as he returned to his spot.

"Told him to keep his elbow up, Coach." Reed grinned at Billy Tomkins.

"I'll do the coaching," Coach Sindoni snarled.

Tomkins looked at Troy and dragged a thumb across his own throat, signaling that Troy was as good as dead. Troy set his teeth and fired another pass at Coach Sindoni, a perfect spiral.

"Nice," the coach said.

When the coach looked away, Troy flipped his fingers under his chin at the two older boys. He knew better than to act afraid, no matter what he felt inside, and this wasn't a joke in the locker room anymore. This was football. The two older players rewarded him by making baby noises, *goo-goo* and *ga-ga*, every time Coach Sindoni got out of earshot. Troy ignored that because it was just stupid, but he got the feeling that Tomkins—the bigger and stronger of the two, even though he was a year younger than Reed—wasn't really into the whole thing. He was simply going along with Reed's meanness.

After a while, the receivers joined them and they began to run some basic pass patterns. Chuku jumped right out at everyone, literally. If the ball was too high, he could launch himself through the air to get to it, and the ball seemed to just stick to his fingers as if they were made of something other than flesh and blood.

Reed had a strong arm and he threw every pass to show it off. When a tall, skinny receiver with freckles named Spencer Gentry—a sophomore—did a short crossing route and Reed fired a bullet two yards behind him, Spencer barely got a hand on it. The deflected ball skittered across the turf.

"Catch the darn thing, will you?" Reed barked. "You get your hands on it, you catch it."

Spencer hung his head as he jogged to the back of the line.

Troy stepped up to take the next turn and whispered to Reed under his breath, "If you want him to catch it, throw it to him."

Troy took the snap, dropped back, and laid a touch pass into Chuku, who had run the same short crossing route.

"Careful, or I'll smash your face in whether you're the coach's little pet or not," Reed whispered back.

"You'd be the coach's pet if you knew how to win a game." Troy spoke loud enough for the others to hear.

"You think the rest of us care because you were on TV?" Reed sneered and raised his voice, too.

Chuku marched right over to where the quarterbacks stood. "Don't have to worry about anyone putting you on TV. They wouldn't know which end was your face and which was your butt."

Some of the players laughed and Chuku grinned all around, but Reed didn't take his hateful eyes off Troy.

"You're a little circus freak, you know that?" Reed growled.

"Loser." Troy snarled right back.

"Hey!" Sindoni shouted. "You two got something to say?"

"What's going on?" Seth stepped into the drill with a tight jawline and a frown.

"These two can't seem to get along." Coach Sindoni pointed to Troy and Reed.

Seth stared at Troy and Reed for a moment with a look of disgust. "Troy, take a lap. Go!"

Troy's mouth fell open. "But—"

"Okay, take two." Seth folded his arms across his chest.

CHAPTER THIRTY-SIX

TROY DROPPED HIS HEAD and took off running. By the time he'd finished, the entire team was together, running plays, offense against the defense. Reed was running the offense with the first team, which Seth had named based on seniority. Troy gritted his teeth. It felt as if steam was pouring out of his ears.

He stood watching the first team run plays against a defense holding padded shields since there was no real blocking or tackling going on. Troy knew the coaches were just trying to get the team to learn a few new plays and line up in the right places. After three plays, Coach Sindoni swapped Reed out for Tomkins. Troy twisted his lips and bit into the side of his mouth.

When Seth appeared beside him, Troy ignored him, staring straight ahead and pretending to watch.

"Relax," Seth whispered. "Trust me. It'll all work out."

"You said I could *start*." Troy's voice quavered with anger.

Seth turned to him. "Do you trust me?"

Troy ground his teeth, but nodded.

"Then relax. I didn't say *when* you'd start. You don't just come in and take over when there's a senior quarterback who started last year, no matter how bad the team is. You gotta ease into it, especially because you're so young. They're gonna be tough enough on you for that alone. *I* know what you can do, but you've got to show your stuff to everyone else. Let it happen. Don't be in such a rush. I know what I'm doing."

Troy felt a bit calmer. He did trust Seth. He had a hundred questions, but the tone of Seth's voice kept him from speaking. He remembered a similar situation when Seth had been coaching the Georgia Junior League All-Star team. He didn't start Troy then, either. Instead, he waited until it was clear to everyone that Troy was the best player at the position. He'd get his chance. He'd just have to wait, something he hated but could do.

Seth wandered away, barking out instructions occasionally but for the most part letting the other coaches take care of business with their individual players.

After about ten plays, Seth shouted, "Okay, get some backups in!"

The coaches started making substitutions. Troy, Chuku, two more receivers—Spencer and Levi Kempka—and some other kids Troy didn't know got to join the huddle. Troy called the play Coach Sindoni gave him and went to the line. Troy took the snap, dropped back, and threw a perfect strike to Chuku down the sideline. The offense hooted and hollered, loving the fact that they finally scored on the defense. Troy showed very little emotion, instead calling the offense back into the huddle. The next play, Troy threw a touch pass to Levi over the middle for a twenty-yard gain. The third play was a deep out to Spencer, thrown on a flat line, and caught by Chuku, who planted the toes of both feet inside the white line before going out of bounds. The two older quarterbacks had run the same plays but come nowhere near Troy's accuracy throwing the ball.

Finally, Troy went back to Chuku on a comeback, perfectly timed, and something they couldn't have done without days of hard work at the Jets practice field with Ty. The defender overran Chuku, who darted into the end zone. In half the number of plays, Troy had scored twice when the older players hadn't scored at all. Seth blew his whistle and shouted for the team to take a water break. On the far side of the field was a water horse, a section of pipe with holes every couple of feet so a dozen players could drink at the same time. Troy jogged over with the rest of the team and took his drink.

When he finished, Troy walked right by Reed. As he passed, Reed whapped him in the back of the head. Troy staggered and nearly fell over. He spun around, red-faced. The rest of the players stared at him to see what he'd do. Reed had three inches on him and about fifty pounds. The veins in his muscular forearms swelled above his fists and the barbed-wire tattoo twitched.

"Come on," Reed snarled. "What you gonna do about it?"

CHAPTER THIRTY-SEVEN

TROY GLARED FOR A few seconds, unblinking.

"Hey!" Chuku stepped up with his grin. "How about a little brotherly love here? I know you all ain't *brothers*, but in Baltimore we'd call each other brothers anyway and it's not a race thing, either. I got plenty of white *brothers*."

Chuku patted Grant Reed on the back as if the two of them were old friends and Reed had no idea what to do.

Troy used the opening to turn and walk away.

He felt the disappointment in the players around him. They were looking for a showdown, but Troy knew better. He wasn't stupid. Getting into a fistfight with Reed could get him hurt *and* in trouble.

"That's right, run, you little wimp."

Troy's ears burned.

"Don't mind him, Troy," Chuku warned. "He's mixing up his bark and his bite is all."

Troy stopped and turned, keeping his head high. "Last I checked, this isn't a fight club. It's a football team, and I bet some of these guys are tired of getting their butts kicked every Friday night. That's where I come in, because you gotta have a good quarterback to *win*."

Reed closed the gap between them, grabbing a fistful of Troy's shirt, his eyes scanning the other side of the field to make sure the coaches weren't looking. "You pencil-necked little wimp, you think you're better than *me*?"

Troy stared right back at him. "I know I am, and so do you . . ."

There was a low, growling noise behind Troy. "Hey. Let him go."

Troy turned and saw Chance Bryant baring his teeth.

"Yeah." Big Nick Lee, the starting center on the offensive line, stepped up. "Let him go. You're not afraid of him, are you?"

"Afraid of *what*?" Reed shoved Troy away from him, dusting his hands.

"Afraid he'll take your job?" Nick Lee said.

"Are you kidding?" Reed said. "This little baby?"

"Good." Chance Bryant rumbled like a belch of

thunder. "Then leave him alone. If he *is* our quarterback, you don't touch him. No one does. You know that. No one touches our quarterback, whether it's you . . . or him."

Troy tried not to grin, but so much delight bubbled up inside him, it had to come out somewhere.

Chuku leaned close, sharing his smile. "Looks like *you* got a pair of guardian angels, brother."

"Who's the second?" Troy asked.

"Do you not realize how close that caveman was to being laid out by the good-looking part of the Killer Kombo?" Chuku made a flourishing motion with his hand before he touched his own chest.

On the far side of the field, Seth's whistle blew, ending the drama.

CHAPTER THIRTY-EIGHT

THE VERY NEXT EVENING, Seth's new team had its second practice, and the obvious separation of abilities between Troy and the two older quarterbacks only grew.

Troy and Chuku each seemed to know what the other was thinking, and they completed every pass. Spencer and Levi, too, quickly developed good rhythms with Troy.

"Okay." Coach Sindoni knelt down in the second-string huddle with a greaseboard. "You guys look like you're ready for something a little more advanced. I call this 'Sticks and Stones,' because it'll break the defense's bones."

The coach drew up a play that had Spencer and Chuku run deep crossing routes with Levi and the other outside receiver running comebacks. Troy repeated the name of the play and gave them a snap count. He broke the huddle and approached the center. Troy read the defense in front of him—the defense they hoped to break.

Troy called the cadence and took the snap. His corps of young receivers took off down the field. Troy pumpfaked to Chuku, drawing the free safety to one side, then launched a strike to Spencer that left him in the end zone with the ball held high.

Troy hooted and he and his receivers all bumped fists on their way back to the huddle. Troy couldn't help overhearing Seth as he walked up to Coach Sindoni. "We're awfully young."

"And we're awfully good, too," Coach Sindoni replied with a grin.

Even though the night went well, Seth lined them up after practice and made them run cross-fields until Big Nick Lee puked. Seth frowned at the mess on his sideline but said nothing. Instead, he blew his whistle to call them all in. The night had begun to cool and bugs whizzed through the glow of the stadium lights above them. The players surrounded Seth on one knee, panting and sweating hard.

Seth asked, "You guys know why I made you run so hard? Big Nick Lee, you okay?"

Nick Lee wiped puke from the corner of his mouth, nodded, and grinned.

The team only huffed and puffed, trying to catch their collective breath.

Seth snorted. "I had you guys run hard to show you how doggone out of shape you are. You've been doing things here the wrong way for a long time. We can turn this thing around—we *will* turn this thing around—but it's gonna take a lot of hard work. You can't be a champion if you don't work like a champion. And champions? Well, they run until they puke. That's just part of it, right, Nick?"

Everyone chuckled at Big Nick Lee.

"Bring it in for a break." Seth held up a fist for everyone to reach for. "'Work like champions' on three. One, two, three—"

"Work like champions!" the team shouted. Then they began to disperse like weary soldiers after a long battle.

As they walked off the field, Seth leaned close to Troy and spoke in a whisper. "See? You can get just as much work done on second team as you can on the first. It'll all work out. You did great."

"Thanks," Troy said. He saw Grant Reed walking in front of them and wished Seth had only spoken the words a little louder so that jerk could have heard.

Chuku fell in alongside them, all smiles. "How was that?"

Seth put a hand on Chuku's shoulder. "Very nice, my friend. You earned your signing bonus tonight."

Chuku laughed at the joke, and only Troy noticed when Grant Reed glanced back at them with a mean smile that told Troy he had heard what Seth said.

CHAPTER THIRTY-NINE

CHUKU'S SIGNED JULIO JONES and Matt Ryan game jerseys arrived the next day at Troy's house. With Tate looking over his shoulder, Troy tore open the box and pulled out the Julio jersey before he noticed that the chunky UPS man was holding out a pen, waiting for him to sign for the package. Troy took it and scribbled his name on the paper attached to the clipboard.

The UPS man's gray handlebar mustache twitched as he spoke. "That's some jersey. Signed and everything, huh."

"Game-worn. Matt Ryan, too." Troy held up the second jersey, proud of his work. "You know Seth Halloway, the Falcons' linebacker?"

"Yeah, he's the coach here now. I saw that in the paper."

"He got these from the team. Everyone in Atlanta loves Seth."

"You're a lucky guy." The UPS man nodded at the jerseys. "The real thing."

"Yeah, they are the real deal." Troy admired it. "Not for me, though I wish they were. No, these belong to my man Chuku Moore, payment in full."

"Well," the UPS man said as he put the pen into the shirt pocket of his brown uniform and turned to go, "it's a good day to be Chuku Moore, then, right?"

Troy thanked the driver and went inside. The truck ground its gears and trundled off down the street.

"Why did you say that?" Tate asked.

"What?"

"'Payment in full.' I don't know, Troy." Tate shook her head. "That didn't sound good."

Troy snorted. "Payment from *me* to Chuku."

"I know that," Tate said, "and you know that, but *that guy* doesn't."

"You know, Tate." Troy growled a bit. "Sometimes you just overthink things. You think that guy even knows who Chuku Moore is?"

"Not now he doesn't," she said. "But if what you want to happen really happens—I mean, you guys turning this football team around—everyone in this town is going to know Chuku Moore."

Troy bit the inside of his lip to keep from saying

something mean. After all, Tate had her father to worry about. Still, it made him mad.

It made him mad because he knew Tate was right.

He'd been stupid.

CHAPTER FORTY

THAT EVENING THEY DIDN'T have practice. It was a good thing because it was the night of the Helena concert. Tate had tried to convince Troy to take Ty instead of her, but Troy just wasn't going to do that. He hadn't even spoken to his cousin since the day at the beach.

"You guys are going to have to talk. The whole thing is tearing Ty up. You guys are family, Troy." Tate held up her phone as if Ty were on the other end of the line.

It annoyed Troy, the amount of texting back and forth Tate did with Ty. In a way he felt that Ty didn't deserve to be friends with Tate all the time if he wasn't even going to the same school as the rest of them. Wasn't Ty a traitor? He opened his mouth to say so but realized it would sound pretty dumb.

Instead, he shrugged. "I don't think he cares all that

much. If he did, his brother could get him in, trust me. Besides, none of that matters to my mom. No way is she going to let me go without you, Tate. You know that. You're not just my best friend, you're our guest."

That ended it, but Troy knew Tate would try again to get him together with Ty. That's just how she was.

Chuku and his dad picked up Troy and Tate in the big white Mercedes. Chuku turned around in the front seat and flashed the tickets and backstage passes like a winning poker hand. Troy handed over the signed jerseys and Chuku handed him and Tate two of the tickets and passes Mr. Cole had given to Troy in the first place. It was a relief for Troy to have them back in his own hands.

Chuku tugged the Julio Jones jersey on over his T-shirt and jeans and stuffed the Matt Ryan jersey under the front seat. "Awesome. I don't know if I should tell you this, but I was going to invite you anyway."

"What?" Troy's stomach squirmed because he thought of what he'd said to the delivery man.

"You're my quarterback, dude." Chuku grinned back at Troy. "And I wouldn't hang you out to dry with the team owner. I'm not that guy. What? Why so glum? It was no big deal for you to get these, right?"

"No," Troy said, "it was easy. Happy to do it."

"What are friends for, right?" Chuku turned back around.

Troy didn't want to do it, but he couldn't resist looking

over at Tate. She wore a frown and Troy looked away.

The parking pass that came with the tickets let them drive right underneath Yankee Stadium. They passed through several security checkpoints and a metal detector before arriving backstage in a greenroom the size of a small warehouse. Silky drapes covered the walls and comfortable leather couches and chairs rested in groups atop thick rugs. Clusters of fat candles flickered and glowed on every tabletop. Off to one side was a huge buffet, but waiters and waitresses dressed in white shirts roamed through the throng of people with silver trays covered with drinks and food. In the center of it all sat Helena, surrounded by a dozen people. Mr. Cole sat next to her, holding her hand and looking at her like a bedazzled schoolboy.

It was the first time Troy ever remembered seeing the owner look relaxed and happy. When Mr. Cole saw the four of them, he waved them over and introduced them to the megastar. Helena was polite but quiet. She wore her long blond hair in a thick braid. She softly praised Mr. Moore for making the team, then turned to Troy.

"So, you're the one who helped the Falcons win the Super Bowl?" Her big eyes seemed to hold the power of the universe and her smile, its light.

"I . . . kind of." Troy lost his ability to speak.

"Oh, good." She touched his arm. "I know you'll do it again for the Jets this year, right?"

"He sure will." Tate stepped forward and extended a hand to shake. "Tate McGreer, ma'am."

Helena laughed. "You're a spitfire."

"I played football with Troy until last year. I've seen what he can do." Tate beamed at the star singer. "I was the kicker, but you can ask Troy. I made some tackles of my own on the kickoffs. My mom's making me be a young lady now, though, so I'm playing soccer."

"I bet the boys are happy you're not out there, knocking them down." Helena grinned at Chuku. "Right?"

"She'd have to catch me to knock *me* down." Chuku thumped his chest, then took out his iPhone. "How about a picture? It'll be worth something someday."

Mr. Cole seemed surprised. "It's worth a lot right now."

"I mean for Helena, Mr. Cole." Chuku grinned. "No offense, but when I'm an NFL star with my own reality TV show, just like T.O., she can say she knew me when."

Mr. Moore rolled his eyes but Mr. Cole only laughed.

Not for the first time Troy wished he had Chuku's easy ability to charm people.

"Helena? You hear that? You better get one while you can," the owner said.

Helena smiled and stood up in her long white dress to take a picture with Chuku, then Troy, then Tate, and finally with Mr. Moore and Seth Cole and all of them together, before a man wearing all black with a wireless headset came fretting into their midst and hustled her off to get into her costume.

They watched her go with the NFL owner hurrying along beside her.

"Wow," Tate said. "I can't believe that really just happened."

"Stick with us." Chuku put an arm around Troy's neck. "This is just the beginning for the Killer Kombo."

Mr. Moore snorted and shook his head. "Come on. Let's get some food. All this bologna is making me hungry."

Troy piled a plate with lamb chops, ribs, and French fries. They ate at a cocktail table standing up and watched the swirl of people moving through and around the big room before Mr. Moore looked at his watch and said they better get to their seats.

They walked down some stairs next to the stage, through a throng of security guards, and sat in the front row. When Helena came out, the roar of the crowd reminded Troy of the Super Bowl. He and Tate plugged their ears, nudged each other, and shared a quick high five.

The night flew by. Like everyone else, they sang along with Helena's most popular songs—and by the time it was over and they were walking down into the parking garage with their ears ringing from the noise, it seemed to Troy as if the whole thing was worth it, no matter what trouble might come down the line.

That's what Troy said to Tate after Chuku and his dad dropped them off, and they waved good-bye, shouting thank-yous from the front porch.

"What do you mean?" Tate asked as the Mercedes taillights disappeared up the street.

Troy shrugged. "It was just so awesome, I can't imagine any trouble big enough to not be worth all that. That was once in a lifetime. I mean . . . Helena. We met her. She called you a spitfire."

"Tonight was great," Tate said, "but don't say that."

"Why?"

"I've just got a feeling those tickets are going to end up costing a lot more than you think."

CHAPTER FORTY-ONE

TROY DIDN'T LIKE WHERE the conversation was going. He opened the door without a sound and stepped inside, stopping in the hallway outside the kitchen, where he heard Seth and his mom talking. He knew he should announce himself, but there was something about their voices—maybe it was their hushed tone, maybe it was a slight strain of their words. Whatever it was, he held a finger to his lips, signaling Tate to be quiet, and stood in the hallway, listening.

"Are you sure?" His mother's voice sounded almost alarmed.

"Pretty much," Seth said, grim.

"I can't even believe this," his mother said. "What about Troy?"

"What about him?"

There was a silence that made Troy worry they either heard or sensed his presence. He slowly turned and began to silently lead Tate back out the front door, planning to reenter the house noisily to erase suspicion. Then his mother spoke.

"I just think . . . shouldn't we tell him?"

"No, don't do that," Seth said. "Let's see how it plays out. We might be making a big deal out of nothing."

Troy's stomach pushed up, crowding his throat and nearly choking him. He thought of the things he'd done wrong lately and their consequences. Nothing jumped to mind that would make them talk like this. The jersey thing with Chuku was kind of a mistake, but nothing that should make them act like this.

Whatever it was, Troy wanted to know. The uncertainty was killing him. He felt his legs coiling to move on their own, ready to burst into the kitchen so he could demand to know what in the world they were talking about.

CHAPTER FORTY-TWO

TROY'S LEGS GREW WEAK instead. Growing up in their tiny cabin back in the pine woods outside Atlanta, he had learned well the lesson of privacy. His mother would erupt like a volcano if she knew he had stood there in the dark hall, listening. So, instead of going forward, he backed up, leading Tate, stepping softly, and letting them back out through the screen door. He took a breath of the night air. Tate stared at him and shook her head with disapproval.

"Just trust me," Troy whispered to Tate before he swung open the door, let it bang behind him, and shouted, "Mom! We're home."

He walked straight to the kitchen door with Tate in tow, swinging it open as well and finding Seth and his mom where he already knew they'd be, sitting at the table with mugs of steaming tea. A plate with nothing but coffee cake crumbs rested between them.

"How was it?" his mom asked.

"Great!" Tate said.

"Awesome. Didn't you get my text?" Troy reached into the fridge for a couple of sodas, handing one to Tate.

"Yes, I got the picture." His mom tapped her phone. "Amazing. She looks beautiful."

"I guess," Troy said, sitting down at the table.

"Not more beautiful than your mom, though," Seth said.

"Please." His mom flicked Seth's arm.

"I'm serious." Seth flicked her right back.

"He's right, Mom." Troy raised his soda can her way. He knew enough to get in on a good thing.

"I'm in on that," Tate said.

"Okay, thank you all. Enough now," she said. "I'm glad you enjoyed the concert. It was very nice of Mr. Cole."

"Yeah, thanks, Seth," Troy said.

"What did Seth do?" his mom asked.

Tate stared hard at the soda bottle she clutched with both hands.

Troy never told his mom about how he'd lost the tickets on a bet with Chuku, or how he'd relied on Seth to get him the jerseys to trade back for the tickets. She wouldn't appreciate either of those things, and it had been a mistake for him to slip and thank Seth. Still, Troy had another gift besides being able to predict plays in the NFL. Maybe it was connected. He sometimes thought so. Whatever the source, he could process information instantly and come up with—well, he didn't like to call them lies; they were more like stories, because they weren't really harmful if you took the time to consider all the facts.

Whatever you called it, Troy didn't even blink before the words were gushing from his mouth. "If it wasn't for Seth in the very beginning, none of these things would ever have happened."

His mom pressed her lips together and nodded at the truth of it. Seth was the one who believed in Troy's ability and brought his talent to the Falcons' coaches, insisting they give him a chance, even when it put his own career in danger.

"Was there something else?" Troy's mom stared hard at him.

"No, just thanks." Troy returned her gaze, knowing that any sign of weakness would alert her to the fact that he was telling a . . . story.

"And I want to thank you, too, Troy, since we're all being so grateful," Seth said. "The way you've handled yourself with the older kids hasn't been easy, but I'm glad you trust me. It'll all work out."

"Everything will, right?" Troy laid the question in there innocently, then watched the unspoken words bounce back and forth between his mom and Seth.

Whatever it was they were hiding, it didn't have anything to do with Troy playing quarterback—of that he was certain. The trouble was, it was killing him not to know where some problem was lying in wait for him, a problem so disturbing that they didn't even want him to know about it.

Finally his mom spoke. "Everything always works out the way it should."

Troy spoke low, recalling his words with the owner. "Mr. Cole says destiny is written in the animals of time. What's that mean?"

"The *annals* of time," his mom said. "Annals are the record books. He means the history for what's going to happen—in the future—is already written someplace and you can't change what's meant to be."

"You believe that?" Seth scrunched up his forehead.

"Most of the time." She stood and began clearing the table.

Seth got up, stretched, and looked at his watch. "Yup, it's getting late. Troy, see you tomorrow at practice?"

"Seven o'clock, but I'll get there a little early to take some extra snaps with Big Nick Lee."

"Tate, will I see you there?" Seth asked.

"I was gonna bring a soccer ball and work on my left foot. I saw that grass field out behind the school. You think that would be okay?" Tate asked.

"If not, you can use the turf. I know the goals are

behind the school, but it'll be better than nothing if the soccer fields are being used."

"Thanks, Seth." Tate raised her bottle toward him.

"You got it," Seth said. "Tessa, lunch at Barelli's tomorrow? One o'clock?"

"That works for me." Troy's mom gave Seth a light kiss and watched him go before she finished cleaning up the sink and putting their mugs into the dishwasher.

Troy glanced at Tate, then turned the soda bottle in his hands, reading the numbers on the label. "Mom?"

"Yes?"

"I heard that John Madden once said winning was the world's best deodorant."

"What?"

"You know, if you win, it takes away the stink of something, no matter how bad it is."

"Was that on your video game or something?" she asked.

Troy laughed. "Nah, I heard it on ESPN Classics. They did this thing on famous coaches. You should've seen the funny commercials he did."

"The one in the bowling alley?" Tate asked. "That's funny."

"What's your point?" Troy's mom crossed the kitchen and put her hand on the back of his neck, rubbing the muscles there.

"Just that winning fixes things, right? I mean, when

you win, people forget about a lot of other stuff, the stinky stuff."

"Well, winning certainly helps . . . except when it doesn't." She gave his neck a final squeeze. "Come on, it's late. Let's get you two up."

"What's that supposed to mean?" Troy followed her out of the kitchen and up the stairs.

She stopped at the top step and looked back at him and Tate, her face pale and almost ghostly in the gloom. "It means that sometimes when you win, people are gunning for you even more."

Troy's mom left them, and he looked at Tate. She shook her head and it made him feel as if all he could ever do was dig himself deeper and deeper. It reminded him of someone else.

It reminded him of his own father.

CHAPTER FORTY-THREE

TROY FORGOT ABOUT HIS father.

He forgot about the UPS man.

He forgot about Thane and Ty and even Mr. Cole.

In fact, the only thing Troy did think about was Summit football, learning the offense so perfectly that he knew what every player's job was on every play in the book. When training camp began in the NFL, it was Chuku, his teammate, and not Ty, who stayed with Troy, his mom, and Tate.

Thane hired a nanny to take care of Ty. The only one who heard from him was Tate. It seemed as if he texted her all the time. Whether they were playing Xbox together or grabbing pizza down on Main Street, Tate would regularly hunch down over her phone with her thumbs working double time. The only relief they had from her constant communication with Ty was when he had to finally go to his own football camp for St. Stephen's middle school team.

"Why can't they text?" Troy muttered to himself, not daring to raise his voice so she could hear him. "It's *middle school* football. It's no big deal, you know."

Troy's mom had enrolled Tate in Summit Middle as expected, and signed her up for the soccer team, because her father hadn't gotten any better. The only positives were that it looked as if Tate would be with them for a while and that her father hadn't gotten any worse, either.

Troy's attention was almost totally focused on learning the Summit offense and perfecting the chemistry with his receivers. He never missed a Summit practice, because his only job with the Jets was to be there on game days during the regular season to inform the team's coordinators what the opposing team's plays would be. So even though the Jets had a month of training camp and preseason games, they had nothing to do with Troy.

Troy tried not to think about the Jets for two reasons. First, he didn't want the distraction from his own football team, and second, because when he *did* think about the Jets, it made his stomach queasy. Why, he didn't know.

On Wednesday, in the last week of training camp, a sportswriter from the Newark *Star-Ledger* came by to interview Seth and Troy.

The next day at breakfast, Troy sat with Chuku and Tate hunched over the sports page. He was disappointed with the article that had been written. It was mostly about Seth and his coaches and their NFL experience. The reporter stressed the unusual opportunity this coaching gave the Summit players, and cited that as the reason why the roster had gone from a paltry nineteen players the year before to just over forty for the upcoming season. He had several quotes from parents talking about how excited their kids were to have someone like Seth coaching the team. The paper even predicted that Summit could be a playoff contender.

Troy read the article again, scouring it for any hint of Seth's plan to make him quarterback. Seth didn't reveal anything in the interview, though. The article even said that player positions were uncertain.

Maybe worse was comparing the size of the small piece about the Summit team to the front-page article about the Jets. The Jets had high expectations for the season, and their new football genius—Troy—was mentioned as part of the reason. It frustrated Troy. The genius thing was a novelty, something that was fun and—if his father hadn't made a mess of things—something to make them rich, but not what he wanted to be known for.

Troy flipped back to the high school section and slurped raisin bran from a big spoon, chewing while he read about the competition. Milk dribbled down his chin when he read about St. Stephen's. People were predicting another state title for them and it burned Troy, even though he knew it would be good for Ty.

"Try not to make so much noise when you're eating, honey." Troy's mom appeared, put a hand on his shoulder, and yawned. "And use a napkin, not your sleeve. I need coffee. Good morning, kids."

"They're predicting we'll have a winning season, Mom." Troy pointed to the spot on the page.

"The Jets?" She rinsed out the parts of the coffee machine in the sink.

"No, *us*, Summit."

"Remember what we say. Don't believe something just because you read it in the paper." She rattled a filter into the machine and began spooning out heaps of coffee. "Did Seth get here?"

Now that training camp had them practicing twice a day, Seth had taken to arriving early, having breakfast with them all, and taking him and Chuku to practice while Tate went to soccer practice.

"He texted me that he had to stop and get some Gatorade mix. Why would you even talk like that?" Troy asked in a low tone, checking to see that his friends weren't paying attention before he went on. "I can throw the ball as good as any high school kid. You should see how good we look in practice. We're even better with pads on."

That didn't seem to impress his mom, so he said, "Me and Chuku are calling ourselves the Killer Kombo, combo with a *k*."

"I'm not talking about the team winning, just be careful with all the killer genius stuff and the media." Something wasn't working with the coffee machine, and she began hitting the bottom of it with the flat of her hand and jiggling the cord. "Be low-key."

"I can't help what they call me, Mom. I want them to remember me as a player. The Killer Kombo, me and Chuku, connecting for touchdown passes. I want to be known as a football player, not a *genius*." He pronounced the word as if it had gone rotten on his tongue.

"Well, I don't want reporters camped out in front of the house like what happened in Atlanta is all," she said, unplugging the cord and putting it into a different socket. "I think I tripped a breaker. You'll get plenty of attention when the Jets start to win."

Troy rolled his eyes and raised his voice. "You're not listening to me, Mom. I'm not even talking about the Jets. Who cares about the Jets? I'm talking about *us*, Summit. You're the one who says you've got to enjoy life. That's all we're doing, having fun. Chuku's made a rap song about the Killer Kombo."

She wrinkled her nose. "Rap?"

"Chuku, play that song, will you?" Troy asked.

"Huh?" Chuku looked up from his phone.

"'Killer Kombo.' Can you play it for her?"

"Uh, sure." Chuku fiddled with his phone and held it up for Troy's mom, bobbing his head to the beat while Tate snapped her fingers in time.

"It's got people watching on YouTube," Troy said. "You believe that?"

The coffee machine light came on. Troy's mom gave it a loving pat and turned her attention to them, doing her best not to frown. "Very nice, Chuku. Okay, I've got to get dressed while this coffee brews. Troy, can you help me upstairs? I want you to move that desk in front of the window in my bedroom."

Troy followed her. It didn't take a genius to see from the look on her face that she wanted him for something altogether different from moving a desk.

CHAPTER FORTY-FOUR

WHEN TROY GOT INSIDE her bedroom, she shut the door. A braided rug covered the wooden floor beneath an old brass bed. Sunlight filtered in through the curtains and dust danced in its beams.

"Listen, mister, you keep your head on straight with all this . . . Killer Kombo." She clucked her tongue and shook her head.

"Mom, I'm the kid who was on *Larry King Live* and *Conan. Today?* You think I don't know? Even you said I'm good with the media."

"That was them wanting to talk to you, not you wanting to talk about yourself."

Troy blinked and looked out the window. His football tire waffled in the breeze, hypnotizing him for a moment before he looked back at her. "It's my dream, Mom."

"I knew a dreamer once," she said.

"Who are you talking about?"

"Your father." She said it like a swear word and stared hard at him. "Have you seen him?"

Troy squirmed. Since jumping off a bridge to escape from the FBI, his father had popped in and out of his life, most recently with some mobsters as his partners. His mom knew about all that, but not that he'd shown up suddenly with a red beard. "No."

His mom bit her lip. "Well . . . I didn't want to tell you this, but I think you should know."

CHAPTER FORTY-FIVE

"KNOW WHAT?" TROY ASKED.

His mom sighed. "I know you've got a lot on your mind, but Seth thought he saw him, your father, watching practice one night from outside the fence. He said the guy had red hair and a pointy beard, but he was pretty sure it was your dad, Troy."

Troy realized that must have been what his mom and Seth were discussing when he'd overheard them talking in the kitchen. It made him mad. He knew his father messed things up in a lot of ways, but Troy loved his father, despite the problems. It was his father— a record holder for touchdowns at the University of Alabama—who gave him his athletic ability. So Troy refused to let it go.

"Not everything is bad about him." Troy raised his

chin. "If I play for five years, and our program wins a bunch of state championships, I'll be a five-star recruit for sure, just like he was. Maybe I'll go to Alabama, too."

His mom put her face in a hand.

"I'm serious, you should see how good we look. You should stop by practice later," he said.

"If your father tries to contact you, Troy, I want to know about it." She looked up and frowned. "You hear me?"

Troy's mind went into high gear because what she just said didn't mean he had to tell if he *had* seen him, only if he *did* see him. "Okay, I hear you, but you haven't even seen us. If you did, you'd understand why I'm so excited, Mom."

"I'd love to. I really would, but the managing partner has his panties in a bunch about the hospital gala we're underwriting and I'm to the wall right now. New girl on the block."

"The guy wears panties?" Troy's upper lip left his teeth. He'd heard all about how odd lawyers could be, but the image of the managing partner in women's underwear stuck in his mind.

"It's just an expression," Troy's mom said. "Tightie whities in a twist. Is that better?"

"It's gross, Mom. Cut it out."

"Speaking of underwear, get back downstairs so I can change for work."

"You don't have to ask me twice." Troy put a hand over his eyes and let himself out of the room.

As he clunked down the stairs, Seth came in through the front door.

"What's up, buddy? You sore from yesterday?" Seth stopped to look him over.

"My legs feel like punching bags," Troy said.

"Good."

"Good?" Troy asked.

"Working hard, right?" Seth gave Troy's shoulder a pat. "I'm gonna get a quick bowl of cereal and we'll get to the school a little early. I've got some Lawton game film from last year I want you guys to see."

The Lawton High Wolverines were the first team on Summit's schedule. It would be no small feat to beat them. They were a strong playoff team year after year and had ended last season ranked fifth in the state.

"Haven't we seen all the tape they gave us two times already?"

Seth put a finger to his lips and nodded. "But I got a source who got me some more. It's a game Lawton played two years ago against Kennedy, which also runs a spread offense. It's the same coach, so I'm sure they'll run the same defense against us, or they'll try."

"It's not cheating, is it?" Troy lowered his voice.

"No." Seth laughed. "It's just being thorough, but I don't like people to know all my tricks."

"I like it."

"And speaking of tricks . . . you're all ready to help me out on the sideline when we're on defense, right? You don't need to see some more film on their offense?" Seth asked. "This isn't NFL football; things might not be as predictable. You know, with their tendencies and all that."

Troy's face clouded over. "Won't I have to be making adjustments with Coach Sindoni on the greaseboard? I need to focus on *that* more than predicting plays, right? I mean, this isn't junior league anymore, Seth. If I'm gonna be a varsity quarterback, I need to pay attention to *that* stuff."

Seth rubbed his chin. "Well, if I really need you, though, right? In a pinch? *Could* you do it? I mean, just pick it up without any preparation at all."

"I keep telling you, it's just a feeling I get. I don't know why everybody can't just accept that. I can call a high school game as easy as an NFL game. I did it in junior league, right?"

Seth shook his head. "The whole thing is pretty freaky, Troy. You can't blame me for wanting to be sure."

"Just trust me. Besides, I want to talk about *our* offense," Troy said.

"You're right. I want to put in our rollout packages today," Seth said. "I'm not sure our tackles can hold up against those Lawton defensive ends—kids are animals—and I want to make sure we've got some plays to get you outside the pocket if they get overrun."

"Seth . . . um . . ." Troy had kept the question inside for the past two weeks and it was killing him. "When am I gonna get to start running the first-team offense?"

"Why? You don't like throwing to Chuku and Levi and Spencer?"

"I *do*. When are we all going to be first team?"

"Trust?" Seth raised his eyebrows. "You got to trust me, too."

"I do, Seth, but . . ." Troy hammered his fist into the wall. "This is getting ridiculous. That Reed is acting like he's some alpha dog, wanting everyone to sniff his butt. I'm sick of it. Lawton is next week. Aren't you going to put that clown in his place?"

Seth sighed. "First of all, he's not a clown, he's your teammate. Well, maybe he's kind of a clown, but the second thing is that I have a plan. I've had it all along. I know just when I want to do it, and I know just how.

"Now let me get some breakfast."

CHAPTER FORTY-SIX

TROY HATED SETH'S PLAN, but there was nothing he could do to stop it.

He changed for practice and went out onto the sun-drenched field early with most of the rest of the team. From there, he could see the entrance to the coaches' offices and team meeting rooms, so he saw when Seth came out with his arm around the shoulder pads of Grant Reed. The two of them arrived at the field together and Seth blew his whistle. Instead of sending the team to get warmed up, he called them all in.

Troy took a knee and chomped on his mouthpiece.

"Guys," Seth said, looking around at them with his eyes hidden behind sunglasses, "you've worked hard. You've had a great camp. This is our last double-session practice day. Tomorrow is a light walk-through and

Saturday is our intrasquad scrimmage. Next week, school starts. A week from tomorrow, we take the field against Lawton, and it'll be the beginning of something special, something Summit football has never been a part of, a championship. We'll be playing one of the best teams around. Summit hasn't beaten Lawton in twenty years, but it starts with them.

"In order to win, I'm going to make some changes. We've allowed guys to play positions they wanted and given the first-string spots based on seniority. That's all over. Every move I make now is so that we can *win*. I told you from the beginning, that's how it would be. If you don't like what I'm about to do, you go to your individual coach and let him know. He'll explain our decision. If you can't work it out with him, then you and he will come to me. Do *not* go home to Mommy and Daddy and gripe about your position or what team you're on. I *will not* discuss any of that with parents unless you've first talked to your position coach, then to me. Everyone understand that?"

Seth's voice oozed with authority and simmered with aggressiveness.

"Good. Now, I've made a decision on captains. It's a great honor to be a captain, and there were several of you who could have gotten it, but not everyone can be one. I picked two, and I want to introduce them to you now. First, Chance Bryant."

Everyone clapped, no one harder than Troy. Chance's

face went red, but he stood, towering over the rest of them, and went to shake Seth's hand.

"Stay right here." Seth grabbed Chance's collar to keep him in front of the team. "Chance is our offensive captain. On defense . . . our captain is Grant Reed."

There was an instant of shock when no one clapped, then Billy Tomkins started a thunderous applause and the rest of the team followed, with some—like Troy— doing only what was required, no more. Reed grinned and it was obvious he already knew his captaincy was coming.

Seth blew his whistle and had the team warm up. They ran through individual drills and then went to team defense. Reed played strong safety with Tomkins right in front of him at middle linebacker. Troy didn't play defense, and neither did Chuku, Levi, or Spencer, so they helped out on the scout team, mimicking Lawton's offense as best they could for the Summit defense to practice against. Reed had always been a loudmouth, but now, as a captain, he seemed even more vocal, howling and barking at his teammates.

It made Troy mad. Reed was such an arrogant jerk, but Seth said Troy had to trust the decision, so he would try.

After one play, when the defensive end let the scout team runner get outside him and gain seven yards up the sideline, Reed yelled at his own defensive player,

"Let's go! You think that's good enough? It's not!"

"Reed!" Seth shouted, but then marched across the field to where Reed was to give him a friendly pat on the back and talk in a cheerful undertone. "You're the captain, not the coach. I'll let you know when my job is up for grabs. Okay?"

Reed grinned at Seth and returned to the huddle.

The camaraderie between them made Troy want to puke. After a couple of dozen or so more plays, the team took a water break and then Seth gathered them together again.

"Okay, the starting offense is going to look a little different today." Seth looked down at his clipboard. "Chuku, you take the Z, you're our fastest guy and the outside receiver on the strong side."

"Now, Coach . . ." Chuku held up both hands and paced a bit. "Correct me if I'm wrong, but the Z is like Andre Johnson and Randy Moss and . . . well, Jerry Rice, too, right! I mean, Z is the *go-to* guy, right?"

Seth blinked at Chuku, then couldn't contain himself. He grinned and nodded. "Yup, that's you, Chuku. The go-to guy."

"I just love this game, Coach." Chuku shook his head. "And the nice thing about it is, this game loves me."

Seth chuckled and turned back to the rest of the team. "Levi, you're the X, outside receiver on the weak side. Spencer is the Y, inside Chuku in the slot. Galbato, I want you at right tackle. The rest of the line stays how it's been, with Molnar and Dranzack at guards, Big Nick Lee at center, and Chance at left tackle."

Seth looked at Troy, then at Grant Reed. Troy's stomach clenched. He knew what was coming and he knew it wasn't going to be pretty.

CHAPTER FORTY-SEVEN

"TROY, YOU TAKE Q." Seth held up his hands, anticipating problems. "I know Reed has been Q. He's maybe our best defensive player, and now he's a team captain, but Coach Sindoni keeps track of everything everyone does at that position, every completion, interception, touchdown, fumble, everything. It's simple. He graded them out and Troy was clearly the top performer."

Seth glared at Reed, as if to remind him of the deal Troy knew he'd made in making Reed a captain. Reed bit his lip and nodded.

"Now, the rest of you guys." Seth looked around. "Before you get yourselves worked up, I know this'll be the youngest high school offense in the country, but it'll also be the fastest, and that's how we're going to turn this thing around. I want the offense lightning fast.

It's like putting a featherweight up against a heavy-weight, but if the featherweight is a Golden Gloves and the heavyweight is a slob, you bet the featherweight is gonna knock him out cold, and that's what we're gonna do. We gotta save our mauling and brawling for when we're on defense. That's how you win games—defense. On offense, like the great Ali said, we float like a butterfly and sting like a bee."

Seth glared at the team and he raised his voice. "Don't you doubt me, not *any* of you."

Troy snuck a look at Reed, who scowled back and clamped down tight on his mouthpiece.

"Listen to what I'm saying," Seth said. "We are going to be champions. Bring it in, 'champions' on three, and then give me that first offense with a scout D."

The team gathered around Seth, holding up their helmets in a cluster above their heads.

"One, two, three . . ."

"CHAMPIONS!"

Players flooded to their positions on the field, Troy in the center of the first-team huddle. He looked around at the older kids, the big linemen with their bulging muscles.

Chance Bryant—who was both huge and in need of a shave—stuck out a hand. Troy took it.

"You're our QB," Chance said. "I don't care if you wear diapers, you better believe we got your back. On the field *and* off, like I said before."

Troy wanted to ask why Chance thought he might need anyone to watch his back off the field. Chance was staring at Troy, waiting for some response. So Troy thanked the older player and tried not to sound scared.

When Galbato stuck out his hand as well, Troy was even more surprised. The enormous player was one of the ones right in there grinning and laughing with Reed and Tomkins whenever they had a baby joke going. Maybe being elevated to the starting team himself gave the big guy a new appreciation for Troy.

As they jogged out onto the field to form the huddle, Chuku grabbed Troy's face mask, pulling him close.

"This is it, bro. It's you and me, the Killer Kombo. This is *our* team. You feel it?"

Troy felt a surge of joy at the sound of Chuku's words. He laughed out loud. "I know. It *is* our team!"

As they ran through the script of plays, Troy got more and more comfortable with his new status. He began marching the offense up and down the field with precision and efficiency, completing nearly every pass and carrying out fakes that stumped the defense.

CHAPTER FORTY-EIGHT

THAT NIGHT THE LOCKER room buzzed with excitement, and Troy knew the older players believed the things Seth had told them. Confidence added a glimmer to their eyes, and, except for Grant Reed, most of them treated Troy like a lucky horseshoe, not quite part of them but something they appreciated even if they didn't completely understand how it worked.

Troy and Chuku said their good-byes and walked out into the evening air. They sat around in the bleachers waiting for Seth to finish meeting with his coaches so they could get into the truck and head for home.

Troy's stomach was rumbling by the time Seth appeared, giving them both a thumbs-up.

"You looked great. Honestly? We are gonna beat these guys!"

CHAPTER FORTY-NINE

TATE WASN'T GOING TO get to see Summit's opening game. This upset Troy, but he certainly understood. Tate's mom had purchased a ticket for her to fly out to San Diego so that she could visit her father in the hospital over the weekend.

After school on Friday, Chuku's dad picked him up from school to have a special pregame meal of grits, eggs, and collard greens doused in hot sauce, something his father did before his own games. Troy waved good-bye, then got into his mom's car to help drop Tate off at the airport.

Troy's mom checked Tate's bag for her and got her ticket at the curbside check-in. Troy stood with Tate, watching, nervous about the first game of the season.

"You sure you're ready?" Tate asked him in a low voice.

"Of course." Troy grinned and hugged her. "Good luck with your dad."

"He'll be okay. He has to be."

After Tate was safely with the JetBlue representative who would help her get to the gate, Troy and his mom got into the car and pulled away. His mom kept both hands on the wheel and she sighed heavily. "You sure have to be thankful for what you've got."

"Is her dad going to be okay?" Troy asked. "Tate thinks so."

His mom glanced at him. "They really don't know, Troy. Say a prayer, though."

Troy did that, then turned his mind to the night ahead. As much as he tried to put football into perspective with something like Tate's father and the accident, he just couldn't make himself feel as if the game they were going to play was any less important. He had so much hope riding on Summit's football season that it felt like a life-or-death situation.

His mom left him outside the locker room and disappeared into the stands. Troy saw Chuku coming and waited so they could go in together.

They bumped fists. "How were the eggs and grits?"

"Dawg, you don't know what you're *miss*ing. My mouth's on fire and I'm about to do the same thing to that football field." Chuku pointed toward the field. "Watch out, I'll be *burning* it up."

"Nothing like a little confidence," Troy said.

"Nothing like a *lot*."

Together, they changed and came out with the team. A warm breeze blew across the field. The sun nestled down into the treetops, promising night and mosquitoes. Fans started to fill the bleachers and two different television crews spilled out of their trucks and down onto the sidelines. People wanted to see if Seth Halloway and Troy White were for real.

Troy was surprised when he saw Ty and Thane up in the stands. Part of him was proud that his All-Pro cousin would come to the opening game, but Troy still resented Thane. He knew if they lost tonight, it could be—in part—because of Thane. But when Troy saw them looking his way, he could only wave and smile because he sure wasn't going to let them know how much it bothered him. It made him even hungrier to do well, to show them both that Troy and Seth didn't even need them to win.

They waved back, and that's when Troy saw Mr. Bryant talking to the tall man Troy had seen on the field the day he arrived. The man wore a suit, which was a strange way to dress for a Friday night football game, but Troy didn't give it a second thought. His mind was churning with all the excitement of the game.

Troy was warming up with the rest of the team when

the Lawton bus arrived. The Lawton players marched like a small army down onto the field in their white uniforms. Lawton circled the field, then ran in two columns straight through the Summit team as they were stretching their hamstrings.

Seth called Summit into a big huddle after the warm-ups. His red face twitched and twisted with rage. "Did you guys see that? They ran right through your warm-up? That's like spitting in your *face*."

One of the older players in the back spoke up. "They always do that, Coach."

"Not anymore they don't," Seth snarled. "Not after tonight. They run through our warm-up? We are gonna run through their world. We are gonna stomp them so hard they'll be wearing their butts for hats. Now get in here and give me three wins because that's what we are going to do. It's a new day and it starts here, tonight."

CHAPTER FIFTY

THE TEAM PUT THEIR fists in. Troy looked over at Chuku's face. His eyes were crazed and his mouth a sneer.

Seth shouted, "One, two, three . . ."

"WIN! WIN! WIN!"

They broke off and finished their pregame routine, throwing, catching, blocking, form tackling, and finally running through a couple of practice plays. Troy could barely catch his breath. He'd played in big games before, but that was with a bunch of *kids*. Surrounding him now were monster-sized players, some who could bench-press three hundred pounds, some with breath and body odor like ogres. Nothing felt like this. On the other end of the field, the Lawton team chanted in perfect time. They not only looked like an army, they sounded like one.

While Reed ran a couple of plays with the second-team offense, Troy studied the opposition. Someone brushed up alongside him.

"They sure make a lot of noise." It was Chuku, also staring at their opponents.

"Big, too." Troy couldn't help marveling at the size of the Lawton defensive line.

"I got a little noise for them." Chuku turned his backside toward the other team and let one rip.

Troy giggled, but with his nerves jangled as they were it didn't make him feel any better. After the national anthem, Chance Bryant and Reed went out for the coin toss. Summit won. Troy's heart rammed up into his throat and struggled like a rat caught in a trap to spring free. They'd be on offense to start the game. Troy looked over at Coach Sindoni, who gave him a thumbs-up. The kickoff team surrounded Seth. They held their hands up high and chanted: "WIN! WIN! WIN!" With a single cry, the cluster broke apart and they flooded the field.

Chuku returned the kickoff, but got only ten yards before a group of Lawton players buried him. Chuku bounced up out of the pile and swung a fist in the air. Troy and the offense swarmed onto the field. Galbato and Bryant flanked him like two towers and they huddled up.

Chuku wedged into the huddle and hooted at them all. "Come on! Let's get these bums!"

Troy felt a strange calm wash over him. He called the play, a rollout pass, deep to Chuku. For an instant, he wished for Ty, knowing that with two speedy receivers, the choice of where to throw would be so easy. He pushed that from his mind, broke the huddle, and approached the line. The noseguard looked up at Troy with a red sweaty face, growled, and spit. He made Big Nick Lee look not so big. Troy glanced out at the defensive ends. They were massive, and he knew they'd be gunning for him, one on one side, one on the other.

"Hey!" The shout came from one of the Lawton linebackers. Troy couldn't even be sure which one. "You guys got an *eighth grader* playing quarterback! You stink, Summit!"

Troy took the snap and started to roll. His line crumbled in front of him. Chuku shot down the field. The safety rolled over the top, double-teaming Chuku, so Troy had to wait. Ty flashed through his mind— he could be running *free* if only he were on the other side. A whisper of sickness passed through Troy at the image of his speedy cousin just sitting in the stands, watching. Useless.

Before Troy could launch the ball, the right defensive end pummeled him into the turf. As the pile cleared, Galbato reached down with a giant mitt and helped him to his feet. The big man clapped Troy on the back. "We'll get them. That one was on us, Troy. That was on us."

Galbato pounded his own chest with a fist.

Before Troy could even catch his breath, Coach Sindoni signaled the next play from the sideline. It was a mirror image of the first play, only running it to the other side so that Levi was running deep. If Coach Sindoni was right, then the safety would roll over the top of Levi, and Chuku would be open on the back side of the play.

"Look for Chuku!" Coach Sindoni shouted through cupped hands.

Troy gave a nod and dipped into the huddle, knelt, and looked up at Chuku. "You're gonna be open on the post."

"Watch me walk in backward." Chuku showed off his brilliant smile. "Killer Kombo."

"Okay, same play, going left this time." Troy glared at Chance, his left tackle, not a boy but a young man four years his senior and nearly a hundred pounds bigger. "You get that guy, you hear me? Don't miss him, Chance. I need four seconds, that's it. Can you give me four?"

Troy surprised himself with the tone of his voice, and he could tell by the looks on his linemen's faces that he had surprised them as well.

Chance grunted. "I got him."

Troy broke the huddle and approached the line. The defenders were pointing at him and jeering.

"Someone change that kid's diapers, will you?" The noseguard chortled.

"Coming for you again!" the Lawton defender who'd pummeled him shouted from his spot on the end.

"Not if I get him first!" the other end shouted. "Gonna send that little boy home to his momma!"

Troy ignored them. He checked the secondary. He saw cover three and knew it meant something. It didn't matter. It was a simple play—Levi up the sideline to draw off the free safety, Chuku cutting into the post from the back side. Simple. He wished it were Ty—that would make the play so much more certain—but Levi would have to do.

Troy shouted out the cadence and took the snap. He spun and rolled left. The line bent but didn't break. No one in his face, but the left end had Chance Bryant on his heels, lifting him and running him back into the backfield. Troy head-faked outside, then ducked back inside his tackle. Chance ran the end past him. Troy kept going toward the sideline. He stopped suddenly, set his feet, pump-faked to Levi, then launched the ball into the post, trusting Chuku to be there.

As the ball left his hand, the end grabbed him from behind and swung him into the air.

The world spun.

In that fraction of a moment, Troy knew something bad was about to happen, and he thought of Ty again.

Just sitting there.

CHAPTER FIFTY-ONE

THE CROWD ROARED.

Troy hit the turf and bounced like a toy. Pain shot through his shoulder.

Big Nick Lee lifted Troy to his feet. Troy winced, but bottled up a gasp.

"You good?" Big Nick Lee grinned and sweat glazed his swollen cheeks.

"Good," Troy said. It was his left shoulder. He didn't need it to throw. He only had to stand the pain.

The other linemen swarmed him, pounding his back so that they propelled him down the field toward where Chuku stood in the end zone with his arms outstretched. The excitement helped Troy push the pain to the back of his mind. It was his first varsity touchdown.

"You got lucky on that one, punk!" a Lawton defender shouted.

The right defensive end tried to get in front of Troy. "You're going down, junior. You won't make it through this game."

Big Nick Lee shoved the defender, who shoved him back until a referee stepped between them both. Troy soaked up the cheers. Chuku hugged him and they both jogged off to the sideline. Seth wrapped his arms around Troy and lifted him off his feet. Troy winced.

"You okay?" Seth wore a look of concern.

Troy nodded. "Banged my shoulder. I'm fine."

"Maybe have Emily Lou look at it. Ms. McLean!" Seth waved the trainer over, then turned away to focus on the field.

Ms. McLean asked Troy what happened.

"When they threw me down." Troy pointed to his shoulder.

Ms. McLean felt up under his shoulder pad.

"Ah!" Troy flinched.

The trainer nodded and put him through a series of tests in which she asked him to hold out his arm and resist her pushing it one way or another. Sometimes he could hold strong. Other things made his arm flop like a dead fish and he growled in pain.

"I think it's a slight shoulder strain," the trainer said.

"Slight?" Panic chocked Troy. It didn't feel slight.

"What does that mean?"

She shrugged. "It's your AC joint. There's nothing you can do. If you can take the pain, you can play. It's not a separation or anything. It won't get any worse."

Troy heaved a sigh of relief.

"It's gonna hurt, though."

"I'm okay," he said.

"It's probably gonna get worse before it gets better."

Troy nodded that he understood. He was playing with the big kids now, the men. He knew what he had to do. He thanked the trainer and walked away.

The Summit kicking team missed the extra point and the crowd went flat. Troy grabbed a cup of Gatorade and found himself standing next to Seth on the sideline. It was time to play defense. Summit kicked off. The ball landed short. A Lawton player returned it, and ended up close to the fifty. Troy watched the Lawton offense take the field. He knew Seth would love it if he could read the offense and tell him the plays.

He watched Lawton and tried to absorb the personnel grouping they sent onto the field. It looked like two tight ends and two backs. He watched as they ran the ball off-tackle for seven yards.

"You gotta fill that, Reed!" Seth shouted at the top of his lungs.

Troy felt only the smallest of pleasures, even though Reed got yelled at good. The Summit defense needed to hold. If they did, it would take some pressure off him and the rest of the offense.

Down the field Lawton drove the ball, running left, right, and center. They threw one pass, a short crossing route that Reed broke up and could have intercepted.

"His hands stink." Troy meant to say it to himself, but Seth heard.

"That was a tough catch," Seth said. "Hey, I see that look in your eye. You got anything for me?"

CHAPTER FIFTY-TWO

TROY LOOKED OUT AT the field. His shoulder throbbed with pain.

He willed his football genius to kick in so he could figure out what Lawton would do next. They came to the line and ran a sweep to the weak side.

Nothing. Troy saw nothing. He probed his shoulder, wondering how it would hold up in the game, then realized that Seth was looking at him.

Troy huffed. "It takes time sometimes. I'll let you know."

Part of him was annoyed with Seth for pestering him. He was the quarterback. He just threw a touchdown pass. Wasn't that enough? Why should he have to read the other team's offense for them to win? Let Reed and Tomkins earn their keep.

And still, he tried.

But nothing happened. Whether it was the pain in his shoulder or the frustration, Troy just didn't feel it. He didn't see it. Nothing happened, and after a couple of series, he shut it down, refusing to waste his energy and focus on *that*. He was a player. He needed to play, and that's what he did. He threw. He ran. He ducked and dodged and made things happen like an All-American.

The problem was that for every score Troy engineered, Lawton returned the favor. It was a back-and-forth game, with both offenses having a field day.

The one thing Troy's team did better at was extra points. After Summit missed the first kick, Seth chose to go for two after every touchdown that followed. Troy completed passes on five of the next six extra-point tries, earning two points instead of the one they'd get for a kick. Late in the fourth quarter, Summit had a 52–48 lead. But with seventeen seconds left, Lawton scored a touchdown to make it 54–52. Instead of kicking the extra point, Lawton went for their own two-point conversion. Lawton's big fullback carried the ball up the middle, plowing right over the top of Grant Reed and giving Lawton a four-point lead, so that a Summit field goal wouldn't be enough. Troy would need a touchdown to win.

Seth grabbed Troy's face mask and pulled him close. "You got to do this. This is it. It all starts here, Troy.

We can win this thing. *You* can win it."

The ache in his shoulder didn't mean anything to him now. It hadn't gotten better, but it wasn't any worse. Coach Sindoni handed Troy a flash card. It had three plays scribbled on it.

"Stick it in your pants," Coach Sindoni said. "Three plays. Use them all. We're not going for the end zone right away. They won't expect us to work our way down the field. They'll leave the underneath stuff open, and if we execute it right, we can do it. Tell Levi to get out of bounds, then use our last time-out after the Y seam."

Troy took the card, looked at the plays, and stuffed it into the waistband of his pants. He bumped fists with his coaches and jogged out onto the field. In the huddle, he told Levi to make sure he got out of bounds at the end of the play to stop the clock so they could huddle before the second play.

"You don't get out of bounds, we lose." Troy held Levi in his gaze before he called out the play to the others.

At the line of scrimmage, the Lawton noseguard snarled up at him. "You're dead meat, little boy. Totally dead."

"You're the meat," Nick Lee growled as he gripped the football. "Hamburger brains."

Troy barked out the cadence, took the snap, dropped three steps, and fired. Levi did a quick out, caught the ball, and surged up the sideline for seventeen more yards before getting out of bounds. The crowd loved it. Troy didn't have time to celebrate. He gathered his guys in the huddle and called the second play. During the game, Summit's only running back, Jentry Hood, had scored two touchdowns, but Troy had thrown for the other five and he could see in his teammates' eyes that they believed in him.

"Spencer, we got one time-out," Troy said. "I'm going to hit you right away, then you get up that seam as far as you can. We'll call time-out and still have time for two more plays. Green Ghost Twenty-Two Y Seam, on two. Ready . . ."

"BREAK!"

Troy took the snap, fired the pass, and Spencer got them twenty yards. Troy called a quick time-out. They were on Lawton's twenty-seven-yard line. Two seconds remained on the clock.

In the huddle, his offensive linemen were gasping for air. They were tired, and they'd begun to break down in the fourth quarter, letting the defense swarm him so that he'd been sacked three times. Normally, Troy wouldn't have needed to look at the card, but with so much at stake he didn't trust his memory. He tugged the card free from his pants, glanced at the final play, then looked up at his line and saw the hunger in their eyes.

"Give me time, guys. I need time, or it won't work." Troy took a gulp of air. "Chuku, you get deep, then come back. I'm putting this thing on your back shoulder in the corner of the end zone. Just be there. Trips Right, Roll Right, Seven Twenty-Nine Comeback, on one. Ready . . ."

They broke the huddle with a roar. At the line, the Lawton noseguard was huffing and puffing and too tired to threaten Troy. Troy took the snap and rolled right. Levi and Spencer broke to the inside. Chuku burst upfield toward the deep zone. Troy rolled right, into the open space. His line battled the Lawton defenders with grunts and bellows of rage. Pads crashed. Sweat sprayed into the air in great gusts.

From the corner of his eye, Troy saw the middle linebacker streaking toward him, blitzing up through the middle of the line, untouched by a blocker. He needed time, but he wasn't going to get it. Chuku was only halfway to the end zone. It was impossible. He couldn't throw the pass. It was just too soon.

In the instant before the linebacker hit him, Troy saw it all in his mind. He saw the glory of a championship: newspaper articles, TV interviews, admiring faces in the hallways at school, melting into a muddle of disappointment and ridicule. Yes, they'd mock him now. That's how it worked.

It burned.

The linebacker hit him so hard, the impact lifted him up and spun him around.

There was nothing—and no one—to break his fall.

CHAPTER FIFTY-THREE

TROY HAD NO IDEA *how* he did it.

He just did it.

His hand broke the fall and the shock of pain in his shoulder flashed like lightning in his brain. Still, the momentum whipped his legs into a cartwheel, so that one foot landed and the other swung around and left him facing the opposite way. He spun, cranking his hips around, and saw more defenders surging toward him. His eyes found Chuku, right where he should be. Troy set his feet and fired the ball.

As they'd practiced time and again for the past several weeks, Chuku broke back at the last instant and snatched the ball.

Touchdown.

Game over.

Big Nick Lee bear-hugged Troy, lifting him off his feet. The rest of the line raised him up and they carried him to the end zone, where they picked up Chuku, too, dancing and cheering, laughing and crying.

It felt like something special.

It felt like it was just the beginning.

CHAPTER FIFTY-FOUR

ADVIL AND EXCITEMENT MADE Troy forget about his pain. His first win as a *varsity* quarterback lifted him like a magic carpet. Cheering and backslapping and laughter carried him through a night that ended with a dozen teammates, parents, and coaches crowded around the TV in Troy's living room to watch high school football highlights and interviews on the eleven o'clock news. Troy and Chuku stood close as they watched, jostling each other and kidding about who looked better on TV.

Even Chuku's dad beamed with pride at the sight of his son and Troy connecting on touchdown pass after touchdown pass. When the highlights ended, the sports announcer's face came back on with a big picture of Chuku frozen in laughter on the screen behind the announcer's desk.

"And get this," the announcer said. "When I asked Chuku Moore if he had a nickname, he told me he and his friend quarterback Troy White are the Killer Kombo, combo with a *k*."

The news anchor, a pretty, dark-haired woman who sat beside him, had a laugh before they went to a commercial. Everyone around the living room cheered. Troy blushed, but Chuku ate it with a spoon.

When the excitement waned, Troy took out his phone and texted Tate in San Diego. He wanted to share the joy of the evening, and also to ask about her dad. Tate texted him right back and replied that her dad was no better, but she was happy for Troy because she knew what the win meant to him. When everyone finally left, Troy's mom told him to go to bed while she and Seth cleaned up.

His mom put her hand on Troy's cheek. "I'm so proud."

Troy went up, dropped into his bed, and didn't move until nine thirty the next morning, when his mom woke him.

"It's time," she said. Her whisper was quiet but businesslike, with no room for complaints.

Troy had to think where he was, not in their cabin outside Atlanta but in New Jersey, where they'd just won a huge game and made believers of everyone. The muscles in his face tightened with joy.

"Time for what?" Troy rubbed his eyes and pressed

his temples. His body felt like a punching bag. Soreness polluted his legs, back, head, and neck. He sat up and felt his shoulder.

"Is it bothering you that much?" His mother studied him from above.

"No." Troy shook his head. "I'm fine. Really. Just a little achy all over."

His mom sighed. "I hate this part of it. It's not junior league, is it?"

"Nope." Pride flooded Troy.

"The charter leaves at noon. It's a half hour to Newark." His mom walked out of his room. He heard her footsteps on the stairs. "Breakfast in ten, pack your bag!"

After swallowing some more Advil, Troy used the bathroom, then pulled on a hat and some clothes, threw more clothes in his duffel bag, and crept downstairs. He'd forgotten all about the Jets and their opening game on the road in Miami. The breakfast table had been set. Resting on the checkered cloth was the morning newspaper.

"There's a picture in the paper." Troy's mom didn't look up from her frying pan on the stove. "Nice, huh?"

Troy studied the full-color shot of him on one leg, spinning to stay upright and make the final touchdown pass. Above the article in bold letters across page five of the sports section were the words: SUMMIT WIN PURE GENIUS.

"Don't let it go to your head, right?" His mom slipped two fried eggs onto a plate, then a third onto another plate for her before bringing them to the table. "Eat up."

"I won't. It's an awesome picture, though."

"That it is." His mom dipped her toast in egg yolk. "How's the shoulder now?"

Troy forced a laugh. "I'm sore all over. The Advil will kick in."

His mom shook her head. "I told you, you should have kept playing soccer. You were a great soccer player."

Troy sighed but said nothing. He'd heard it all before.

"I saw your ball out in the yard." His mom looked past him and out the window. "You better not leave it. It's supposed to rain."

Troy finished eating, cleaned off his plate, and loaded it into the dishwasher. He limped out onto the back porch and spotted the ball. He retrieved it and climbed back up onto the porch, stopping before he went inside to study the spiderweb in the window. Strung up in its middle hung what looked like two white cocoons. He looked closer. One might have been a housefly, the other a moth, dead and wrapped in webbing so that their killer could feast on their fluids at a later time.

The spider was nowhere. He checked the hole in the casing where he knew it hid. Empty. Not knowing where it was sent a little chill down his spine. Maybe it wasn't the spider that was creeping him out. Maybe it was the idea of his father, out there somewhere.

He stepped away from the window and heard his mom calling him from inside.

"Coming!" he called.

This was the first time he wasn't excited about going to an NFL game to help his team win. He sucked in a quick breath. He wasn't just not excited.

He was dreading it.

CHAPTER FIFTY-FIVE

AFTER HAVING SPENT AN entire season with the Atlanta Falcons, riding on a charter flight with an NFL team was as natural to Troy as taking the school bus. He sat next to his mom in the front of the plane with the other people who made up the support staff for the team. The players sat in the back. Thane stopped on his way past.

"Hey, Troy. Sorry we didn't come over for the party after. Two nights before a game is the most important sleep you get, so I had to turn in. That was some game you played last night." Thane held out a fist for Troy to bump.

Troy's mouth dropped open. He was still so excited by the big win that he hadn't even considered what he'd say to his older cousin. In that moment, he wanted to tell Thane that if he'd let Ty play at Summit, Troy likely wouldn't *have* his shoulder injury. But that wasn't fair and he knew it. Besides, how many high school quarterbacks got congratulated for their performance by an NFL player?

"Thanks." Troy forced a smile and bumped fists. "When's Ty's first game?"

"Thursday," Thane said. "He's playing on the eighth-grade team. He's looking good."

"He *is* good," Troy said, unable to keep the sharpness out of his voice.

"Well, hopefully we'll get you guys together next year," Thane said. "It'd be a great connection."

Thane gave Troy's mom a friendly handshake and he kept going toward the back. If Thane knew Troy was miffed, he sure didn't show it.

"I told him we were a good connection, but he wouldn't listen." Troy watched Thane go.

"You're not still mad about all that?" his mom asked.

"I am, a little." Troy broke out into a grin. "But winning like we did sure helps."

Troy watched the seats ahead as the coaching staff filled up the first-class cabin. When the plane backed away from the gate, Troy asked his mom in a whisper where the owner was.

"Probably taking his own plane," she said, then returned to her magazine.

"Good." The word slipped out of Troy's mouth.

His mother gave Troy's hand a pat.

Troy thought about Mr. Cole, zipping down to Miami in his private plane. Troy rode on the owner's plane back when the Jets were trying to sign him to a contract, back when Troy's father was in the picture. His mother looked over at him and—as if she knew what he was thinking—took his hand and gave it a loving squeeze. Troy forced a smile and remembered the briefest of times when he had both a father and a mother in his life. He reached into his bag for his book and dipped his head into it so he wouldn't have to talk.

"Excited?"

Troy looked up at his mom. "Excuse me?"

"Are you excited?"

Troy stared at her for a beat and lowered his voice. "Mom, I'm not even getting paid."

"Well, you *got* paid." She wore a sad smile.

Troy just shook his head.

"Come on, Troy." She touched his arm. "I remember a day when you dreamed of doing this. Remember showing Seth during that Monday night football game? You were dying to do this."

"Mom, that was for the *Falcons*. They're my team, Mom. This is a job and the money is *gone*. I know that's not the team's fault, but it's not my fault how I feel. I want to *play* football, not predict it."

She didn't seem to have anything more to say, and Troy retreated, gratefully, into his book. He read on the plane, the bus, and in his hotel room to pass the rest of the day.

One thing the Jets did insist on was that Troy attend the defensive meetings the night before the game. Even though they were asking him to help Coach Crosley, the offensive coordinator, too, his main focus was helping the Jets' defense by predicting their opponent's offensive plays, and that's why they wanted him in the defensive meetings. His mother brought him down to the meeting room and left him in the front row sitting next to Antonio Cromartie. He turned around and waved to Chuku's dad, who waved back but was all business.

"Hey, it's the genius," Antonio said.

David Harris and Antonio Cromartie held out fists for Troy to bump. Troy appreciated them being so friendly, but he couldn't help comparing it to the thrill he had when he helped Seth and the Falcons. Those were players he followed with his gramps since the time he could talk. These guys were sure nice—and talented—but it was vastly different from mixing with his childhood heroes.

Coach Kollar, the defensive coordinator, came in and gave Troy a curious look before addressing the team. The coach went over the defenses they'd play the next day, then put on some Dolphins film from the game when the Jets played them the year before. The Miami team hadn't changed dramatically, so the film would give the players one last example of what their opponents should look like tomorrow.

Instead of ignoring the screen, Troy decided he'd try to get a feel for what was happening. It was something he didn't have to do for the Falcons last season, but he'd seen every Falcons game there was to see. The Jets were something new, so even though he'd watched lots of their game films, he figured this one could help him get the job done tomorrow. After a dozen or so plays he began to try to predict the coming plays in his head. The first guess was wrong. So was the second, and the third. Ten more plays went by—plenty now for him to have a feel for what was happening, and still, nothing.

An alarm went off in his head.

He didn't realize he was tapping his foot until Antonio Cromartie leaned over and asked him if he was okay.

"Yeah," Troy said. "I'm good."

"Relax, little man," Antonio said. "It's not your neck they're gonna try to break tomorrow, just mine."

Troy forced a grin at the joke. He wasn't worried about Cromartie or the Dolphins.

What worried Troy was the Jets' owner, and that dark scowl when he found out that his team's fifteen-million-dollar secret weapon was broken.

CHAPTER FIFTY-SIX

TROY SAT NEXT TO Coach Kollar on the bus ride to the stadium the next morning. He wore official Jets clothing the team had given him: shorts, a cap, and a collared shirt. The coach shed the wrapper from a stick of Big Red gum, then attacked it with his teeth before offering Troy a stick. Troy's mom sat behind them next to Thane.

"So, you're just going to tell me what the play is? That's how it works?" Coach Kollar shook his tan, shaved head as if he still couldn't believe it.

"Once I know," Troy said.

"It won't do me any good if I have to wait until they get to the line."

"I should know when I see what personnel group they run into the huddle. Sometimes it may be when they're coming to the line. Usually before." Troy jammed his hands into his armpits. "Once I get a feel for everything."

"I heard about that." Coach Kollar spoke as fast as he chewed. "The whole thing is unbelievable, really. How long does it take?"

"Depends on the game. I've had it happen halfway through the first series on a long drive." Troy bit his lip. "Once it wasn't until late in the second quarter."

"Any rhyme or reason to *that*?" the coach asked.

Troy rubbed the back of his head. "Not really."

"Well, I'll call it my way until you start telling me the plays. Once the light goes on, it doesn't go out, right?"

"It never has before." Troy was very close to confessing his fears, but when the brakes hissed and they came to a stop inside the stadium, Mr. Cole stepped up into the bus, found Troy with his eyes, and motioned for Troy to follow him.

"See you out there," Troy said to the coach as he left his seat.

Troy's mom signaled for him to go ahead. "I'll be up in the box. Have fun."

Troy looked to see if she was joking, but she smiled and blew him a kiss.

Outside the bus, Troy walked beside the owner through the cool concrete tunnel and out into the muggy air of Florida's midday heat. Wet grass baked beneath their feet. Only a handful of Dolphins players stretched or stood on their end of the field. Troy looked around the stadium. Seats stretched for the sky. At its brim, a necklace of green and orange pennants snapped in the wind.

The owner wore a dark suit with sleek leather shoes. Cuff links and a silver watch glittered below his suit coat sleeves. He looked calm and cool, even in the heat. The intensity of his stare made Troy uncomfortable even in good circumstances. Today it made Troy stuff his hands in his pockets and shift his weight from one foot to the other.

The owner shaded his eyes with one hand and looked around. "Last time you were here, you helped the Falcons win the Super Bowl. Lots of good luck for you in this place, right?"

Troy swallowed.

"Nervous?" the owner asked.

"It always happens." Troy looked up into the luxury boxes for any sign of his mom.

"Good." Mr. Cole put a hand on Troy's shoulder. His grip tightened until Troy looked at him. "Means you care. You've got to care about what you do to really do it well. Don't you think?"

"I care a lot." Troy nodded, hoping to make up for the false ring in his tone. "I want to win. This means as much to me as . . . my own team."

Troy looked down and scuffed the grass, because his words continued to sound off-key.

The owner seemed to read his mind. "I read about that . . . Friday night, I mean. Big win for Summit. Seth Halloway's coaching, right?"

"He coached my junior league team in Georgia." Troy shaded his eyes and looked up at the owner, thinking he might lobby for Seth to get hired one day by the Jets. "We won the whole state. He wants to coach in the pros, but Seth says he's not afraid to start at the bottom."

"One thing jumped out at me, though." The owner's mouth twisted into a curious smile. "I was surprised to see that other team scoring on you guys at all. I'm sure Seth couldn't come up with five million dollars, but I thought you might give him a discount, you know, to let him know what the other team was going to run on offense."

The owner's words startled Troy. It was as if Mr. Cole knew Troy's dark secret, and that wasn't good.

CHAPTER FIFTY-SEVEN

TROY'S MIND SPUN LIKE a blender and spit out a story quick as a blink. "Yeah, well, it's a whole new system for everyone and the coaching at Summit before was pretty stinky. It's hard for these guys just to get the signals right. We're working on it, though. Seth says he'd rather have everyone lined up for sure than guys scrambling like a fire drill at the last second and leaving a big hole in the defense."

Mr. Cole looked at him for what seemed like a very long time, even though it was no more than a brief pause, before he nodded. "That makes sense. Well, have fun today. I can't imagine making a quarter-million dollars a week at the age of thirteen. I thought it was a fortune when I earned my first six-figure salary after law school."

"You were a lawyer?" Troy asked, thinking of his own father.

Mr. Cole gave him a funny look. "In another life. Oh, and I'm sure you've figured out that I've used what influence I have to keep the media off your front porch and from haunting the school yard, but after the game today, I think it's only fair if you talk at the press conference. It's in your contract, but I wanted to ask anyway. You okay with that?"

It suddenly felt hard for Troy to breathe, but he managed a nod and grunted in a way that promised he'd be there.

"Excellent. Well, up to the box."

The owner walked away, leaving Troy to stand alone in the bench area until Coach Kollar wandered out and slapped him on the back. "Stay close, buddy."

Troy stayed close, following Coach Kollar around through warm-ups, in the locker room for the head coach's pregame speech, and finally out into the packed stadium for the big game.

The Jets earned boos from the crowd as they sprinted out onto the field. Troy clenched his hands and worked at his gum, wanting the whole thing to begin already. His mom called his cell phone and directed his attention to the luxury box where she sat just two seats behind the owner. Troy waved up at her and Mr. Cole raised a hand before giving him a thumbs-up.

Troy said good-bye to his mom on the phone, but then,

in a growing state of panic, he got Tate on the line.

"How's your dad?" Troy couldn't keep the tremble out of his voice.

"Same." Tate's voice was flat, but then she came to life. "Hey, aren't you getting ready for the Jets game?"

"I'm on the sideline right now." Troy covered his mouth and the phone with his other hand, speaking softly. "Tate, I don't know if I can do it."

"Try to relax. What's the worst thing that can happen?"

"They find me floating in the Passaic River?"

"Stop. You're talking about an NFL owner, not some mobster."

"This guy is scary. I've got a contract to call the plays for his team and he paid me five million dollars to sign it—which is already gone thanks to my father."

"Just . . . I don't know. It'll work out," Tate said.

"How do you know, Tate?"

"I don't know, Troy, but I'll be watching. They have Direct TV in my dad's room. He still can't talk, but my mom says she knows he's happy when football is on."

Troy went quiet. When he thought of Tate's dad, it made him feel a little guilty for making such a fuss.

"Anyway," Tate said, "I'll be watching . . . Good luck."

The players lined up along the sideline and took off their helmets. The crowd stood for the national anthem.

Troy fumbled with his phone and spoke into it before hanging up. "Thanks, Tate. I think I'm gonna need it."

CHAPTER FIFTY-EIGHT

AN ELECTRIC CURRENT FILLED the air, adding a charge of excitement and thrill to the face of every player, coach, equipment man, and even the trainers on the Jets sideline. Troy felt it, too. He'd felt it before, never as intensely as at the Super Bowl seven months ago, but this was a close second: opening day for two bitter AFC East rivals. For Troy, though, the current didn't lift him or put sparkle in his eyes. The current went to ground in his stomach. Only one thought clawed away in his mind.

He didn't want to be there.

For the first time since he had discovered his gift and dreamed of using it to help the Atlanta Falcons win a Super Bowl, Troy had no interest in being on an NFL sideline. Troy wanted to *play*, not call plays.

That's where his heart was now.

Under the lights, slinging the ball downfield like Friday night, dodging defenders—*that's* where he wanted to be. *That* was his real dream. Now that he'd had a taste of real football, high school varsity football, he could clearly see the path that would take him to the NFL. He wanted to be Drew Brees, or Aaron Rogers, or Eli Manning on opening day, not a kid who got paid to help give a billionaire's team a strategic advantage.

He finished mouthing the words to "The Star-Spangled Banner" and looked around. In the energy overload, no one even noticed him. He felt like slipping away. He looked up into the box where his mother sat. Her eyes, unlike anyone else's, were on him. She smiled and gave him a thumbs-up. He waved back and groaned, turning his attention to the field and the kickoff the Jets were receiving.

Coach Crosley, the Jets offensive coordinator, caught his eye and motioned him over.

"So, word is you're gonna start telling me what coverages they're going to be running at some point?" Coach Crosley asked.

"Once I get a feel for it," Troy said.

"Well, I'm not counting on it, so anything you got is a bonus. You tell me and I've got hand signals worked out with McElroy and Thane. Just don't give me the wrong coverage. That I can't have." Coach Crosley wore a deadly serious face.

Troy nodded. He stood next to Coach Crosley with nothing between them and the players on the field but the chain stretched between the first-down markers. Troy watched the Jets as they marched down the field then sputtered, throwing two incomplete passes in a row. On third and eleven, Coach Crosley gave him a questioning and hopeful look. If Troy knew what coverage to expect, it could help him call a successful play. Troy could only shrug and shake his dull and heavy head.

The Dolphins double-covered Thane and the Jets pass fell incomplete. The kicker went out on fourth down and made the field goal, so that was something.

"I could have used you on that third down," Coach Crosley said, obviously frustrated. "Maybe you'll do better for our defense."

The coach marched off toward the bench to make adjustments with his players.

Thane passed by on his way off the field. "How'd it go, buddy? No feelings yet?"

Troy had a feeling—a lump in his gut. "Not yet."

"Don't worry. We're up three already." Thane messed his hair and went to the bench.

Troy didn't do any better for the Jets' defense. Nothing came to him, and the Dolphins drove down the field. Coach Kollar gave Troy a questioning look when the Dolphins crossed the fifty-yard line, but Troy could only shrug and look at his feet. When the Dolphins scored to take a 7–3 lead, Coach Kollar turned without saying anything and walked away.

Troy stood dutifully beside each coordinator who called the Jets' plays—one for the offense, the other for the defense—without giving any help as the game went on.

Halfway through the second quarter, with the Jets losing 13–10, Troy's cell phone rang.

It was his mother. "What's wrong? You look like you're having trouble."

Troy huffed into the phone. "Sometimes it takes time. You know that, Mom. I haven't done this since the Super Bowl."

"Do you feel it, though? Are you close?" His mother was whispering into the phone. "Mr. Cole keeps looking over here at me. I'm sorry. I shouldn't have called. Just do your thing. I gotta go."

She hung up and so did Troy. He watched the game, trying to see it, trying to feel it. When David Harris came off the field after Miami scored the next touchdown, he whipped off his helmet and cast a glare at Troy. Harris marched his way and Troy expected a chewing-out before Chuku's dad stepped in front of Troy, stopping the fellow linebacker in his tracks. Mr. Moore whispered something to Harris that ended with "Come on, dawg, he's just a kid."

Mr. Moore flashed a smile not unlike Chuku's.

Harris clenched his teeth, nodded at Mr. Moore, and

turned for the bench. When he passed by, Troy heard Harris curse under his breath.

"Don't worry, Troy. This is a rough way to make a living. People get tense." Mr. Moore patted Troy's shoulder and walked away with his helmet under his arm.

Troy nodded. He knew that as the starting middle linebacker, no one could have benefited more from Troy's gift than David Harris. Harris had been expecting to have the plays fed to him with a series of hand signals Coach Kollar had devised to go along with the defense he'd want to shift to—if he knew the play. For a cost of five million dollars a year to the team, David Harris was supposed to know where the ball was going. If it worked—as it had for Seth Halloway until his knees gave out—David Harris would have more tackles than any other player in the NFL and be a shoe-in for the Pro Bowl, maybe defensive MVP.

When Troy turned to watch Harris stalk toward the Gatorade table, he found himself staring into the lens of the CBS handheld camera behind the bench. Three red lights glared at him like a deadly, three-eyed alien and Troy knew his face was live on network TV and the announcers were probably talking about him. He pretended not to see and turned away to watch the game.

When halftime came, Troy pinched the bridge of his nose and jogged into the locker room with the rest of the Jets. Except for a friendly wave from Thane before he headed for the trainers' room to get retaped, the players and coaches ignored Troy. Even Mr. Moore and Antonio Cromartie didn't look Troy's way, so he sat in a lonely corner on an empty stool, out of the mix. Mr. Cole appeared unexpectedly, still calm and cool-looking in his dark suit, but he found Troy immediately and motioned him toward the showers.

Troy stood and followed, marching like a convict.

Inside the vast empty space, the clicking of the owner's shoes echoed off the tiled walls. He stood facing a soap dispenser on the wall. Troy stopped in the middle of the showers and waited. Mr. Cole sighed and turned to face him. His eyes were dark and empty and his face might have been made from wood.

"So tell me," the owner said. "What do I need to do here?"

CHAPTER FIFTY-NINE

TEARS STREAMED DOWN TROY'S face. That turned his distress into anger.

He gritted his teeth and spit his words. "You don't think I'm trying? You think this is fun for me?"

"Okay." The owner nodded, as if he'd made an important decision. He spoke with soft intensity. "Story time. Once there was an Onondagan named Running Deer. He led his people into one of the most brutal and famous battles against the Hurons, defeating them, and bringing a peace that lasted throughout the Iroquois nations for hundreds of years. My mother used to tell me his blood ran through my veins. I don't know if that was even true, but she told it to me at a time when I thought *I* was still a boy . . . Running Deer led his people into battle when he was only eleven."

"And, what, this is my battle?" Troy asked, uncertain where the owner was going with all this.

Mr. Cole stared hard at Troy. "Yes, this is your battle. You're a boy, but you're being treated like a man. We have an agreement, a contract between two men, and I want to know what the problem is . . . Maybe I can help."

Troy took a deep breath and said, "I don't feel it."

The owner stared for a moment, then nodded slowly. "And this affects your abilities."

"I think so, but it's taken time before, so I wasn't sure. I'm not sure."

"Into the second half?" The owner's look remained steady.

Troy returned the stare. "No."

The owner frowned and nodded. "I'm not happy, I've got a lot riding on you, a lot of plans to get this franchise to a championship, but I appreciate the honesty. Dishonesty makes me see red. Okay, let's see what happens in the second half. Get a Gatorade or something. Are you hungry?"

Troy shook his head. The owner gave Troy's shoulder a squeeze, but the only sound he made was the echoing click of his shoes on the shower floor as he left Troy to think.

Troy took out his phone. He had no service. On the other side of the wall Coach Ryan, the head coach, shouted at the players, telling them they were better than what they'd shown so far. Troy slipped back into the locker room, past the yelling, and out into the guts of the stadium, where he got two bars on his phone. Two state troopers looked at him curiously. He felt their eyes scoping out the all-access pass hanging from his belt loop. One of them—he could tell by the look on his face—recognized Troy as the Jets' "football genius"; the other did not. Troy's face reddened as if he were standing naked in front of the troopers.

He turned away and headed toward the tunnel, stopping just short of the sunlight, where he got three bars on the phone and dialed Tate. He knew she was watching on TV.

"What's going on?" she asked.

Troy's eyes darted around him at the security people, who kept their eyes up on the crowd surrounding the tunnel. "I feel like getting out of here, calling my mom, and catching a cab to the airport. This stinks."

"You're not feeling it?"

"Does twenty points look like I'm feeling it? Seth Cole just threatened me with I don't know what."

"What's that mean?"

"He said he paid me a lot of money. He wants results."

"Maybe it will come to you." Tate's suggestion sounded weak.

"I feel like I'm gonna puke. I don't even want this anymore. I want to *play* the game, not predict it."

"Fight or flight," Tate said.

"What are you talking about?"

"Remember Mr. Dunn's science class last year? When a mammal is faced with danger, it just reacts. The adrenaline starts pumping and it either puts its back up and fights, or it turns and runs. You can't run. That's not who you are, Troy."

"Why is that not who I *am*?" Troy wanted to smash the phone against the concrete wall.

"This whole thing is about football, being a great player." Tate sounded urgent. "I know that's what you want. A great player is someone who *fights*. There's no room for flight in football."

Troy wanted to tell Tate she was just a girl and what did she know, but she did know. Tate was right. Troy bit the inside of his cheek until he tasted blood.

"It still stinks."

"If it was easy, Jamie Renfro would be doing it."

Troy couldn't help smiling at the mention of his old nemesis, a bully who had ridiculed Troy and made his life miserable on and off the football field. "He's probably having a good laugh at me right now if he's watching this game."

"How many touchdowns did you throw Friday night?" Tate asked. "Six, right? Let him laugh at that. Now go do your job. Do the best you can. If it's not good enough, work at it. Maybe it will take another week."

Troy took a deep breath. "Thanks, Tate."

"Hey, that's why I get the big bucks."

Troy laughed. A metal door crashed open from the direction of the locker room inside the tunnel. Troy heard the growl of angry NFL players. He hung up the phone and let the tide of green-and-white Jets sweep him out onto the field and up the sideline.

CHAPTER SIXTY

THE PLAYERS STRETCHED AND threw and darted about to get loose. Troy stood on the fifty-yard line and waited for Coach Kollar. The big, rangy coach put on his headphones and shucked a fresh stick of Big Red. Keeping his eyes on the field as he studied the Dolphins sideline, he offered a piece to Troy.

Troy took it and chewed hard, determined to focus with all his might and see or feel—or smell if he had to—what the Dolphins' plays would be. He remembered his mom and turned to find her staring at him from the box. The owner wasn't back yet. Troy forced a smile and gave her a thumbs-up. The Jets received the ball and Coach Ryan's halftime speech fueled enough excitement for the offense to score a field goal. Grim faces shouted encouragement to one another as the offense jogged off the field urging the defensive players on to the same success.

Troy put his hands on his knees and bent over, studying the Dolphins intently. The Dolphins' offense moved the ball down the field with ease. Coach Kollar gave Troy a look that bordered on panic. All Troy could do was shrug and look away. He had no better luck with helping Coach Crosley.

The game ground on, and by midway through the fourth quarter, the Jets began to lose hope. They were three touchdowns behind and nothing seemed to be working. Coach Kollar wore a pained look and he avoided Troy's eyes. Coach Crosley didn't even bother with him. Troy kept at it, hoping—even though the cause was all but lost—that he could reignite his talent and prove to them that he was for real.

It never happened.

With thirty-two seconds left in the game, the Dolphins got the ball back. Coach Kollar looked at Troy with a deadpan face. "What do you think they'll run? Kneel-down?"

Troy watched as the Dolphins snapped the ball and knelt down to run out the clock.

"Maybe I should be getting five million a year," the coach said under his breath as he threw down his headphones and walked away.

The sting of Coach Kollar's comment cut through Troy's fog. Thane slapped him on the back as he jogged past and told him not to worry, but that didn't help. Ritchie Anderson, the Jets' PR director, appeared at Troy's side and took his arm, guiding him toward the locker room. "Mr. Cole said to give the media five minutes with you while Coach talks to the team. That way, you don't have to wait around."

Troy swallowed hard but kept walking. His mom met him in the tunnel and he had a ray of hope that she'd somehow save him.

"Mom?"

CHAPTER SIXTY-ONE

TROY'S MOM SHOOK HER head and lowered her voice. "It's in your contract, Troy."

"And I'm supposed to say what?" Troy tried to keep the panic out of his voice.

"You hurt your shoulder Friday night. You're in some pain. Distracted." His mom threw her hands up. "I don't know, but don't tell them you don't *care*. Just say you're trying. I know it's hard, but let's just get it done and over with. They'll hound you anyway if you don't give them something. Come on. You can't run from it."

Troy looked at her suspiciously, wondering if she'd spoken to Tate.

His mom walked with him past the locker room and farther into the concrete tunnel toward the media interview room. With the PR guy beside him, Troy stepped into the crowded room and up onto the dais with a huge green-and-white Jets banner behind him. Cameras flashed. Red lights blinked on. An excited murmur rose up like an angry mob as the reporters fired questions. Troy gripped the edges of the podium. Ritchie Anderson adjusted the microphone and held up his hands.

"Stop! Just stop!" Anderson scowled at them. "One question at a time, or this is over. I want to start out by saying on behalf of the team that Troy was unable to assist the coaching staff in today's game. We are hopeful that will change between now and next week. This is going to be very brief, so I apologize to you in advance because only a couple of you will get to ask questions. Now, Mike Lupica."

All eyes turned to the ESPN and *New York Daily News* commentator.

"Troy, when you helped the Falcons win the Super Bowl, I called it magic. What happened? Is the magic gone?"

Troy swallowed. "I don't . . . I don't think so."

Lupica stared.

"I don't know," Troy said. "Maybe."

"What happened?" Lupica asked. "Is it possible you're just outgrowing this genius thing? You look like you're five or six inches taller than you were at the Super Bowl," Lupica said.

Troy glanced at his mom but got no help. He leaned

into the microphone. "I don't think so. Maybe. I got hurt in my own football game on Friday night. My shoulder. It's bothering me. Maybe that's it."

Murmurs rose like a fast tide.

Anderson held up his hands, then pointed. "Pam Oliver."

The Fox NFL reporter wore a sad look and it seemed to Troy as though, besides his mother, she was the only person in the room who actually cared about him.

"If *playing* football is making it . . . hard for you to do your genius thing . . . well, will you stop *playing*?"

"I hope I can do both." Troy rubbed the back of his head. "But *playing* football is my dream. One day all the way up to the NFL if I can. I mean, you can't get to the NFL if you don't play in high school. That's step one. Helping the Jets win games is . . . well, it's a job, not a dream."

The room exploded with questions. The PR guy held up his hands, but it didn't work. Troy couldn't have answered another question if he wanted to. Anderson and his mom escorted him out of the room and he bumped into Greg McElroy, who was on his way in. Troy stumbled, but McElroy caught him and held him up straight. "You okay?"

"Thanks," Troy said.

McElroy glanced into the media room and chuckled. "Thanks for the distraction."

"Huh?"

"No one's gonna be asking me about my two picks today."

"Oh," Troy said.

"It'll work out." McElroy pointed up and flicked his eyes at the ceiling. "He's got your back."

Before Troy could reply, McElroy waded into the storm of reporters and the room grew quiet. Troy's mom took him by the arm and led him past the locker room.

He followed her march through the stadium tunnel and outside. Instead of leading him to one of the players' buses, his mom steered him toward a long black limousine whose rear door she swung open for him.

"Whose is this?" Troy asked. "Where are we going?"

CHAPTER SIXTY-TWO

A VOICE CAME FROM inside the limousine. "I thought it might be easier for you to ride back with me. Get in, Troy."

Troy recognized the owner's voice. He hesitated because Mr. Cole was the last person he wanted to see. His mom waved him on and he slipped inside. The bright sunshine left him seeing only dark shadows and vague shapes inside the back of the cool, dark car. His mom got in beside him and closed the door. The owner's expressionless face began to materialize before him as his eyes adjusted.

The limo pulled out of the lot behind two police cars with their lights flashing. They quickly slid into an empty lane meant for emergency traffic, whisking past the long line of cars waiting to exit the stadium and pulling out onto the open highway.

The owner removed three bottles of water from a small refrigerator, offering one to Troy and his mom before cracking open his own and taking a swig. Mr. Cole sat studying the water bottle. Finally, he sighed and lowered it into his lap.

"Look, Troy, I heard what you said in there."

Troy held the owner's gaze and swallowed hard.

"Do you remember when we talked about how you could help this team? I took a huge chance. I outbid everyone else before the bidding even started, and there was a lot of excitement when I gave you a contract. The team hasn't won a championship since the sixties. Getting it this year is *our* dream. It should be yours."

"Are you going to fire me?" Troy gripped his water bottle so that the plastic crackled.

"Are you going to stop playing high school football so I can at least get my money's worth out of you?" the owner asked, his voice suddenly like steel.

Troy's mom cleared her throat. "Mr. Cole, my son wants to play football."

The owner looked as if he was holding back laughter. "In your wildest dreams, did you ever imagine fifteen million dollars?"

Mr. Cole's tone made Troy hot and without thinking, he said, "I did. Peyton Manning makes a lot more than that."

The owner finished his laugh. "Peyton Manning? Is that who you are?"

"Maybe." Troy glared at him. "I'll make millions playing football."

"You like to talk about contracts." Troy's mom turned her mouth into a flat line and fired up her eyes before she continued. "Troy's got one and nothing in it says he can't play football. I'm not going to stop him, and neither are you."

Troy's heart swelled with love for his mom.

The owner stewed on that while they rode in silence to a private airport. The limo pulled out onto the tarmac and they all got out, stiff and quiet, right beside a big white jet. A flight attendant in a dark blue uniform led Troy and his mom up the stairs, through one compartment into another in the back the size of a living room, where a leather couch and chairs faced a big flatscreen TV.

"Just let me know if you'd like sandwiches or drinks," the flight attendant said.

Mr. Cole stayed in the front room by himself. When they took off, the jet seemed to go almost straight up. Troy's mom gripped his hand as the force pushed them into the backs of their leather chairs.

After they leveled out, Mr. Cole appeared in the doorway leading to his area. In his hand was a green bottle of sparkling water. Whatever dark thoughts he'd been brooding on seemed to have vanished.

"I'm used to getting what I want, so you'll have to excuse me. I hope I wasn't rude. You're right about the contract." He smiled and pointed at Troy's mom with his bottle. "It also says that after the first season the contract can be nullified if there is a failure to perform. The lawyers will have fun arguing over that clause if it comes to that. Let's hope it won't. I will say, though, that I know about your current financial situation and your issues with the IRS and Troy's father. So, no, I can't make you stop playing football, but if you can't perform . . . well, it won't be good for anyone, will it?"

Before Troy or his mom could say anything, the owner slipped away.

When they landed at the airfield in Morristown, Mr. Cole was gone before they left the plane. A car waited for them on the tarmac and the driver headed toward Summit.

CHAPTER SIXTY-THREE

TROY AND HIS MOM had dinner together alone. Seth was with his coaching staff working out the Summit game plan for next Friday night. Tate landed at Newark Airport late and fell asleep on the way home in the car. The next day, Troy's shoulder felt a bit better and that was a relief. The kids at school cheered when they saw Troy and thanked him for the big win.

During lunch, Chuku dragged Troy up on the stage at the far end of the cafeteria and with his mouth so close to the microphone that it boomed through the room he announced that Troy was the savior of Summit. The entire cafeteria broke out into applause and Troy pulled away, blushing and returning to his seat, even though Chuku proceeded to bow like a boxing champion after a big fight and drone on about how their team was on a mission and the Killer Kombo couldn't be stopped. Troy wasn't sure who'd turned the microphone on for Chuku, but the principal was the one to turn it off, even though she did it with a smile, accepting a hug from Chuku.

Everything was positive, but Troy had a feeling some of the older players might not be so happy about Chuku's show, especially Grant Reed. When Troy walked into the locker room after school it didn't surprise him to hear Grant Reed's loud voice. It took Troy a minute, though, to realize he was being made fun of by the older player and that it was about his failure with the Jets in Miami.

"Ha *haa*!" Reed's eyebrows danced and he acted as if he was surprised to see Troy. "You're not as smart as you think, are you? What happened in Miami? I thought you were a football *genius*? That's what you call yourself, right?"

Troy bit his lip and kept pulling on his pads. Thankfully, Chance Bryant appeared from around the lockers. Chance had all his pads on already and his hands were taped like a fighter's. He hammered a locker with one of his fists.

"Who farted?" His voice was mean and serious. The locker room got quiet, and Chance spoke in a low growl. "Oh, that wasn't a fart. That was you, Reed . . . talking."

Grant Reed drew in a breath and puffed up his chest. He was about to say something when Chance took three quick steps, closed the gap, and lifted Grant Reed up off his feet with a single handful of shirt.

Chance banged him up against a locker, put his face close, and whispered through his sneer, "I want to win a championship, you got that? I want to play football in college, and you're not gonna be the reason it doesn't happen. You got that? You're a *captain*. *This* kid is our quarterback. We just beat a team we haven't beaten since your daddy was in diapers. I want to keep winning. So you just leave my man here alone."

Reed opened his mouth. "I—"

"No." Chance shook him, banging Reed's head into the locker again. "Don't even try to explain, Grant. You just leave him alone or the next time you won't even see me coming. You got that?"

Reed just stared, but Troy could see that the light had gone out in his blue eyes.

"Nod if you got that," Chance said, slow and mean.

CHAPTER SIXTY-FOUR

REED NODDED.

Chance dropped him and stalked away.

Troy had to bite down on his lip to keep from grinning, and that was the last anyone mentioned anything about the Jets or any of the painful stories in the newspapers about Troy losing his magic.

Before practice, Seth approached Troy during stretching and asked how he was feeling.

"Good to go," Troy said. "Shoulder is much better. It only hurts a little. I'm fine."

"Yeah, your mom called and told me you were feeling a lot better, but I wasn't talking about your shoulder. I meant, you know, all this business with the Jets . . ."

"I'm fine, Seth." Troy buckled up his chinstrap. "I mean it. Really."

"Nice," Seth said, and walked away clapping his hands. "Let's go Summit Centurions! We got Morristown this week and we will *crush* them!"

Practice ran hot and fast with players still feeding off the excitement of beating a team like Lawton. The coaches stayed on them, though, and the theme for the week became one of not letting up. No one tried to pretend that Morristown was anything close to Lawton, but it was thrilling to go to the game as a championship-caliber team and stomping someone the way Summit had been stomped for so many years.

Practice that whole week went well, and between that, school, and the dinners that he, Seth, his mom, and Tate would have later in the evenings, the week flew by. Troy was obsessed with Morristown. After beating Lawton, the Summit team and coaches knew they could beat anyone. That made some of the players dream—dream and even talk—about the chances of going undefeated, a perfect season.

Troy forced the Jets and his deal with Mr. Cole to a back corner of his mind, and even his mom agreed that it was the best way to handle the whole thing. She stood behind Troy's decision to focus on his own football team, even if it meant the end of his NFL contract.

"We lived in that tiny cabin for twelve years," his mom had said. "I don't see any reason we can't live there for twelve more."

"Or this place." Troy had no intention of moving.

"Or this place," she had said.

"Then, after that," Troy had replied, "I'll sign a huge NFL contract and buy you a place in the Cotton Wood Country Club."

"Or maybe you'll be in law school." His mother never could help herself from quickly bringing Troy down to earth.

CHAPTER SIXTY-FIVE

THE FRIDAY NIGHT CROWD for Morristown was even bigger than it had been for Lawton. The smell of sizzling hot dogs floated up from the concession stand in thick clouds. Banners and pom-poms appeared like dormant wildflowers after a desert rain, waving over the throng of fans dressed in gold and blue. Many of the Summit residents wanted to see if the football team was for real, and a lot of outsiders came with hopes of seeing Troy and Chuku play brilliantly. He figured there might be a grump here or there who wanted to see if he'd fall on his face the same way he had for the Jets last Sunday, but he sensed that the crowd was firmly behind him.

Troy stood on the edge of the field in his equipment and drank in the crowd like an actor peering from behind the curtain before a big show. His mind skipped a beat when he saw the tall man in the suit again, the one with the surveyors on the field his first day at the school. For the second game in a row he was wearing a suit. This time, instead of talking with Mr. Biondi, he had someone next to him who looked familiar.

The tall man suddenly pointed behind Troy. Troy turned and saw Chuku coming down the steps. He looked back to the stands. The man next to the tall man was chunky with a thick gray . . . mustache.

"The UPS guy," Troy spoke under his breath. Baffled and slightly alarmed by seeing the two of them together, he began to scan the crowd again. Tate had gotten a text from Ty saying he might come with Thane. *Might*. Troy spotted Tate, but she was sitting alone with his mom. He wondered if his failure with the Jets had anything to do with his cousins not showing up.

Either way, people spilled out of the bleachers and onto the grass outside the fence surrounding the field. The night was room temperature, and anticipation crackled in the air. It reminded Troy of the Helena concert, lots of happy talk and laughter, but plenty of anticipation to see a big show.

The difference for Troy was that now he felt it running *through* him, not just around him.

"I'm the quarterback." He whispered the words inside his helmet so only he could hear. Still, they sent a shiver through his frame.

On the way out to the field, Seth put a hand on Troy's

shoulder pad and pointed to the crowd. "Football is officially alive and well in Summit. We keep doing this,
they're gonna have to build a new stadium. Did you
know they were talking about tearing this down and
just folding the program?"

Troy laughed out loud. "Tell 'em to save up their
money. It's gonna have to be twice the size."

"I'll let the school board know." Seth slapped Troy
on the back. "Hey, enjoy yourself out here tonight. We
are gonna bury these guys. I want all the backups in
the game halfway through the third quarter. I want
everyone to play."

The team ran like a high-performance engine during warm-ups, with Troy connecting to Chuku, Levi, or
Spencer on every single throw. The receivers' feet were
quick and precise and their hands sure. Their running
back, Jentry Hood, had a spring in his step that promised touchdowns. Troy's head had cleared completely, so
he was feeling razor sharp.

He roared with the rest of the team when Seth gathered them in the team room and said, "Let's go out
there and smash Morristown! Right now! Let's go!"

CHAPTER SIXTY-SIX

SMASH MORRISTOWN IS EXACTLY what they did. Troy and his teammates played with fury, and by the final minutes of the third quarter, the score was 70–12 and the Morristown players just wanted it to end. When the backups went in, Seth found Troy on the sideline and draped an arm over his shoulders. "Nice win, buddy. Everybody plays. You did it."

Troy looked up. "*You* did it, Seth. You made this all happen."

Seth gave Troy a one-armed squeeze. "You're the one throwing touchdown passes."

Troy shook his head. He knew Seth was modest. He'd been that way as a player, always talking about what his teammates did instead of himself. "You moved up here from Atlanta. You've got a huge mansion and now you're living in some crummy apartment in Summit."

"Hey, it's got running water and electricity," Seth said.

"Your game room is bigger than the entire apartment," Troy said. "I just want you to know how much I appreciate it. I think all these guys do. This is . . . amazing."

Seth looked out over the field and his eyes glazed over with a dreamy look. "You know, buddy, I'm with you on that. This is amazing. I love it."

"Let's just hope we can keep it up."

CHAPTER SIXTY-SEVEN

TWO DAYS LATER, THE Jets played at home against the Bengals.

Troy attended and felt awful.

Whereas the week before players and coaches had looked at him with a mixture of curiosity and wonderment, he now got treated—except from Thane and Chuku's dad—like one of the ball boys. People were polite, but no one really cared. Mr. Cole *wished* him good luck before the game. At the beginning, Coaches Kollar and Crosley glanced at him hopefully from time to time, but Troy had nothing to give them and they stopped before the first half ended. Afterward—even though the Jets won and people were happy—the owner was nowhere to be seen.

The reporters ignored him, too. That was a relief

anyway. Ritchie Anderson didn't ask him to talk at the press conference. The football-genius story seemed to be officially dead. Troy found his mom in the tunnel. She had a parking spot in the players' lot underneath the stadium. They got out of there before anyone else.

When they pulled out onto the turnpike, Troy's mom frowned at the road. "I'm sorry, Troy."

"I just want to get as far away from this place as I can." He thumped his head against the window.

"If he hadn't already paid you—"

"The money my father *stole*?" he interrupted.

She gave a short nod. "I'd say you could just quit. I hate seeing you have to go through all this. I'm your mother. I'm supposed to make the hurt go away.

"But I feel like you've got to try."

CHAPTER SIXTY-EIGHT

FOR THE NEXT COUPLE of weeks, Troy did try.

He didn't focus on his job with the Jets as much as he did learning the game plan for his opponents on Friday nights, but he tried. That's what he told Mr. Cole, and Troy was grateful that the owner seemed almost to have lost interest in him. The coaches and players certainly had. Troy looked at his Sunday outings as the price he had to pay for the joys of playing on a winning football team on which he was the star quarterback.

His own Summit team seemed to only get better with each passing week. Troy was certainly a huge part of the reason, because—along with his line and receivers—he kept improving. Articles began to appear in the smaller, local papers about him and Chuku, the

Killer Kombo. Troy's timing on passes, his fakes on bootlegs and play-action passes, made Coach Sindoni pucker his lips from time to time and let out a low whistle that filled Troy with joy.

He was so thrilled that the bad stuff seemed to be nothing more than minor annoyances, like pesky mosquitoes on a wonderful summer evening.

On the morning after the Summit team's sixth win Troy sat undefeated at the kitchen table and opened the Saturday morning newspaper to read about himself. He chewed on the words and gulped them down as if they were the marshmallows in his breakfast cereal.

"Mom." Troy tapped the paper until she put down her pencil and looked up from a Sudoku puzzle. "This guy called me a 'phenom.' How about that? I'd rather be that than a genius. Geniuses are a dime a dozen. And they're saying I'm a candidate for the *All-State* team. Can you imagine? As an eighth grader? It's never been done, Mom."

"Let me see." Tate leaned over his shoulder. "That's awesome, Troy. Phenom. Cool."

Troy searched his mind for something enthusiastic to say to Tate, something to return the compliment. The trouble was that things for Tate weren't going so great. Her mom was still stuck in San Diego with her dad, who wasn't doing any better at all. She had made the JV soccer team, which was a pretty big deal as an eighth grader, except for the fact that even though she was evolving into the star player, the team itself had won only two games.

"Thanks, Tate." That was all Troy could think of.

Troy's mom smiled at the "phenom" news, but something was missing.

"What's wrong, Mom?" Troy asked.

"Well . . ." She took a sip of coffee. "I just wish the Jets were winning as much as Summit."

Troy frowned at her for raining on his parade. "They've won a couple of games . . . and I'm *trying*, Mom. I am. I said I was, and I *am*."

"Oh, I'm proud of you, Troy." Her smile lost its baggage for a moment. "All those touchdowns. Don't think I'm not. But I worry about the Jets. Mr. Cole had such big plans for the team, and all that money. Don't look at me like that—I'm your mom. I'm supposed to worry."

Troy nodded because he guessed he understood. It wasn't going to dampen his enthusiasm, though. With the team winning and him playing so well, even an annoyance like Grant Reed and his continued wisecracks about the kindergarten corner had become as meaningless as a raspberry seed stuck in his teeth.

"Do you know if we win our next three games it'll be a perfect season?" Troy's voice bubbled. "That's never been done before in Summit High School football history. After that, it'll be on to the playoffs. Think about it, Mom. Seth said Mr. Biondi told him that if we do that, he *knows* we'll get the support for a new stadium. When that happens—with the record we'll have—St. Stephen's isn't going to be the place to be anymore . . . Summit is!"

CHAPTER SIXTY-NINE

THE FOLLOWING WEDNESDAY, THEY were at the breakfast table when Tate got a text from Ty, inviting all of them—including Seth—to join him and Thane at a charity party in Manhattan at the Guggenheim Museum.

"Me, too?" Troy craned his neck to see if he was really mentioned in the text or if Tate was making it up. He felt a bit guilty for having let Ty fade from his life. "We haven't even spoken."

"Chuku is probably going. His dad's on the list." Tate kept reading her phone. "I guess the mayor is going to be there, and the cast from *Glee*. Wow. That's cool."

"Chuku doesn't like *Glee*." Troy just couldn't see Chuku getting excited about some stuffy charity event. "Me neither."

"Can we go, Ms. White? He's picking us up in a limo." Tate showed her phone to Troy, practically glowing with delight.

"I love that cheerleading coach. Jane Lynch, right? Sounds fun," Troy's mom said.

"We've been in plenty of limos," Troy grumbled.

"Do you want me to ask him who else is gonna be there? Maybe Eli Manning." Tate started to text Ty back.

"Naw," Troy said. "Who cares?"

His mom let her spatula clatter into the sink. She set plates of eggs and toast down in front of them both. "Eli Manning? You love Eli Manning, Troy, and you know it."

"Yeah, but I don't need to be glomming onto him in some crowd." Troy picked up his fork and broke open his eggs so that orange yolk gushed onto the plate. He didn't want to say how much he loved Eli Manning because the idea of being Ty's guest just didn't sit quite right.

Tate stopped texting. "You don't want to go?"

"No, I'll go." Troy stuffed some egg into his mouth and talked while he chewed. "It's just no big deal, that's all."

Tate's phone buzzed. "He sent me a screen shot of the invitation. It's five thousand dollars a couple. *That's* a big deal."

"Tate, it's not polite to talk about money." Troy stared at her until she blushed and shrugged and started to eat.

"Tell him we'd love to go, Tate." Troy's mom sat down and she shot Troy a disapproving look. "*All* of us."

CHAPTER SEVENTY

THEY DIDN'T EAT DINNER that night because Thane talked with Troy's mom and said they'd have a ton of food at the party. Troy's mom made him put on some church clothes, which gave him something legitimate to grumble about. He wasn't sure why he wanted to grumble, but he knew part of it was that *he* should be the one picking people up in limos. *He* was the one with a multimillion-dollar contract, not Ty.

When the limo pulled up and beeped, Tate dashed out onto the front porch, then sprang back inside the door. "Check it out! It's a huge Humvee! White! It's like the one on *The Bachelorette*!"

Seth and his mom walked out into the front hall from the kitchen looking like movie stars.

"Nice," Seth said, peering out the open door and smiling at Tate.

Troy felt as if it was going to be a long night.

Thane and Ty sat in the backseat facing forward, with a space between them. When they all climbed in, Thane said, "Here, Tate. We saved this seat for you, right, Ty?"

Ty's face practically turned purple. When Tate slapped his knee and said hello, all he could do was stutter and mumble something about being sorry to hear about her dad. Troy felt pretty satisfied that the whole way into the city, Ty couldn't find his tongue.

When they climbed out in front of the big museum that looked like an upside-down wedding cake, Troy leaned close to Tate. "A limo can't make you smooth, right?"

Tate shot him a scowl, then turned to Thane. "Thank you for inviting us."

"Hey." Thane laughed. "You guys are family."

Inside, waiters carried trays covered in white linen and loaded up with drinks and fancy stuff to eat that Troy gobbled down: scallops wrapped in bacon, deep-fried shrimp, little triangles of fried cheese, and even mini hot dogs wrapped in puffy blankets of golden dough.

Several players from the Giants and the Jets were there, including Mr. Moore and Chuku, who wore a white Polo shirt with red pants and some Converse sneakers.

Troy fist-bumped Chuku before Chuku spread his grin all around.

"What's up, dawg? I didn't know they let just anybody into this place." Chuku raised his eyebrows and everyone laughed. Encouraged, Chuku proceeded to work the room, introducing himself to TV and sports stars alike as an equal. It made Troy laugh.

Ty hung back during it all, his eyes rarely leaving Tate, acting so timid he could barely speak. Troy had to admit that he took advantage of the situation by following Chuku's lead, talking with the Giants' massive defensive lineman, Jason Pierre-Paul, and joking with them about who was going to get more quarterback sacks this season as if they were old buddies.

Behind it all, Troy wasn't only trying to put himself on equal footing with Ty, he wanted to send a secret message that Ty *needed* him. If Ty wanted to be close to Tate, being Troy's valued teammate was the best way to do it.

When Eli Manning appeared, though, it was Troy whose tongue got tied. The famous quarterback seemed shy himself, but other people swarmed him, and before Troy knew it one of the PR people was tugging Eli's arm and saying they had to go. Troy stood frozen, missing his chance.

It was Ty who stepped right into the fray and stuck out his hand so that Manning could only knit his brow and shake.

"Eli, you need to meet my cousin. He's the football genius. You know, Troy White?" Ty grabbed Troy's arm and dragged him in front of Eli Manning before putting their hands together to shake. "Wait, let me get a picture."

Ty stepped back and snapped off a photo on his phone. "Thanks, Eli!"

The PR person looked insulted and quickly hustled Eli away through the crowd. Troy could only stare at his cousin.

Ty gave a small shrug and a cautious smile. "I knew you'd want a picture, and I really feel bad about us not playing together, Troy. Really."

In an instant, Troy remembered how much he liked his cousin and why.

"Hey, Ty. You know what you gotta do?" Troy put an arm around Ty and steered him toward Tate. "Show Tate that YouTube video of a talking cat you showed me. Tate loves cats."

When Tate giggled at it, Ty broke out into a monster smile and Troy nudged him even closer.

There was more food on the next level and Troy began to really enjoy himself. When he and his friends found themselves beneath a painting by Marc Chagall, Troy remembered something from his reading and told his friends that the painter was once a poor Russian peasant.

"My man is more than a football genius." Chuku

pulled Troy close in a one-armed hug.

Troy accepted the praise then continued to mingle. His interaction with Ty lifted a weight free from his heart. He felt at home among the colorful lights, the tinkling of glasses, the soft murmur, and the eruptions of polite laughter from rich and famous people raising money for a children's hospital. It was as though he was meant for things like this, meant to be outstanding and live an above-average life. By the time they emerged from the Lincoln Tunnel and looped around a bridge so they could clearly see the bright lights of New York City in their wake, Troy was confident that things were once again going his way.

So when he shook Ty's hand, he grabbed it with the other as well and coaxed another smile onto his cousin's face before he slid out of the car.

CHAPTER SEVENTY-ONE

SUMMIT FOOTBALL *WAS* THE place to be a high school player.

They won again and, even though Troy had to suffer through another Jets loss that weekend, it couldn't dampen his spirits about football.

Seth had stopped asking Troy to predict plays in their games, and Troy's heart swelled with affection for his coach, friend, and father figure for not pushing him on the subject. Instead, Seth urged Troy to spend as much time as he possibly could with Coach Sindoni, studying the other teams' defenses and preparing game plans to defeat them. Troy loved it.

The only person Troy spent more time with than Coach Sindoni was Chuku. The Killer Kombo was official. In school, they walked the halls together in a league of their own, two eighth graders who were the stars of the varsity football team. Troy led the league in passing, and Chuku led the league in receiving. The two of them had big dreams, and they liked to dream them out loud, together.

"Man," Chuku said one day in the lunch room, wrinkling his face, "I know you like this UCF team, but I'm thinking Alabama . . . maybe Texas."

Troy could only laugh, partly from embarrassment at Chuku talking about such things in front of people, and partly from the thrill that it really *might* come true.

The whole town of Summit, in fact, was abuzz with football, the team, its coaches, and especially its very young star quarterback and wide receiver.

The football team was undefeated, 6–0, and other people besides Troy and his teammates were beginning to whisper about a perfect season, something Summit had never achieved in the school's entire history. The better Summit did, the easier Troy found it to forgive Thane. The one he felt bad for was Ty, relegated to a middle school team that played on Thursdays after school when almost no one could go and watch. Certainly there weren't any TV cameras, newspaper articles, or highlights on the eleven o'clock news.

On the Friday night of their big game against East Orange, Troy was thinking about Ty, surveying the crowd as he liked to do right before warm-ups, and wondering if he'd see his two cousins at tonight's game.

Ty's text to Tate had again been vague, so when he saw them sitting with Tate and his mom, he smiled and waved to all four of them. Troy appreciated the way Thane had continued to treat him well during his Sunday afternoons with the Jets or on the charter flights when the games were away. Even though the Jets' season was seriously floundering, Thane gave no indication that he blamed Troy in any way. Troy wasn't quite sure that if he were in Thane's shoes he'd manage to be so friendly and forgiving.

Knowing Ty and Troy were in the stands gave Troy an added boost and his passes seemed to fly during warm-ups with some extra zip. That didn't bother Chuku. He liked it when Troy heated up his passes, and he was prancing around the field like a stallion ready to break out of the gate. Troy had a light sweat as he marched with the team up the steps alongside the bleachers and toward the locker room for Seth's pre-game speech. He had to admit that the sight of the tall man in the suit didn't shock him, because it was normal for Troy to see the man whether the team played home or away, and he always stood out because of his towering height and his suit and tie.

What did shock Troy was the look on Mr. Biondi's face as he left the tall man's side and tapped Seth's arm. The tall man disappeared into the crowd as Mr. Biondi tugged Seth away from the team toward the side entrance to the school. Troy slowed his pace and hung back by the door to watch them talking before Coach Sindoni grabbed him and pulled him inside, closing the team room door and sealing in the smell of sweaty shoulder pads, body odor, and Icy Hot.

"Seth's out there," Troy said to Coach Sindoni.

"I know, with the AD, probably something about the national anthem or the team introductions," said the coach. "Don't worry about that nonsense, you've got a game and I've got some things I want to go over with you, last minute, on the greaseboard."

Troy tried to concentrate on Coach Sindoni's words and the diagrams on the board, but something told him—maybe it was the look on Mr. Biondi's face—that things just weren't right. To confirm his thoughts, the clubhouse door banged open. Seth stamped inside and banged it shut.

"Bring it in!" The pressure built up behind Seth's face as if he was going to explode. "Everyone! Now! Quiet!"

The team crowded into the benches in front of the main greaseboard at the center of the room. Seth seemed to compose himself, but spasms plagued his face, twisting it from anger to disgust to despair and back again.

"Okay. Here's the deal." Seth's voice quavered. "When you work hard, when you succeed—I mean, we've got a perfect season going here—people will always be gunning for you. And if they can't beat you, they cheat you . . ."

Seth looked around. No one spoke. No one moved.

"Right," Seth said. "You guys have no idea what I'm talking about. I wasn't sure I even wanted to tell you, but I'm going to. I'm going to tell you because it might mean that everything we've done is for nothing, but most of all, I'm going to tell you to make you mad."

Seth's eyes traveled over every face. "We have done nothing wrong, but someone says we have. Guys, the AD just told me that we're under investigation by the league for rules violations, recruiting or something. I can't even imagine where they got that crazy idea, but the league is talking about suspending us and making us forfeit our games."

No one spoke.

"I know," Seth said. "What can you say? Nothing. But guys, whether this game counts on our record or not, it *might* be our last, so let's make it good . . . Let's make sure people know that Summit football is for real. Summit football is the best. Let's go prove that against East Orange. I WANT YOU TO PUNISH THEM!"

The team rose with a single roar and flooded toward the door.

CHAPTER SEVENTY-TWO

AS THE CLOCK WOUND down for another victory Seth stood with Troy at the edge of the field while the second-string offense slogged across midfield.

"Nice win," Seth said.

"I hope it counts." Troy couldn't keep the misery out of his voice.

"I hope so, too. I don't even know what we supposedly did wrong. They won't tell Mr. Biondi. We're probably going to have to get some lawyers involved, and that's never good."

"Some perfect season . . ." Troy ground his teeth.

"Yeah, well . . ." Seth looked down at him. "Hey, I don't want to bring up another sore subject, but I was wondering about . . . you know . . . could you read their plays tonight?"

Troy kept his eyes out on the field. "No. I couldn't."

"You tried?" Seth asked. "I know we haven't even talked about it."

"I didn't *try*, but I didn't feel it, either. It's like I've tried to forget about it. You know, to focus on playing."

"No matter." Seth slapped him on the back and walked over to Coach Sindoni to congratulate him.

When Seth gathered the team in their end zone after the game, his voice cracked as he told them all how proud he was.

"You played like champions tonight, boys." Seth's voice was hoarse from yelling and his words were raspy with emotion. "This thing with the league is not fair, and I will do everything I can to get it fixed. I promise that. But it's also a good lesson, guys. That's life. You can't count on things being fair, so when someone cheats you or mistreats you, you have to remember to keep your head up and just plow forward. Don't let them stop you. Never quit. That's what winners do, they never quit."

Troy was exhausted from the game. Only two of the smaller, local papers had reporters there. People were used to Summit being a good team now, and the novelty of Troy working for the Jets—especially because he was a flop—had worn off. Troy spoke to the reporters after he changed. The coaching staff was going out to the Blue Water Grill for some nachos. Seth had invited

Troy and his mom to join them, along with Tate.

When he finished answering the handful of reporters' questions, Troy accepted hugs from his mom and
Tate and they all got into his mom's VW Bug. Seth was
nowhere to be seen, but the team room door was closed
and all the coaches' cars were there, so Troy knew the
coaches were having a meeting. Most of the other cars
were already gone when they pulled out of the lot and
headed for Blue Water.

"Did you hear what's going on?" Troy asked her.

She pinched her lips together and nodded. "Mr.
Biondi was in the stands and told us. Everyone knows.
The league is saying they have some information that
could make the team forfeit some games, maybe all of
them. Supposedly they have to verify the facts, but Mr.
Biondi says he has a bad feeling."

"I bet it was that Grant Reed." Troy clenched his
teeth. "That jerk."

"Grant Reed?" Tate tilted her head. "Why?"

Troy sighed. "One night during the summer workouts Seth was kidding with Chuku about earning his
signing bonus. I know Reed heard him. He probably
blabbed about it."

"Yeah, but why would he do that?" Tate asked. "Grant
Reed is your top defensive player. He's been puffed up
like a peacock."

"Because he's a jerk." It was all Troy could think of.

His mom shook her head. "Mr. Biondi says it isn't. He said it's an adult. He thinks someone in the school."

"That just doesn't make sense," Troy said.

"I'm just telling you how it is, Troy. Try to be calm," his mom said. "That isn't even the worst part about the whole thing."

"Not the worst part?" Troy tilted his head. "They're talking about us having to forfeit games, games we've already won, and that's not the worst part? What are you talking about?"

His mom held on to the steering wheel as if it was a bucking bronco. She waited until she pulled up to a red light before she looked over at him. "He said the school board is talking to the league about getting rid of Seth."

CHAPTER SEVENTY-THREE

TROY'S MOM PULLED INTO the Blue Water Grill parking lot and shut off the motor. She didn't get out.

"But . . . we're *winning*," Troy said.

"And in most places, that would matter." Her laugh was bitter. "Not here. I don't know why. Something's going on. Something we don't know about."

"It's more than just winning," Troy said. "Seth tells our team nonstop about doing good in school and being nice to people—I think some of the players are really doing it. They believe in him. They look up to him."

"Whoever is behind this doesn't care about any of that. I know, it's twisted, but they don't, whoever they are. Come on, let's get a table." Troy's mom got out of the car.

Troy followed her inside. A hostess took them to a

table big enough for twelve by the window. Troy's mom accepted a menu and began to look it over. "Maybe I'll get some steamed clams."

"Mom, what are you doing?" Troy asked.

She peeked over the menu. "Getting something to eat. I worked all day, skipped lunch, and hurried to the game."

"You're acting like it's no big deal."

She set the menu down. "You can't predict what's going to happen with something like this, and you can't control it. When some people get a little power, they go crazy."

"They need to be stopped!" Troy pounded a fist on the table, jangling the silverware. "It's garbage!"

"Right, but things happen. This is a high school football team. Exciting to you and me, but most people don't really care. People are busy. Life goes on." His mom ducked back behind the menu, leaving Troy to fume.

When Seth arrived with the other coaches, Troy felt a sense of relief. Seth didn't look as if he was going to let anything slide. He wore a deep scowl, sat down, and slapped the table.

"Can you believe this?" he asked Troy's mom.

She put the menu down and sipped her ice water. "I was just telling Troy that, yes, I do believe it."

"I can't," Seth said. "These guys can't. You look so calm."

"There's nothing we can do," she said. "Do you guys want to order?"

"Nothing? What do you mean, 'nothing we can do'?" Seth asked.

"It's a sports league committee," she said. "They answer to no one. It's their game. They've been playing it long before we got here, and my bet is that they'll be playing it a long time after we're gone."

"I've played a few games," Seth said. "I'm not going to just sit around and take it, that much I promise."

"And you'll do what?" Troy's mom asked.

The waitress came and took their order. When she left, Seth said, "I called Thane's agent on the way over here. He's in Manhattan. Morty Wolkoff. He's got this woman lawyer, Ellen Eagen—she used to be a federal prosecutor—and she'd going to take my case. I'm not messing around. They want to investigate my team, me? They better watch every move they make, because if this is about lawyers, I'll outspend them ten to one."

Troy's mom shook her head. The rest of the coaches said nothing.

"What, Tessa?" Seth asked.

"I hope you're not making it worse, that's all," she said.

"I got reporters asking me if I broke any rules. I got people talking about lies and rumors like it's the truth," Seth said. "I've got to protect myself, and I'm not going down without a fight."

They ordered food and tried to talk about the game, but no one could break through the dark cloud that had settled in.

Troy turned to Tate as the waitress cleared their plates. "You're pretty quiet. What are you thinking about? Your soccer game tomorrow?"

"No." Tate came out of her trance. "I was thinking about a bunch of things, who's behind this, why they're doing it, and what they've got—you know, evidence."

"They have no evidence." Troy spoke low so only Tate could hear. "Seth didn't do anything wrong."

Tate looked around, making sure the adults were all talking to each other. "I know he didn't, but what about those jerseys you got from Seth to give to Chuku?"

"Tate," Troy whispered, "no one knows about that but you, me, and Chuku."

Tate shook her head and kept her voice low, too. "There's one other person, Troy. You know it. Stop trying to pretend it didn't happen."

CHAPTER SEVENTY-FOUR

TROY MOVED SO CLOSE that Tate's long dark hair tickled his lips. He tried to keep his words to a whisper. "You mean the UPS guy? How can he be connected to all this? You're crazy."

Troy's heart didn't match his words. It was pounding with panic because he remembered now seeing the UPS man at the stadium with the tall man, and his instincts told him there was a connection.

Tate narrowed her eyes. "People talk, Troy. It's not like you're not in the news or anything. That guy could have told anyone."

"Stop trying to blame me, Tate," Troy growled.

"I'm not blaming." Tate raised her chin and spoke louder than Troy liked. "But if we're going to figure out what's going on here, we've got to look at all the facts."

Troy folded his arms tight across his chest, signaling an end to the discussion. No way was he getting into this mess with his mom and Seth and the other coaches sitting right there, so he clammed up.

It wasn't until later, when they were home and Troy lay alone in bed, staring at the ceiling and unable to sleep, that Troy realized Tate was right. If they were going to have a chance to stop all this nonsense, he didn't want to leave it in the hands of some lawyers. He wanted to *do* something, and he would.

Quietly he crept out of bed and slipped into the hallway.

The question he had to have answered was whether Tate would help.

CHAPTER SEVENTY-FIVE

THE DOOR SQUEAKED, THEN let out a low groan as Troy eased it open. Moonlight fell in a thick beam across the dresser and the rug next to Tate's four-post single bed.

She bolted straight up. "Who's there?"

"Shh. It's me."

Troy sat on the edge of her bed and told her what he was thinking.

"Of course I'll help," she whispered. "Why do you think I'm lying here awake? I've got practice tomorrow at nine and I can't even sleep."

Tate swung her legs out of the bed, put her feet on the floor, and rested her chin on one hand. "When I first got here, Troy, you said there were some people at the football field doing surveys or something."

"Yeah, because the stadium is falling apart, you

know that. If we do good, though, they're going to have to build a whole new one. Stands, a press box, hopefully a couple of twenty-five-second clocks in the end zones like they have in the NFL stadiums."

"But . . ." Tate scratched her ear. "What happens if the team doesn't do well?"

"Well, they were talking about shutting it down before Seth came. That much I know," Troy said.

Tate sat there nodding slowly to herself. "So if Seth wasn't around, football might be finished in Summit?"

"That's the way it was looking."

Tate looked up sharply at him. "Troy, what if those surveyors weren't measuring for a new stadium?"

"What do you mean?" Troy wrinkled his nose.

"What if they were measuring for something else?" Tate's voice was a mixture of excitement as well as danger. "Something that would go there if they knocked it all down?"

CHAPTER SEVENTY-SIX

"YOU KNOW WHAT, TATE? There's this guy. I don't know who he is, but I see him around all the time. I saw him with the surveyors. I see him at our football games. I saw him with Mr. Biondi before he told Seth the news about the league and . . ." Troy looked down at his guilty hands. "I saw him with the UPS guy before a game pointing out Chuku."

"What? Who?"

"That's what I'm saying. I don't know who. He's tall, though, like NBA tall, six eight or six nine. Huge. He's always wearing a suit."

"I think I *have* seen that guy," Tate said, "but I have no idea who he is or what he does. Maybe there's a connection."

"There *has* to be. I know it."

"Know it like you know what plays a team runs?" she asked.

Troy looked at her and saw she was serious. "Yes. Like how I *used* to know. This guy is behind it all. I'm sure. But what is it? What could it be?"

"I have no idea, but there's that big empty field next to the stadium," Tate said. "What if he wants the stadium torn down so they can use the land? What if they were planning on the football team being its usually crummy self, hardly enough kids to field a team, losing all the time, no one showing up for the games, so the program gets folded? The stadium comes down, and they get the land to use for . . . I don't know, whatever it is they want it for."

"Tate, why would anyone want that land?"

"I have no idea," Tate said, "but I think I know how we might be able to find out."

CHAPTER SEVENTY-SEVEN

THE NEXT DAY, TROY and his mom dropped Tate off at the back of the school for soccer practice before he headed for the football meeting rooms. The football team watched film, lifted weights, then went out onto the field for a brief walk-through practice where the players didn't even have to change clothes, but merely to walk to the spot on the field where they had to be when certain plays were called. Seth said every college and NFL team did this to correct the big mistakes they made during a game.

"But Coach?" Chuku had said the first time they did it. "We didn't make any mistakes. We *won*."

Seth had laughed at that. "Even when you win, you make mistakes, Chuku. Trust me, you always need to improve."

Halfway through their walk-through, Troy saw a flash of gold from Tate's jersey through the fence. He looked just in time to see her wading into the tall grass on the empty lot next to the field in her soccer uniform.

As the practice slogged on, Troy lost sight of her, but when the team wrapped up their session, Tate was waiting at Seth's truck for a ride home. Her cleats and long soccer socks were soaking wet. Troy could see the streaks of mud on her shoes, even though she seemed to have wiped most of it away. When he started to ask what she was doing, Tate put a finger to her lips to quiet him.

When Seth pulled into Troy's driveway, he didn't even get out, but texted Troy's mom instead. Troy and Tate climbed out and thanked him for the ride. Troy's mom burst out of the house and gave him and Tate kisses before she swung open the truck door.

"I left you two some raviolis you can heat up," Troy's mom said as she climbed in. "There're two plates in the fridge, just put the microwave on three minutes and pop them in."

"What's your hurry?" Troy asked.

His mom glanced at her watch. "One of the lawyers gave me tickets for a two o'clock show at the Museum of Modern Art and the tunnel is down to one lane. Love you. Bye!"

Off they went, with tires spitting stones.

Troy shook his head. "Jackson Pollock. I swear, I

could do one of those paintings. Give me a couple of cans of paint and a spoon."

Tate rolled her eyes. "Really? First you tell us about Chagall at the Guggenheim, and now you think you could paint a Pollock? Don't pretend you know what you're even talking about."

"What? Have you seen what one of those paintings looks like? They're a mess."

Tate got dreamy-eyed and looked to the sky. "They make you *feel* things. They're not supposed to *look* like anything."

"Come on, you need a soda or something." Troy marched into the house. "Give your brain some sugar. What were you doing in the weeds, anyway?"

Troy got two sodas, put them down at the kitchen table, then slid one of the ravioli plates into the microwave. He noticed the peas next to each mound of ravioli and wondered why his mom never mentioned the vegetables. Did she think he wouldn't notice a pile of peas and would just eat them by mistake? When he turned, Tate was already at his mom's computer.

"Well?" Troy asked.

With her fingers dancing on the keyboard and her eyes on the screen, Tate said, "Checking it out."

"Checking what out?"

Tate huffed. "The lot next to the football field. There're new orange markers all over the place. They go for a ways, but when I got to a certain point the plastic flags were faded, like they were old."

"I see markers like that all over the place." Troy took the first plate out of the microwave and popped the other one in. "Are you gonna eat?"

"Don't you get it?" Tate looked up from the computer.

"Uhhhh." Troy tilted his head. "I guess not."

Tate huffed again. "Look, those markers are for when you're going to build something or dig something. You have to get permits to do that kind of stuff. You can't just build anything—not even a shed—without permission from the town. And towns keep records of everything. I think it's like a law or something. So if I can find the records . . ."

"You think you can find out who's trying to build something there?" Troy asked, seeing the value in that.

Tate scratched her ear and nodded toward the computer. "I don't know if I can get it off the computer. But trust me. I'm on it. If the information is out there, I'm gonna find it."

CHAPTER SEVENTY-EIGHT

ON MONDAY MORNING TROY woke to a thump at the front door. The clock beside his bed said 5:57. It was still dark outside and he had another half hour before he had to get up for school. He rolled over but couldn't get back to sleep. He kept hearing that thump over and over in his head.

The windows in the old house leaked heat like rusty buckets leak water. Troy shivered as he dressed, then tiptoed down the stairs and eased open the front door. There was no need to wake his mom or Tate. On the porch the morning paper lay wrapped in a plastic bag. The sky spit cold drops of rain at random and a breeze tossed handfuls of them onto the porch in little fits. Troy stepped out and looked down the street. Through the fog of his breath the paperboy was nowhere to be seen.

Troy wondered if it was someone new and decided to have his mom call the paper company and tell whoever the delivery person was not to throw it at the door from now on. Usually, it was delivered without any noise.

Troy bent down, picked it up, and extracted the sports page as he flicked the lights on in the kitchen. What he saw was a big picture of Seth in his Summit Football coaching cap.

What he read made him sick.

CHAPTER SEVENTY-NINE

"MOM!" TROY BOUNDED UP the stairs, threw open his mother's bedroom door, and flipped on the light.

She blinked and pawed her eyes before peering at the clock beside her bed.

"Look!" Troy smacked the newspaper with the back of his fingers.

"What's wrong?" She spoke in a scratchy voice as she studied the picture and the headline. "Why are you up?"

Troy said nothing.

He watched her lips move as she read then muttered to herself. "You've got to be kidding."

"It's not even true!" Troy tugged his hair. "How can they put this in the paper?"

His mother twisted her lips. "It says they have a

witness, Troy. Someone who works for UPS? A Falcons jersey for Chuku Moore? And an unnamed player on the team who heard Seth talk about a signing bonus?"

Troy clenched his jaw so hard he thought his teeth might break like candy. His voice was too low and guttural for his mom to understand. "Reed, that rat."

She looked up. "I thought Chuku moved here on his own. Do you know anything about all this?"

Troy's mind worked quick. He stabbed his finger at the paper. "Forget about the jersey, Mom. Look at this bull!"

Her lips moved as she continued to read. Her face rumpled and then she laughed. "A *car*? Seth offered some kid named Dennaro a car to play high school football? That's the stupidest thing I've ever heard of. Who is this kid? Do you know him?"

Troy huffed. "He's a goof. Dennaro couldn't play his way out of a wet paper bag. He showed up the first week we started over the summer. He said he played on the line at St. Stephen's. He showed up for only a couple of nights for workouts before everyone knew he was a joke. He kept flapping his mouth about how he knew Seth would want him at Summit."

"Do you think Seth . . ." His mom shook her head. "I don't know . . . do you think he might have just asked this boy to play here? I know he didn't offer him a car."

Troy rolled his eyes. "Mom, come on. Seth didn't get

anything for anyone, especially not some sloppy kid like that. That kid's a clown."

Troy felt almost giddy knowing that he'd thrown his mom off the track about the jerseys, but his outrage was real. "How can they put that in the paper? Don't they have rules about telling the truth?"

"It's called defamation." His mom frowned. "Slander is when you say something untrue, libel is when you print it in a newspaper. The problem is that, either way, Seth's a public figure."

"What's that supposed to mean?" Troy asked.

She shrugged. "A politician. Movie star. An NFL player. You."

"Me?"

"You've been in the news. You've done interviews on *Larry King*, *GMA*, all that. You're an entertainer, at least for the stuff you did for the Falcons, and now . . ."

Troy's voice dropped as he continued her thoughts. "For the stuff I'm supposed to be doing for the Jets."

"Sort of." His mom waved a hand in the air to dismiss it. "Anyway, newspapers and TV shows get a lot of slack when it comes to what they say about public figures. It's slander only if you can show that they intentionally lied. So if they can get someone to say something crazy—like this Dennaro boy—they can repeat it and make it sound like news, even if it shouldn't be."

Troy felt bile streaming up into the back of his throat

as if he was going to be sick. "This says the league is planning a vote to suspend our whole team because of this stuff. It'd be over. No playoffs. Nothing. That is so not fair."

"Yeah." His mom frowned at the paper. "Who said life is fair?"

CHAPTER EIGHTY

"WHAT'S GOING ON?" TATE wandered into his mom's bedroom rubbing her eyes.

"Look." Troy handed her the paper.

"I gotta call Seth." Troy's mom snatched her phone
from the nightstand. "They quoted him in this story, so
he must have known this was coming."

"Yeah, one quote," Troy said. "'I did nothing wrong.'
Big deal. They write a two-page article with a bunch of
bull and he gets four words buried at the end."

While his mom dialed, Troy read the story again
along with Tate.

"They make it sound like Seth's doing all this stuff to
get kids to come to Summit when he's not." Tate put the
paper down. "They've got one kid, this Dennaro, and
then it's all these unnamed sources and anonymous

289

phone calls to the league, and 'serious complaints' from other school districts."

"The league doesn't think they're so silly." Troy pointed to the paper. "They're talking about suspending our team."

"Seth must be sleeping with his phone off." Troy's mom put the phone down. "The thing I don't get is where this is all coming from. It can't be just a fluke that people are all saying these things, but who would do all this? Who would care?"

Troy's mom stared at him. "Troy, why are you looking at me like that?"

Troy sighed. "Tell her, Tate."

CHAPTER EIGHTY-ONE

THEY BOTH STARED AT Tate.

"Everything?" Tate tilted her head at him and he knew she was thinking about him blabbing to the UPS man about Chuku Moore.

Troy scowled, knowing that Tate always wanted to get the truth about things out on the table. He didn't want her to bring the Falcons jerseys into the whole thing, and he bet she knew that. "What do you mean, 'everything'? Just tell her about who you think is doing all this."

Tate sighed. "Well, we think someone *is* behind all this. Someone *wants* the football program to go down."

"Down?" Troy's mom furrowed her brow.

"Finished. Ended." Tate drew her fingers across her throat. "No more. Remember when Seth got hired? The team had a losing streak a mile long."

Troy's mom narrowed her eyes.

Tate kept going. "We think someone wants the football program to end so the district will demolish the stadium and the property can be used for a development. If they'd kept losing, no one would care when the football stadium got torn down."

"What development?" Troy's mom asked.

Tate winced. "That's the part I can't figure out . . . yet."

Troy's mom raised her eyebrows. "So, there's a developer who wants the program to end, or there isn't?"

Tate lowered her voice and looked at her feet. "I don't know. I thought so. I *think* so. I just can't find it."

"Because if they were planning something, it would be public knowledge," Troy's mom said. "They'd have to show the town their plans."

"That's what I was telling Troy." Tate looked at him. "I got the meeting notes from the planning board online and I read through them all, going back to August, but I didn't find anything."

"I mean, three months you went through?" his mom said. "They'd have to have a bunch of meetings about something like this. There are woods behind that abandoned shopping center and I think a stream runs back through there."

"Tate knows," Troy said. "She said there were a bunch of old plastic flags all over the place."

"Wait a minute!" Tate slapped her own forehead and did a little jig on the wooden floor next to Troy's mom's bed. "Oh, my gosh! I'm so stupid!"

"What, Tate?" Troy asked. "What are you talking about?"

CHAPTER EIGHTY-TWO

"THE FLAGS," TATE SAID.

"That's what I just said," Troy replied.

"The old ones." Tate was breathing fast. "*That's* why I couldn't find the meeting notes. They haven't *had* a meeting, maybe in a couple of years. They surveyed everything a couple of years ago. I bet they tried to get the development approved but didn't have enough land, then they went to work on figuring out how they could do it. They came up with the football field, but they didn't put a new application in or have any meetings yet because . . ."

Troy felt the same thrill Tate obviously had. "Because they didn't want anyone to know what they were doing!"

"Because probably something fishy is going on," Troy's mom said. "But wait a second, you two. Before we get too excited, we have to find out. Some old plastic flags don't prove anything."

"And some new plastic flags," Tate said.

"Remember, Mom?" Troy said. "The first day we went to the school? Those guys out on the field with the survey stuff?"

"There are new flags all over the property next door, too," Tate said. "They probably got started with their plans because everyone knew Summit football was going down the drain."

"Until we showed up," Troy's mom said.

"Until *Seth* showed up." Troy felt kind of proud about the whole thing, even though it was a mess.

"We can't just think it," Troy's mom said. "We need to *prove* it."

CHAPTER EIGHTY-THREE

SETH ARRIVED AS THEY were all sitting down to breakfast.

Tate stared up at him from her seat, unsure what to say. Troy felt as if he were in a dream, everything was so quiet and weird. The toaster rang. Seth poured himself a cup of coffee from the pot on the table, ignoring the folded-up newspaper. Troy was busting to ask, but something on Seth's face told him not to.

When Troy sat down, Seth said, "I'm thinking about putting in a double-reverse pass for Friday night. You like that?"

Troy's mouth hung open for a minute before he could speak. "Yeah. Sure."

It wasn't until Troy's mom served up four plates of eggs and sat down beside Seth with her own cup of coffee that she pointed to the paper. "Well?"

Seth sighed and sipped his coffee. "It's worse online."

"Online?" She wrinkled her brow.

"The comments. People are nuts." He picked up his fork and started in. "A car? Really? It's high school football. You should get a look at the kid who's saying that. He'd have a hard time making our second string."

Tate had her phone out and she began typing in a search.

Seth shook his head at her and talked through a mouthful of eggs. "Don't. Seriously, you shouldn't even read this stuff. It's poison. The people writing it are like something you'd scrape off the bottom of your shoe. What they say with their anonymous posts doesn't matter, so don't even give it life by looking."

"I heard about some Dennaro kid and a car." Troy's mom nodded at Troy, then cleared her throat. "What I didn't hear about—and what's really bothering me—is this fuss over these Falcons jerseys . . . Troy?"

Troy winced.

CHAPTER EIGHTY-FOUR

"I . . ." **EVEN THE FAST-SPINNING,** well-worn wheels in Troy's brain couldn't spit out an answer.

"I got the jerseys for him." Seth sipped his coffee and everyone stared at him.

"For Chuku?" Troy's mom wrinkled her face like a dried prune.

Seth spoke before Troy could say anything. "Not Chuku. For Troy. I didn't ask Troy who he wanted them for, or why—I just got them. You know Whitey Zimmerman loves me. That's all I did, called Whitey and had them shipped up."

"Just like that?" Troy's mom stared.

Seth stared right back. "Yup. Just like that. There's nothing wrong."

"The whole thing is innocent, then." Troy's mom got

excited. "Troy can just tell the paper and—"

"Ha!" Seth slapped the table. "You think the paper is going to print that? No way. They love this mess. Besides, the really juicy thing isn't the jerseys."

"But it's the one where they've got this so-called witness," Troy's mom said. "And a player from your team heard you talking about a signing bonus?"

Troy and Seth glanced at each other.

"Reed," Troy muttered. "I hate him."

"You hate Reed because he's a big, aggressive—and sometimes obnoxious—teammate," Seth said. "But you don't know who talked to him or what they asked him. He probably didn't mean to add to the mess."

"But he did." Troy didn't want Reed to be forgiven so easily.

"The jerseys, and the fact that they've got two people to support that part of the story, make the whole thing seem like you really *are* recruiting," Troy's mom said.

Seth scratched his chin. "I guess I ought to sue that Dennaro kid. A car . . ."

"Why don't you sue him?" Relief washed over Troy at the turn the conversation had taken—away from the jerseys—and he wanted to keep it going that way.

"You don't sue a kid for saying something stupid just so he can get some attention," Troy's mom said. "You just let it go."

"He deserves to be sued, or something," Troy said. "A pie in his face."

"If everyone got what they deserved, your mom would be married to Prince William instead of dating a broken-down football player," Seth said.

"I like broken-down football players." She gave his arm a pat and started clearing the table. "Especially the strong, silent type."

"Then I'll stop talking." Seth grinned and sipped his coffee. "You kids want a ride to school? I'm meeting Mr. Biondi about all this mess."

"What does he think?" Troy's mom asked.

Seth set his fork down and wiped his mouth. "Honestly? He thinks we're in trouble."

"We've got a plan." Tate proceeded to tell Seth her theory on the football stadium being targeted as part of a development plan and how they were going to follow through on getting some proof so the league wouldn't suspend the team.

"What did Troy say Helena called you?" Seth nodded at Tate. "A spitfire, right? I like that about you, Tate."

"She's super." Troy's mom went to the fridge and handed Troy and Tate the bag lunches she'd made. "Now you guys get going. School."

They got their backpacks and climbed into Seth's truck and drove to the school. Seth was quiet. He chewed a piece of gum as if he was trying to kill it.

"I'm meeting Mr. Biondi in the football team room, but do you want me to drop you guys in front?" Seth asked as the school came into view.

"No," Troy said. "The back entrance is closer to our lockers anyway."

Seth pulled right up next to the football clubhouse door. No sooner had they left the truck than Mr. Biondi burst out of the team room with a look of disaster.

"Seth, I'm sorry, I can't talk right now. The league isn't even waiting until tomorrow night anymore. They called an emergency meeting to vote."

"Vote?" Seth's tone was a blend of anger and disbelief. "Vote on what?"

Mr. Biondi looked away for a moment, then squinted at Seth. "This thing is getting too hot for some people, with everything in the paper."

"It's all lies," Seth said.

Mr. Biondi spoke quietly. "But it's *in* the papers. Listen, I'm your biggest supporter, you know that, but I don't like how this is shaping up. The people on this league committee are from the schools you've been beating up on every Friday night."

"But vote on what?" Seth asked.

Mr. Biondi frowned. "A suspension for recruiting violations."

"Suspend me?" Seth laughed out loud. "Let them try. I'll sue their pants off. I recruited no one. That's slander."

"Not suspend *you*." Mr. Biondi shook his head sadly. "They're clever, the snakes. They want to suspend *us*, the school. The football program."

Seth tilted his head. "So we'd be out of the playoffs?"

Mr. Biondi blinked at him. "Seth, before you came, this football program was on its last breath. We barely had enough kids come out to field a team, and no one cared about football. The board has to make a decision. If they keep football, they have to build a new stadium that would cost at least a couple of million dollars. If they let football die, they could not only save the money on the new stadium, they'd make money by selling the land. That's what *was* going to happen. It was practically a done deal. Everyone knew it. Then you came and . . . it's all different. But this?

"If they suspend us, it's over, Seth. This isn't about the playoffs. This is about Summit not even having a football team."

CHAPTER EIGHTY-FIVE

SETH STARED FOR NEARLY a minute. Troy heard the first bell ring and he knew if he didn't go, he'd be late for homeroom. He didn't care.

"Tell me you're kidding. You're kidding, right?" Seth said.

Mr. Biondi shook his head, slow and sad, again.

"You're acting as if this can really happen." A note of alarm rang in Seth's voice.

"I'm hoping it won't. Look, I've got to get to that meeting. I'll call you as soon as I know anything." Mr. Biondi pushed past them, got into his car, and drove off.

Troy shifted the backpack from one shoulder to the other. Seth watched the car disappear before turning his attention to Troy. "Don't worry. It'll be fine."

"Is there something I can do?" Troy asked. The hollow sound of the words made him even more helpless.

"Throw five touchdowns Friday night. That's all you have to do." Seth patted Troy on the shoulder. "Leave the rest to me. Don't worry. You guys better get to class, right?"

The second bell rang. Troy cast a glance at the brick building. "We're already late."

"Well, I'm fine, so stop looking at me like that," Seth said. "I'll see you at practice. Bye, Tate."

They left Seth just standing there and hustled inside.

Troy's homeroom teacher, Mr. Chapman, didn't even look up from some papers he was grading when Troy came in late. Chuku was frowning at something on his desk, his eyes so intent that he didn't hear Troy's greeting. Troy slipped into his seat, but before he could ask what was wrong, the bell rang, ending homeroom.

At lunch, Chuku grabbed Troy by the arm as soon as he saw him, pulling him close.

"Did you see the paper?" Gone was Chuku's brilliant smile and easygoing manner. He scowled as Troy had never seen him do before.

"I know about that." Troy kept his voice low. "Listen, the league is having an emergency meeting. Seth says it will all work out. I don't know. Mr. Biondi didn't look so good."

"Yeah, but why are they talking about *me*?" Chuku's voice crept up a notch and he shot a glance all around them, as if people might be listening. "I *paid* for those jerseys. I took you to Helena. And who's this unnamed player who heard Seth talk about a signing bonus?"

"Reed, that jerk. It had to be."

"I didn't get a signing bonus. What's he talking about?" Worry weighed down Chuku's face.

"Remember when Seth was kidding with you about it? It was the first time we had practice."

"I didn't think I could hate Reed any more than I already did." Chuku shook his head.

"Look, all that doesn't even matter," Troy said.

"It matters because I can get suspended." Chuku's voice rose. "Even if it's not true. If they say it's true, it doesn't matter what the *real* truth is. I'm in deep crap."

"Chuku, relax." Troy hushed him. "Please. It's bad enough already. They aren't after you. Trust me. They're after Seth. They don't want to end *your* season. They want to end it for everyone."

Tate came over, and between her and Troy, they explained everything that was going on. Instead of Chuku calming down, he grew even more visibly upset. When the bell rang, they got up to go. Chuku put a hand on Troy's shoulder. "Can't somebody stop them?"

"Sure, where's Superman? Maybe Thor." They moved into the tide of kids flowing through the halls for the afternoon classes.

CHAPTER EIGHTY-SIX

IN THE LOCKER ROOM after school, Seth told Troy in a whisper that Mr. Biondi hadn't surfaced yet.

"All day they've been meeting?" Troy asked. "That's gotta be good, right?"

"I have no idea," Seth said.

Troy marveled at Seth's acting ability. At practice, he carried on as if the upcoming game against Glen Cove was his only care in the world. He worked on the defensive signals with Reed as if the traitor was a wonderful teammate. Seth was the same as always, and when he called them all in to take a knee around him at the end of practice and Spencer raised his hand to ask about the suspension rumors, Seth played it off as if it were nothing.

"You guys let me worry about the nonsense." Seth

smiled; he actually *smiled*. "I got everything taken care of. None of that is true, and I'm sure we'll all be fine. We win two more games, it's a perfect season and we're off to the state playoffs. Now let's go. Let's focus on winning."

They all raised their helmets up and chanted together. "WIN! WIN! WIN!"

Troy slogged along beside Seth. With the sun already down, the air had a chill and steam curled up from Troy's bare arms in the glow of the stadium lights. Troy looked around and was careful to speak low enough so only Seth could hear. "How can you be so nice to Reed? How can you be so calm?"

"We need Reed to win." Seth laughed. "He runs our defense, in case you didn't notice. And I spent the last fourteen years of my life having three-hundred-and-fifty-pound giants trying to take out my knees. You think these people worry me? Naw. They're nothing."

"But . . ." Troy reached the last concrete step of the bleachers and his cleats clacked on the blacktop.

"But what?"

Before Troy could explain, a vehicle zoomed into the parking lot and came to a stop with its lights blinding Troy and Seth, so that they tried to block it with splayed hands at the same time. The engine went dead. The driver hopped out and slammed the door.

"Sorry." It was Mr. Biondi—Troy could see that now. The AD glanced around as he approached Seth. Most of the players and coaches were already in or near the locker room door. Mr. Biondi leaned close to Seth and whispered in his ear.

Seth's back went rigid. "No way. You're joking."

Seth's laugh came out in a twisted cackle of disbelief.

Mr. Biondi took a step back. "I wish I was, Seth, but I'm not. The vote was unanimous.

"The season is over."

CHAPTER EIGHTY-SEVEN

TROY, HIS MOM, TATE, and Seth sat at the kitchen table staring at one another.

"I was so close," Tate said. She had already told them about the meeting notes she'd found that very afternoon online from a planning board session from a year ago. The town had actually taken a vote on a shopping center project proposal by a company called Maple Creek. The project was denied because they didn't have enough room according to the zoning laws. What they needed was the football field.

"Too little, too late." Troy's mom sighed. "You tried. We all did."

Their talk faded into nothing and the only sound was the wind rattling the brown leaves of the big trees out back.

Seth jumped up all of a sudden and disappeared into the living room, saying, "I've got to make a call."

Tate looked at Troy's mom. She only raised her eyebrows and shrugged.

When Seth returned to the kitchen, his lips were pressed together so tight they lost their color. "Well . . . I think we just might be able to play."

"Really?" Troy's jaw went slack. "What happened? How come you're not smiling?"

"First of all, it's not done, but if it works the way Ellen Eagen—my lawyer—thinks it will, we can get a TRO, a temporary restraining order. That'll keep the league from suspending us until the court hears the arguments."

"Court?" Troy's mom looked worried.

"Yes," Seth said, "we're asking the court to stop the league."

Troy never heard so much talk about courts and suing people, but he felt a blaze of hope. "So they'll listen? I can tell everyone I was the one who gave Chuku the jerseys and me and the other guys can tell them about what a goof that Dennaro kid is?"

Seth held up a hand. "I know this is a bit complicated, but Ellen says the court isn't focused on whether I did anything wrong. The only question the judge is willing to rule on is whether the league can suspend us without a fair hearing, like a trial of sorts."

"Of course they have to give you a fair hearing!"

Tate burst out, then froze and stared at Seth. "Right? I mean, don't they?"

Seth frowned. "Maybe not. That's what the judge has to decide."

"So people don't *have* to be fair?" Troy let out a bitter laugh. "Seriously?"

"That's exactly it," Seth said. "We need to get the judge to force the league to hold a hearing, *then* Troy can tell them about Chuku and we can prove Dennaro is just a silly kid. If the judge agrees with the league and says they don't have to have a hearing, then we're finished."

"I can't even believe this!" Troy couldn't contain himself.

"There is one other way," Seth said. "A way that guarantees we'll win. If we can show intentional malice, the judge will make the league reverse the suspension."

"Malice?" Troy frowned.

"It means evil," Tate said.

"Ellen tried to argue that someone—some group or individual—is behind this and doing it for another reason, a malicious reason, something that's wrong."

"Like to ruin everything so the football team gets shut down?" Tate asked.

"We all think there's something going on," Seth said, "but that won't hold water with the judge. We have to *prove* it."

Troy's mom's cell phone rang and everyone stopped talking.

She shrugged and answered it. "Oh, hi. Yes, Tate is doing just fine . . . No, please, it's our pleasure. She's a wonderful young lady and we're happy to have her . . ."

Troy watched his mom's face drop.

"Yes. I understand. No, she's right here. Do you want me to put her on?" Troy's mom nodded and held her phone out for Tate. "Your mom wants to talk to you, Tate."

The look on his mom's face made Troy forget about malicious intent, the football program, and even a perfect season.

CHAPTER EIGHTY-EIGHT

STARS RIDDLED THE SKY like a billion pinpricks of light. Troy and Tate were side by side on the back porch. After Tate spent ten minutes on the phone with her mom from San Diego, she said she needed some air.

"I'm sorry about your dad." Troy felt Tate shrug in response.

"They said he still has a chance," she said. "My mom says we have to be hopeful and pray."

"Well, there's a chance. That's good." Troy knew he sounded lame, even though he put a lot of spark into the word *good*.

"Thanks for having me," Tate said. "It makes it better to be here with you and your mom."

"You're like my sister anyway," Troy said.

The stars flickered and they were quiet for a while.

Finally, Troy couldn't stand it. "So I have to ask you, Tate. I know this football thing isn't even close to being as important as your dad, and I don't want you to think I think it is . . . but do you want to talk about it to, maybe, I don't know, get your mind off things?"

After a minute of thinking, Tate sighed. "Sure. I think that's actually a good idea."

"So," Troy said after a beat. "What do we do now, then?"

"I'm thinking," Tate said, and her voice did sound somewhat relieved. "The thing that bothers me is that your mom and Seth can't figure it out, and if they can't, I don't know how I can."

"Yeah, but you've got a devious mind," Troy said.

Tate elbowed him in the ribs. "You're the one who can lie with a smile on your face."

A breeze rattled the dying leaves above them. One broke off and drifted in a crazy swirl, disappearing into the darkness beyond the fence.

"I don't *lie*." Troy tried not to sound too defensive. "I bend the truth sometimes. I . . . I tell stories to protect the innocent."

"Innocent? You mean, you?"

Troy laughed.

Tate went quiet for a minute before she spoke again. "*Someone* ought to be able to . . . I don't know, get bank records or something. Something to show someone is getting paid off."

"See?" Troy said. "Anything's possible to you. My mom doesn't think like that, getting someone's bank records."

Tate snapped her fingers. "Wait, not bank records. *Tax* records."

"Tax? What, like the IRS?" Troy huffed. "The guys who say I owe them two million dollars?"

"Yeah." Tate's voice drifted up into the night sky, fading and hopeless. "Not much of a chance at that. Like we know anybody in the IRS or the FBI or something.

"Hey." Tate popped up into a sitting position and she slapped Troy's knee. "What about Ty? Didn't he and his brother know that FBI agent down in Miami pretty well? Maybe him."

Troy sat up, too. The words burst from his mouth like coins from a jackpot. "Not Ty, someone else! Tate, I know someone who's got a friend in the FBI who'll do it for us! He'll do it for me! He said he would!"

"Easy, easy." Tate slapped Troy's knee with the back of her hand. "What are you talking about?"

Troy looked into Tate's dark eyes and saw the dull glint of starlight. "I'm talking about . . . my father."

CHAPTER EIGHTY-NINE

TATE FOUND TROY'S DAD, or Sam Christian, on Facebook. Troy sent a friend request and a private message, asking him to call.

Troy was disappointed, but not surprised, when nothing happened that evening. The next day they went to school, and in anticipation of getting the TRO from the judge, Seth held football practice. The team was flat, though, even with Seth and the coaches acting as if they'd get the temporary restraining order and be able to play Friday night.

Troy tried to hold out hope, but by Thursday night it had faded to a dying flicker. They were just finishing dinner when Troy's mom's phone rang. She lifted it off the table and scrunched up her face before she answered it.

Troy wondered if it could be his dad.

After a pause, his mom said, "You're a lawyer for who? The Jets?"

Troy studied his mother's face as she spoke to the Jets' lawyer on the phone.

Her frown deepened and she became angry. "Yes, we'll be there . . . I don't know, do I *need* a lawyer?"

Troy's stomach plunged as he wondered what more could go wrong.

"Then it will just be us," she said, and hung up the phone.

"What was that?" Troy asked.

His mother bucked up and cranked out a smile. "Just your contract. It's all fine. Some formalities. We'll work everything out. I already talked to Ellen Eagen, Seth's lawyer, about this. There are things we can do."

"What things? What are they saying?"

Her face softened. Moisture in the corners of her eyes reflected light from the brass lamp over the kitchen table. She reached over and took his hand. "I miss your gramps."

"I . . . do, too, but . . ."

"And Nathan. I bet you'd like to play on his team again, right?"

"I like Chance and these guys, too," Troy said.

"Ha!" Her laugh was more like a short bark. "I'm glad I didn't sell the house. They can't take that. I'm pretty sure that's one of the rules. They can't take your house."

"Take our house? In Atlanta?"

"We'll have to move back." Troy's mom spoke as if she were in a trance, then she turned to Tate. "Tate, I bet you'll be glad. Not now, but after your soccer season."

Troy's mom looked around the kitchen, at its peeling wallpaper and the water stains on the ceiling. She sighed as if to say good riddance.

"Mom, you're not making sense."

She focused on him again and raised her chin, defying the world. "Well, the contract with the Jets has those performance clauses in it. We owe the IRS and it looks as if we'll owe the Jets, too. There's no way we can pay everything back.

"We're going to be bankrupt, Troy."

CHAPTER NINETY

TROY STARED AT HER until he realized that it wasn't a joke.

He pounded a fist on the table. "I *can't* do it. I just don't know why. It's gone, Mom. It's just *gone*."

His vision grew blurry. Tears split the light into shattered fragments. A sob escaped him. "I'm sorry, Mom. It's just gone."

She squeezed his hand. "Don't. It'll all be fine."

"But I don't *want* to go back to Atlanta."

"Don't you miss Nathan, and Gramps?" She spoke softly.

"I'm the quarterback. We're having a perfect season. Seth's the greatest coach ever. Everything is here."

A growl gurgled up from Troy's throat. "Why did I have to bet Chuku for that stupid jersey? I don't even care about Ray Lewis!"

Troy pounded his fist on the table, jangling the silverware. His mom said nothing. Finally he looked up at her. He knew what she was going to say before she said it, and he winced at the sound of her voice.

"Some things are meant to be. Come on, you two, let's clean up."

She got up and he and Tate helped her. They worked together, clearing the table and loading up the dishwasher, drying and putting things away. When they were finished, they read books silently in the living room, Troy and Tate on the couch, his mom with her legs curled up under her in a recliner. They shared the light of a single floor lamp. Outside, dead leaves rattled across the porch.

After a while, Troy's mom closed her book with a thump. "Come on, let's go up. We've got to meet the Jets' lawyer before school."

"Mom, do you know something I don't?"

"I think I told you everything," she said. "No money is no money."

"Not about that, I mean about this stuff in court with Seth and the league," he said.

She stood up and put a hand on his shoulder. "You know how they always say in football to play every game as if it's your last?"

"Yeah. Seth says that."

"I think tomorrow night, if Seth can even get this restraining order," she said, "that's what you should do."

CHAPTER NINETY-ONE

TROY HAD NO IDEA Mr. Cole would be at the meeting, and he could tell by the look on his mom's face that she didn't, either. Still, there he was, sitting at the head of the table in a conference room at the Jets facility. The lawyer, whose name was Ben Bolt, removed papers from his briefcase and dealt them around the table like cards.

"I've highlighted the specific clauses." Bolt seemed almost apologetic. "The contract calls for written notice. I have that here for you. It's a formality, but we have to do things like this in the event . . ."

"That I sue you." Troy's mom wore a dark brown business suit. She had pulled her hair back into a tight bun and added just a touch of lipstick—something she rarely did—and she looked like someone who'd sue you.

"We'd like to avoid all that." Bolt glanced at Mr. Cole, who showed no response either way.

Troy's mom turned her attention to the owner. "And you're here to intimidate us?"

Mr. Cole didn't even blink. "I'm here because I like you. That doesn't mean I'm going to make a bad business decision. That's all this is, business."

Troy's mom scowled at him. "My son is thirteen years old."

"I paid your son five million dollars, Tessa. That's twice what Justin Bieber made when he was thirteen. Look, the papers are all in order. I didn't have to be here, but I wanted to. I'd like to see this thing work, but it's not. We need to beat New England Sunday, or we will be officially eliminated from any chance at the playoffs. That, along with those documents that put you on legal notice, will terminate this deal. Under the performance clause, you'll owe the team two million dollars."

"I can't—"

Mr. Cole held up his hand. "I know you can't pay me back, but if the money your husband—"

It was Troy's mom's turn to interrupt. "That man is *not* my husband. He never was."

"I apologize . . . If the money Troy's father lost to the FBI is returned—and that might happen, right, Ben?"

The lawyer nodded. "I've seen it before. It is possible."

"Right," the owner said. "So, if that happens, I do

want my money back. You'll have to pay the IRS, and you'll *still* have a million dollars. I, on the other hand, have gotten nothing. This is not a bad deal for you. I'm agreeing not to execute a judgment against you unless the money comes back."

"Is this supposed to make you feel good?" Troy's mom asked.

"I'm trying to be nice, Ms. White."

"What happened to 'Tessa'?" she asked.

He stood up and addressed Troy. "I'd still like you to try to help us this weekend. I know something about last chances . . . Sometimes they pay off."

Troy bit his lower lip and shook his head slowly. He wasn't going to get into it with the owner because he had no idea what had happened to his special ability. He knew only that it was gone and it wasn't coming back. Instead of saying that, he thanked the owner quietly and watched him leave the room.

"If you'll just sign these?" Ben Bolt handed his mom a pen. "We didn't want to have some stranger show up at your door."

Troy's mom signed the papers in a fury. She slapped the pen down and stood to go.

"Mr. Cole doesn't normally take this kind of time," Bolt said.

"Yeah." Troy's mom motioned to Troy that they were leaving. "He's a real peach."

Troy's mom took him to school. They rode in silence.

When her phone rang, he could tell by her voice that she was talking to Seth.

"On our way to the school, why?" she said after talking for a minute.

Troy's mom glanced at him as she listened. "Sure. We can meet you in the parking lot."

"What is it?" Troy asked.

"He wouldn't say. Something. Some kind of news."

"Good or bad? What did he sound like?"

His mom curled her lower lip beneath her teeth. "Honestly? I have no idea."

Troy could barely stand it. As the school came into sight, he couldn't help staring at the barren fields and wooded property someone had staked out with orange flags. It made him so mad that people could do something so wrong—spreading lies about Seth and destroying the football program—for money.

Seth stood outside his parked truck with a paper in his hands. Troy barely waited for his mom to stop her car before he jumped out.

CHAPTER NINETY-TWO

AS HIS FACE BURST into a smile, Seth practically shouted. "The judge came through, buddy! TRO! How'd you like to play a football game tonight?"

Troy floated through school because it all seemed like a dream. All the students, not just the football team, were buzzing with excitement, so Troy was surprised to see Chuku sitting at their lunch table with his head in his hands.

"Chuku, what's up? We're *playing*, man." Troy sat down beside him and put a hand on his shoulder.

"Yeah, we're playing." Chuku had none of his usual spark. "But you ain't the one being singled out."

Troy huffed. "Yeah, but Chuku, you can't let that drag you down. You can't let people undo the Killer

Kombo just by spreading some stupid lies. Killer Kombo is *deep*, right?"

Chuku's mouth curled at the corners. He nodded slowly. "Yeah. Yeah, you're right. Killer Kombo. That's *you* and *me*. We don't need no one else. No chump newspaper writer or anyone else can stop Killer Kombo."

"That's what I'm talking about." Troy slapped him on the back.

Chuku dug into his lunch and began talking now, nonstop. It was as though Troy had uncorked a bottle of noise and Chuku had to make up for lost time with some serious chatter.

When Troy saw him between classes in the hallway, Chuku spoke so fast and so incessantly that Troy wondered how he could even catch his breath. "They can't stop *us*. They can't stop Killer Kombo. Not on the field. Not off the field. Right, Troy? Right, dawg? They can't stop us . . ."

Troy didn't feel his feet hit the earth until he arrived at the locker room to dress for the game. The smell of old sweat and new mixed with the hint of plastic from the padding in his helmet brought him to the here and now. Teammates around him hooted with glee and barked out tough talk about what they'd do to the visiting team from Glen Cove. Troy didn't know why, but all the chatter reminded him of a handful of stones banging around in the bottom of a metal trash can.

When he went out with his team to warm up, Troy

just couldn't get his mind to focus on his throws.

"Come on, dawg," Chuku said after even his extraordinary leap in the air didn't get him close enough to catch a post route Troy had overthrown. "Don't *you* get distracted now. Killer Kombo is a *com-bo*. Right now it's just a *com*. Come on, dawg, give me some *bo*."

Troy shook his head, frustrated, but continued to make one mistake after another before Seth pulled him aside.

"What's up?" Seth asked. "You look like a junior league backup."

Troy opened his mouth, but the words about bankruptcy and performance clauses and Atlanta logjammed in his throat. "Nothing."

"Something. Your timing is off. Your throws look like wounded turkeys. You're hanging your head. So tell me. What is wrong? Because I can't have you like this if we're going to win this game."

"What's wrong?" Troy suddenly felt consumed with anger. "What *isn't* wrong? Tell me that. What *isn't*? This restraining order thing? Great. Good. But I'm not stupid, Seth. That judge is going to rule against us next week and it'll be over after tonight. Up and down, back and forth. It makes me feel like puking."

Seth looked around before laying his arms across Troy's shoulder pads and bringing his face so close to Troy's that his nose touched the metal cage of Troy's face mask. "Listen, forget all that. Let me worry about all that. I got a great lawyer and there's still a chance. You just play."

Troy shook his head. Seth didn't know that Troy felt terrible about causing Chuku so much grief by blabbing about the jerseys. Seth didn't know about the Jets and Troy's contract trouble, either. His mom insisted that Seth had enough to worry about without piling that onto his shoulders.

"That's what you keep saying, but things keep going in the wrong direction," Troy said.

"Are we about to play a football game?" Seth lifted his eyebrows.

"Yes."

"That's not the wrong direction."

"I'm talking about off the field."

"But we're not off the field right now, are we? We're on the field. Troy, I need you sharp." Seth's voice bubbled with enthusiasm. "Don't let these people ruin it for you. Don't let them *win*. You can't. Are you with me?"

Seth's voice was like an updraft. It lifted Troy above his funk, like an airplane rising above the clouds.

"Are you?" Seth shook him.

"Yes." He really felt it.

"Good, let's get us some Glen Cove Wildcats."

CHAPTER NINETY-THREE

GLEN COVE WERE AS vicious as they were well coached. Their defense was simple, but they played it well, using man-to-man coverage and bringing the heat on Troy by blitzing on almost every play. By the end of the first quarter, Summit had a 14–10 lead, but on both touchdown throws, Troy had been smashed to the turf by the middle linebacker coming right up through the middle of the line.

"You okay?" Seth had real concern in his eyes as Troy jogged to the sideline after the second touchdown pass.

"I'm fine." Troy didn't hide his annoyance. He wasn't a bird's egg. He was a football player.

"Okay, just asking, Troy. Great throw." Seth turned his attention back to the field.

The Summit defense got the ball back four plays later. After a long punt, Troy snapped on his chinstrap, got the call from Coach Sindoni, and jogged back onto the field. Chance Bryant played both ways, starting at right end on their defense and left tackle on offense. As he limped into the huddle, Troy asked him what was wrong.

Chance clenched his teeth. "I'm good. Pulled my hammy a little, but I'm fine."

Troy knew, like everyone else, that Chance wouldn't come off the field if he broke his leg, let alone pulled a muscle in it. Troy couldn't help smiling. He loved having someone that big, strong, and tough protecting his blind side. He called the play—a drop-back pass with Chuku as the primary receiver—and took his team to the line. Troy surveyed the defense. They were blitzing their cornerback off the right-hand side. The pressure would come at a price. But without the cornerback in coverage, the safety would have to cover Chuku Moore deep all alone.

Troy grinned and looked over at Chuku. Troy tapped the top of his helmet and made a throat-slash gesture. That told Chuku to forget the play that was called and just run deep for the end zone. Troy would do the rest. Chuku's teeth flashed out at him through the face mask. He was on board.

Troy barked out the cadence over the roar of the crowd. They knew that every time Troy touched the ball, a touchdown was possible and he intended to give them just that. An eleven-point lead this early in the game might just punch a hole into the balloon of Glen Cove's spirits.

Troy took the snap and faked a handoff to Jentry Hood. He dropped five steps and saw the blitz coming. Chuku was already closing in on the safety. Troy chortled to himself. The blitzing cornerback would never get to Troy in time. Chuku was past the safety now. Troy cocked his hips and arm, the cornerback a good five yards away.

That's when something hit him from behind.

CHAPTER NINETY-FOUR

"HEY." TROY TRIED TO sit up. "Wow."

Strong hands held him down.

"Just wait a minute," Ms. McLean said. She squeezed his fingers. "You feel that?"

"Sure."

She squeezed his toes. "Can you move your feet?"

Troy moved his feet.

"Does your neck hurt?"

"No," Troy said. "My head a little. I'm fine."

"Well, you're not fine," the trainer said. "You just took a huge shot from the blind side."

Panic filled Troy, but he choked it down. "I am fine. I got dinged. That's it."

"Dawg, you okay?" Chuku pushed through the faces.

"Get back in the huddle, Chuku." Seth's command

didn't allow for argument.

Ms. McLean shone a light in Troy's eyes. "Come on, let's get him up."

Seth and Coach Sindoni helped him to his feet. He put one foot in front of the other and staggered just a bit.

"Whoa." The trainer grabbed his arm.

"Please, I'm fine." Troy tried to shrug her off, but she had his arm and wasn't letting go. He walked off, intent on keeping his head held high. The crowd broke out in a polite patter of applause from both sides of the field. It made Troy want to puke.

They led him to the bench. Behind him, a whistle blew and the game resumed. He looked over his shoulder and saw Grant Reed take a snap and hand the ball off to Jentry Hood, who ran for a first down. Troy's mom appeared, wide-eyed and firing questions at Ms. McLean.

The trainer tried to calm her. "He's okay. A little dizzy maybe. I'm just being cautious."

"Does he have a concussion?" Troy's mom's voice had the shrill quality of an auto accident victim.

"Mom, stop." Troy looked directly at her. "I'm fine. Don't do this."

Troy spoke with enough force to stop her in her tracks. She blinked and looked at the trainer.

"I think he's going to be all right," Ms. McLean said.

"He's not going back in?" Troy's mom raised her

voice. "You don't mean that?"

"Please, Ms. White, let me and the doctor evaluate him."

Thankfully, his mom stepped back behind the bench. Troy took a seat and a doctor arrived. Together, he and Ms. McLean began to poke, prod, and question him. The doctor shone a light in his eyes. Troy did his best, aware of his mom hovering over his shoulder, and also trying to follow the progress of the game. Grant Reed dropped back and threw a pass. The ball arched up over the heads of Troy's teammates standing on the sidelines before it came down again deep in the secondary.

The Glen Cove crowd suddenly went wild. Troy arched his neck to see a defender sprinting down the sideline with the football. Interception, and a touchdown.

Troy's instincts told him that if he didn't get back in the game they were going to lose and the whole thing would be over.

Troy bounced up off the bench.

"Oh, no," Troy's mom said. "He's not going back in. You need to make sure he's okay."

The doctor rumpled his brow and nodded. "That's the safest course. We can do a full evaluation tomorrow morning, first thing. That way, if he's fine, he'll be able to play next week."

"Next week!" Troy shook his head. "No. I have to go in now! Mom, you can't."

Seth appeared, looking worried. "How is he?"

"I'm fine," Troy said. "Tell her, Seth. She's saying I can't play. She can't do that. Tell her."

"I can and I *am*." Troy's mom folded her arms. "You might have a concussion. We're talking about your *life* here, Troy. Your well-being. I'm your mom."

"I'm *fine*, Mom! They said so." Troy looked to Seth and knew by his expression that he'd get no help.

"Doctor, will you explain this to my son?" Troy's mom said.

The doctor put a hand on Troy's shoulder. "This way we'll know for sure. It's the safest way. If you test out fine, you'll be ready for next week."

"Next week?" Troy's voice rose to a panic. "There might not be a next week! We've got a perfect season going. We need to win these next two games to get into the state playoffs. That's if we're even *allowed* to play. It's not just this game. It's our season."

"Troy." Troy's mom growled. "Look at me. You're done for the night. That's final!"

CHAPTER NINETY-FIVE

TROY'S MOM GAVE SETH a concrete look, then walked back up into the stands.

Seth patted Troy's shoulder pad and told him it would all work out before he returned to the coach's box on the sideline.

The doctor left and Ms. McLean was called away to deal with an offensive lineman who needed her to retape his sprained ankle.

Troy slumped down on the bench and turned his attention to the game. They'd taken his helmet away so he wouldn't even try to go back in. It was painful to watch. Grant Reed was a lousy quarterback and their defense seemed half a step away from stopping Glen Cove's offense on every drive. As the game went on, Chuku and all the rest of Troy's teammates came over to him to express their concern. Chuku didn't mention the Killer Kombo, but Troy could read the doubt in his teammates' eyes and the fear that without him, the whole thing was about to crumble. By the time the whistle blew signaling halftime, Summit was down, 31–21.

Troy marched with the rest of the players into the team room just inside the school. The Glen Cove players filed into the visitors' locker room a few doors down, hooting and slapping high fives and banging on the metal door as they entered the building.

Troy found Seth and pulled him close. "You can't keep Grant Reed as quarterback."

"Troy, you're not going back in." Seth gave his head a violent shake. "It's not an option. Your mom makes that decision, not me. Please, don't even talk about it. Are you okay?"

"I'm . . . yes, I'm fine. This is ridiculous. If you can't put me in, you've got to put Tomkins in. You see that, right? Reed is *terrible*."

"I know you're sideways about him talking to the paper, but he's better than Tomkins, Troy." Seth kept his voice low so only Troy could hear him. "If I put Tomkins in, Reed will fold and I won't be able to switch them back. I've got to try Reed in the third quarter and hope he can get something going."

"This is my mom being crazy."

"Look, it's done. Hopefully you'll be okayed for next

week—if there is a next week." Seth's eyes lost their focus for a second. "I've got to talk to the team."

Seth turned to go, then stopped and put his face close again. "Troy, I know this is crazy, but . . . what do you think about predicting their plays? Have you tried?"

Troy froze and shook his head slowly. "No. I can't . . . it's gone."

"But you didn't try in the first half, right?"

Behind Seth, the team was all assembled on the benches in front of the big board. The ball boys were passing out bottles of Gatorade and bananas.

"No," Troy said.

"Okay," Seth said, "forget it. It's just . . . I can taste it, you know? With all the junk against us, I still think it's gonna work out somehow. If we win next week, it's a perfect season. We'll be in first place, qualify for the playoffs, and from there, hey, we could win it all. It's just . . . we need something to get by this one, but, hey, I understand. I do. Heck, it wasn't working before. I don't even know what I was thinking."

Seth turned to go.

"Wait." Troy grabbed his sleeve. "I can try, right?"

Seth wore a painful smile. He held up a hand, and crossed his fingers.

CHAPTER NINETY-SIX

TROY WANTED IT SO bad, it hurt.

It reminded him of when he was back with the Falcons and he was helping Seth and the team—he'd grown up absolutely *loving* the Falcons—and he was hungry for them to win. Troy marched out onto the field with the rest of the team, only without his helmet, and watched from the sideline as Glen Cove did a set of perfect jumping jacks in a huge circle before roaring into the center and shouting out a war cry. The captains went out. Glen Cove would get the ball.

Seth appeared beside him. "What do you think?"

"Even if it comes back," Troy said. "How can it help? I mean, when we were with the Falcons, you had all the signals worked out. You could change the defenses half a second before the snap."

Seth gripped Troy's neck. "You think I'm just an ex-football player? I'm a coach. I've been working with Reed on signals for three months. I told you, he's important to the team. Not as complex as we used in Atlanta, but I can signal left, right, center, and run or pass, and he's not bad."

"I hope better than he plays quarterback," Troy said.

Seth laughed. "Yes, better. Good, actually. I talked to him about it just now. He'll be ready. You get me their plays and I'll take care of the rest."

Troy took a deep breath. He didn't trust Reed in any way, but he turned his attention to the field.

Summit kicked off and Glen Cove's offense jogged out onto the field. Seth looked at Troy, and signaled in the defensive play to Reed.

Troy tried to relax, to forget about everything—Reed, the league, his contract with the Jets, Tate's dad, his mom yanking him from the game. He narrowed his eyes as Glen Cove broke the huddle and jogged to the line, willing it to happen. Two tight ends lined up on the same side of the formation. Slot receivers were on the other side. The back was offset.

As the ball was snapped, Troy's mouth opened. "Pop pass to the inside tight end."

Before Troy finished the sentence, the quarterback had set up and rifled a pop pass to the tight end up the seam. Tomkins lambasted the receiver, but not before Glen Cove had gotten a first down.

Seth's head snapped over in Troy's direction. "What did you say?"

It happened so fast Troy almost wasn't certain if he'd said anything at all. "I said . . . pop pass."

Seth grabbed the front of his jersey and pulled Troy within inches of his grin. "You did! I *heard* you. You said, 'Pop pass to the inside tight end.' Troy, you did it! You knew the play!"

"I know, but . . . it was too late."

"Too late for that one. Look! Watch!"

Out on the field, Glen Cove was breaking the huddle. They were in two backs with a tight end and a receiver on one side.

"Twenty-four lead." The words just came out. Troy blinked up at Seth.

Seth cupped his hands and screamed at the top of his lungs out to Grant Reed. "Base D! White left run! White left run!"

Reed nodded, called the defense, broke the huddle, and the Summit D lined up. As the quarterback started his cadence, Reed yanked Tomkins by the arm over to the left side of the defense. Neither of them belonged there, and it put two extra men exactly where the ball was going.

On the snap, Reed didn't even wait. He shot through the gap, swam past the fullback, and tackled the runner as he got the handoff. The ball spurted free and Tomkins, who was right behind Reed in the hole, jumped on the fumble and recovered it.

Seth whooped so loud, Troy thought his eardrums would be torn to tatters. Seth grabbed him and lifted him up and spun him around. "We did it! We did it!"

Seth set him down and got close. "No, *you* did it."

Troy smiled so hard his cheeks started to cramp.

CHAPTER NINETY-SEVEN

SETH STOOD UP IN front of the team. They knelt or sat in a semicircle around him in the team room. His hair was a mess and his voice was a ragged whisper from screaming out signals and then shouting for joy when the final whistle blew and the scoreboard read: HOME 35 VISITORS 31.

"I have been in some incredible football games in my life." Seth's voice sounded like the dying gasps of an old man. "But I have *never* been part of a win more exciting. I want you guys to remember this moment, right here, right now. I want you to remember what you've done, taking a sad-sack program and turning it into a winner. We got one more game, boys, and it's a perfect season. From there, it's on to the state playoffs. And

I'm telling you, if we get there? This group is gonna be state champs!"

The team all hollered and cheered.

Troy felt a mixture of joy and sadness. The win wasn't as sweet after having spent most of the game on the sideline, but he was thankful that he could help.

Troy didn't know how to react when Grant Reed came over to him and hugged him, gripped the back of his neck like a long-lost brother, and kissed him on top of the head. "I was a jerk, man."

Troy blinked and sputtered. "I . . . me, too. Who cares? We're undefeated."

"And I want you to know that stuff in the paper wasn't me," Reed said. "I mean, it was me, but that's not how it was. They asked me a bunch of tricky questions and I didn't know what was going on. I didn't know it was gonna end up in the paper, and then I didn't want to say anything."

"What people?" Troy asked. "Why would you talk to them?"

"They called me down to the school office to talk to some reporter. I couldn't really say no."

"Well, like I said, we're still undefeated." Troy held up a hand and slapped Reed high five.

Reed grinned. "And we're gonna be *state* champions. You get well and run the offense and—heck, if you can do that again—I'll run the defense and we will *crush* people."

They both laughed together. Spencer, Levi, and Chuku came over and the five of them did a group hug.

Chuku's eyes followed Grant Reed as he walked away, and his mouth hung open in a state of confusion before he whispered in Troy's ear. "Looks like miracles *can* happen, dawg. Who knows, maybe the next thing is my name gets cleared?"

CHAPTER NINETY-EIGHT

THAT NIGHT, TROY LAY awake in bed.

The thrill of the win and the discovery that his genius had returned when he felt passionate about winning wouldn't allow him to sleep. His mind ranged over the Jets players, McElroy, Cromartie, Harris, Chuku's dad, and especially Thane. If he could get psyched up, maybe he could help them save their season, too. Maybe he could save his multimillion-dollar contract and they could stay here in Summit. Maybe, just maybe, he could turn things around. It would be so nice to put things right.

That made him think of Chuku. How could he ever put that right? His feet were sweating and the covers seemed too tight. He flipped them off just as something plinked against his window.

Troy froze. "Tate?"

Plink.

He jumped up from his bed, retreated toward the door, maybe instinctively heading for the safety of his mother's room.

Plink.

He stopped and slowly made his way toward the second window, the one not under assault. Below, in the grass next to the big maple tree in the middle of the front lawn, a dark figure fired again.

Plink.

Troy peered into the darkness. The figure moved closer to the house and into the glow of the lamp beside the door on the front porch. A gold loop glinted in the light.

"Dad." The word escaped his lips in a whisper. His heart soared and he had to control his movements to keep from flinging open the bedroom door and racing down the stairs. Instead, he moved with the stealth of a barn cat, breathing in long, slow draughts. He paused only for a moment outside Tate's bedroom door before continuing on his own. He opened the front door's hardware with a series of soft clicks, sweeping it aside to be greeted by a great waft of cold air and the grinning, orange-bearded face of his father.

"How you doin', boy?"

CHAPTER NINETY-NINE

"SHHH." TROY MASHED A finger to his lips, slipped outside, and eased the door shut.

"Oh." His father whispered and looked up at the second-floor windows. "She's not in on this, huh?"

Troy clutched his own torso and shivered, some from the chill, but more from the thrill of the night and his outlaw father, who just might be able to save his football team. "Can we go someplace?"

"My car is out on the street. You got no shoes."

"I don't care. Let's go," Troy said.

"Here. Hop on." Troy's father turned around and crouched down, patting his back with one hand and reaching for Troy with the other.

Embarrassed but cold, Troy hopped onto his father's back and bounced along as they marched toward the dark street. His dad put him down beside a shabby and faded yellow Porsche convertible and opened the passenger door.

"Hop in."

Troy did, closing the door behind him. His father got in, too, and fired up the engine, which vibrated the car's frame with a low rumble. His father twisted the controls to pump up the heat. "It'll get warm fast. What's up?"

"Have you . . . do you live around here? Do you know what's been happening?"

His father smiled, exposing the gold front tooth. "Probably the less you know about me, the better, but I've been following you. Chip off the old block. Maybe you'll be down in Tuscaloosa yourself one of these days. Roll Tide."

Troy knew "Roll Tide" was Alabama's battle cry and he knew his father had set rushing records during his time there, a couple of which still stood. "I got a lot of work to do before that."

"But you got a good start." His father winked. "That's the key. Especially for a quarterback. It doesn't happen overnight."

"These people who are trying to wreck our season," Troy said. "We know who they are. Well, we don't know *exactly* who they are, but we know the name of their company and their lawyer."

"Ahh, the lawyer always leads to the client."

Troy wondered if his father still considered himself a lawyer. He had to believe that given all his own trouble with the law, he probably wasn't allowed to be a lawyer anymore.

"You said you'd help if I needed you."

Troy looked, and waited.

CHAPTER ONE HUNDRED

HIS FATHER'S HEAD WENT up and down like the paint-can shaker Troy had seen in Home Depot one time. "I told you you'd need me. I had a feeling, especially when I started reading about all this recruiting stuff and the league suspending you guys and then Seth Halloway fighting them and getting a TRO. That's how you handle these rats. You sue 'em."

"You said you had someone at the FBI," Troy said.

"You don't stay two steps ahead of the law without friends. Guy I played with at 'Bama. He's a special agent in charge, pretty high up."

"Couldn't he get in trouble?" Troy didn't want to get sidetracked, but the question just popped out.

"Troy, I know I've made a mess of some things, but I never hurt anyone. He knows that. Sometimes good people . . . they just get sideways with the law. Bankers and lawyers and CEOs, the good ones all play the edge, and the lucky ones end up rich. They're just lucky. Not me. I used up all my luck when I met your mom."

"But you wouldn't even marry her." Troy tried to tamp down the scolding sound of his voice.

His father looked at him for a long moment. "I told you, I didn't know about you. I was going through some things. The luck was because I got you, a son. I always dreamed I'd have a son, and look at you. You guys could have a perfect season. You're not even in high school."

Troy felt the blush on his cheeks. Part of him doubted the full truthfulness of his father's words—he thought of his own slick way of telling tales—but he couldn't help basking in their warmth. "So, this development company called Maple Creek wants Summit to get suspended so the program gets canceled. If that happens, the football stadium gets sold to them so they can build a shopping center. Everything was all set and going their way until I showed up and got Seth to coach the team."

Troy's dad put a hand on his arm to interrupt Troy so he could speak. "And then you and Seth and this Moore kid started lighting people up and everyone's talking about Summit football now. No one's going to shut down a championship program with half the town coming out to the games."

"You've been there?" Troy asked.

His father smiled. "So, how can I help?"

"Tate—you remember Tate, her father got into a bad accident in San Diego, her mother's out there, and she's staying with us—she's real smart. She did all this research. The notes from the meetings of the town planning board are all online. She found the name for the company behind the development—Maple Creek. She thinks if we could get someone from the IRS or the FBI to check into their tax returns that maybe we can find some kind of payoff. If we find a payoff, then the court will realize the whole thing with recruiting—which is a lie, but that's another story—is just because these people are crooked. That's intentional malice. That's what we need to show."

Troy finally took a breath and studied his father's face.

"So I use my contact at the FBI to look into Maple Creek's bank accounts and tax returns to see who's getting paid off?" Troy's father raised an eyebrow. "I can do that."

"Really? It's that simple?" Troy just stared.

"Really." His father snapped his fingers. "I got it."

Troy wanted to hug his father, so he did. The grip was so warm and strong that it brought tears to Troy's eyes. He looked away when they separated.

"What's wrong?" his father asked.

Troy sniffed. "Nothing. I'm happy. I appreciate you helping me."

"But . . ."

"I just wonder what it would have been like, that's all." Troy tried to look at his father's face, but knew if he did he'd start bawling, and this was no time for that. He tried to make his voice sound rough. "When can you get this stuff?"

"Give me a few days."

"Dad, the judge hears the arguments Tuesday."

"Tuesday?" Troy's dad frowned. "Troy . . . that's not much time. It's the weekend."

Troy's heart sank.

"I'll do my best, really." Troy's dad forced a smile.

"Can you give me a phone number?"

His father gave Troy a worried look.

"For Sam Christian?" For some reason, Troy felt short of breath. "I won't give it to anyone and I'll use it only if I really need you."

"Here, I'll text it to you." His father sent the contact and Troy's phone buzzed.

Troy added the contact to his phone. "Okay. Thanks. I better go."

Troy popped open the door and his father moved to get out, too. "No, don't. I don't want Mom to see you. I'm good. I'm warm now."

Troy stood outside the car but bent down so that his head was inside. "Thanks. Really. I appreciate it, whether you can get it in time or not."

His father held out a hand and Troy shook it.

"I told you I'd be here for you," his father said.

Troy shut the door and retreated toward the house. Behind him, in the blackness, he heard the engine growl and the clatter of stones as his father rolled down the street into the night. And, despite the warm feelings and the kind words, as he slipped back inside their rented home Troy knew the odds were fifty-fifty at best whether he'd ever even see the man again.

CHAPTER ONE HUNDRED AND ONE

THE NEXT DAY, TROY saw the doctor and Ms. McLean early in the morning. In the end, even Troy's mom agreed that he was fine and on the drive home, Troy's mom said, "I'm sorry I made you sit, but I think it was the right thing, Troy. I wouldn't have been able to live with myself if I let you go in and something happened. You understand, right?"

Troy felt as if he was ready to burst. He wanted so badly to tell his mom about how his father just might be going to save the day. Instead, he nodded vigorously. "That's okay, Mom. It all worked out. We won the game, and I got a good feeling about the court."

"You do?" Her eyebrows shot up and she glanced over at him.

"I just got a feeling, Mom." Troy looked out the side

window to keep her from reading his thoughts. "If I can do what I did last night for the Jets tomorrow, do you know how many of our problems will be solved?" Troy clenched both his fists.

"Do you really think you'll be able to help?"

Troy thought for a minute, then spoke quietly and slowly. "I think what happened was I didn't really *care* about the Jets. That's what happened last night. I wanted it so bad, and all of a sudden, it was just there. I didn't care if the Jets won or lost. I was getting paid to do a job, and I just got into a slump. Last night, I think I figured it out. And I *want* the Jets to win, Mom. I want it *bad*."

"As much as the game last night?" she asked.

Troy frowned at her. "I don't know about *that* much, but pretty bad. I don't want to let those players down. And I want to be here, not just for the next four weeks, but for the next four *years*. So yeah, I want it pretty bad."

"Well." His mom turned the VW Bug onto their street. "We'll see tomorrow."

CHAPTER ONE HUNDRED AND TWO

TROY TOLD TATE TO ride in front with his mom. He didn't talk on the way to the Jets stadium. Tate and his mom left him outside the Jets locker room. When he looked back, his mom gave him an anxious wave. "We'll see you after. Good luck, Troy."

Tate gave him a wink, clicked her tongue, and gave a thumbs-up.

Troy nodded and stepped past the two state troopers, entering the locker room. Players moved about in quiet preparation, some listening to music with headsets, others reading the Bible or simply sitting with their heads in their hands. Troy didn't say anything to anyone.

Mr. Cole was talking to Mark Sanchez and smiled and waved at Troy from across the locker room, but his gestures held no hope or expectations. It was a smile born from politeness. Thane stood at his locker, dressed in only his lower pads. The muscles in his naked torso rippled as he bound his wrists with tape. Troy was going to walk right past him, not wanting to interrupt his game preparation.

Thane must have sensed he was there. He looked up from taping his wrists and playfully grabbed the back of Troy's neck. "Ty told me you guys won again Friday night. Nice work."

Troy looked around and leaned close to his cousin. "It worked."

"It worked?"

Troy nodded. "I called the other team's plays Friday."

"So it's back? You're good to go?"

Troy winced. "I don't know for sure. Don't say anything, okay?"

"I won't. We could sure use it, though. We lose this and we're out of the playoffs." Thane began taping his wrists again.

"I know. I'll try. Um . . . Thane?"

Thane looked up. "Yeah?"

"I just want you to know that . . . well, part of the reason I think I *couldn't* do it—the genius thing—was because I . . . well, I didn't really care. And, honestly, I was pretty mad at you about the thing with Ty. I really wanted to play with him."

Thane smiled. "I know."

"You knew?" Troy felt his mouth drop. "But . . . you just kept being nice to me."

"Hey." Thane reached out and gripped Troy's shoulder. "You're family. You've been through a lot. I felt terrible about the whole thing. I wish your mom would have just let me pay for St. Stephen's for you, but I get why she didn't. She's a great girl, your mom, and you're pretty special, too."

Troy felt a trembling warmth spread through him and he sniffed to keep tears from flooding his eyes. "Thanks, Thane."

"Good luck today, buddy." Thane winked at him and went back to his tape.

Troy left his cousin and sat down dutifully in the coaches' meeting room in the back corner. The coaches were clustered around their greaseboards, making last-minute adjustments and talking about the depth chart, who was hurt, how bad, and what they'd do to replace them if they couldn't continue playing.

Troy might as well have been in a bubble. No one spoke to him. No one came near him. He wandered out onto the sideline like a ghost, invisible to everyone— the crowd, the cameras, the New England Patriots, and even his own team, the Jets. As the national anthem played, he stood with a Jets cap over his heart and for some reason the music stirred something inside him. Maybe it was a country born out of a desperate band of good people who believed in themselves.

Those thoughts held him in a trance, despite all the growls and war cries and pad-smacking around him. New England won the coin toss and received the ball. Troy watched Tom Brady drop back and throw a hitch pass to his outside receiver. The next play, they ran a zone run off-tackle for a first down. Coach Kollar didn't even look Troy's way. Troy ached inside. He wanted this. He wanted to help. He *had* to help. He wanted to help Thane and the team. But if the Jets lost this game, it was over for him. This was his last chance and he knew it.

The Patriots broke their huddle. Tom Brady stepped to the line.

Troy took a deep breath.

CHAPTER ONE HUNDRED AND THREE

"Z COMEBACK WITH A Y corner." Troy said it out loud, but no one heard.

Brady took the snap and dropped back. The Z did a comeback. Brady pump-faked to him. Antonio Cromartie jumped the Z and the Y came open on the corner route behind him. Brady threw a strike and the Patriots gained twenty-three yards, crossing into Jets territory. The crowd booed.

Troy moved closer to Coach Kollar, who was yelling into his headset about the safety who should have kept outside position on the last play. Troy tapped him on the arm. Coach Kollar was caught up in his yelling and deciding the next defense to run. Troy watched the Patriots send a wide receiver out onto the field and the tight end run to the sideline. Coach Kollar signaled in the play he wanted. Brady broke the huddle. Troy saw three wide receivers to one side and the running back offset.

"Coach!" Troy grabbed his arm and wouldn't let go. "Backside screen."

Coach Kollar glared at Troy. "Someone get this kid out of here!"

A 350-pound backup lineman lifted Troy off his feet and carried him out of the coaching box, back toward the bench.

Troy shouted, "Coach! Backside screen!"

Coach Kollar heard him, and when the Patriots ran a backside screen for another first down, the coach turned and found Troy with his dark, close-set eyes. He wore an angry scowl and he gritted his teeth so hard the muscles in his jaw flexed.

"Get him back here. Now."

No one touched Troy, but the players and staff parted to make a clear laneway for him to walk back into the coaching box between the bench area and the sideline.

"You . . ." Kollar's eyebrows nearly met above his nose. "You know?"

"I think so." Troy turned his attention to the field. Two tight ends came on, along with a fullback, replacing three wide receivers who jogged off. "Weakside counter."

"Weakside counter?" Coach Kollar's eyebrows disappeared beneath his cap. "They don't run a weakside counter."

Troy shrugged. "Weakside counter."

Coach Kollar bit his lip. He signaled a play into David Harris, then shouted, "Harris! Play signal! Play signal!"

Coach Kollar then held out his arm with his hand pointing down to signal weak side run. He made a zigzag with his finger in the air to signal counter. Troy could see David Harris's confusion through his face mask.

"Do it! Be there!" Coach Kollar screamed hard enough to make a vein jump out in his neck.

Harris nodded, called the defense as the Patriots broke the huddle. The defense lined up. The Patriots set up in a strong I formation with a pair of tight ends to the strong side. Brady took the snap. The entire Patriots team went left, but he handed the ball off to the back, darting back to the right on the counter.

David Harris was already there, waiting. He lowered his shoulder pads and blasted the runner, lifting him up off his feet and driving him backward and then into the turf. The crowd went wild.

Coach Kollar went wild, too, pumping his fist in the air before he grabbed Troy and hugged him, howling.

"Coach. Coach." Troy pointed at the Patriots, who were hurrying players on and off the field. Brady wasn't even huddling his team; he was calling the play at the line.

"What do they got?" Coach Kollar stood rigid, staring out at the field.

"ZX cross with a Y hook," Troy said.

Kollar signaled and shouted to David Harris. The Jets' defense scrambled for their positions.

"Bait the hook, Harris!" Coach Kollar hollered. "Bait the hook!"

Even Troy knew Harris would lay off the hook, making it seem wide open, to bait Tom Brady into throwing it. Whether Harris could pick it off was another story.

Brady dropped back. The Jets' D line, knowing from the signals that it was a pass, got quick pressure on Brady. The Patriots quarterback saw the open hook and fired. Harris stepped in front of it, just a split second too late to catch it, but enough to tip it into the air. Antonio Cromartie went for it, scooped it out of the sky, and took off like a real jet for the end zone.

The Jets were on top, 21–3, by halftime. Mr. Cole met Troy outside the locker room, along with Troy's mom and Tate. They all hugged him. Troy's mom had tears in her eyes.

Mr. Cole stuck out a hand for Troy to shake. "Glad the genius is back."

The Jets won, 45–10.

CHAPTER ONE HUNDRED AND FOUR

TROY AND TATE STAYED up as late as they could, watching from Troy's window, hoping his father would appear in the front lawn with the papers they needed in hand. When he woke the next morning, Tate was gone, and he was fully dressed on top of his bed. He got up quick, checked out the window for good measure, then changed and went downstairs, trying not to act as jittery as he felt.

School was a nightmare. At football practice, Troy felt like a zombie. Seth was distracted, and Troy wasn't surprised. At dinner that night, Troy asked if he and Tate could go with Seth to court the next day.

Seth put down his fork and looked at Troy's mom. "It impacts him as much as anyone."

"We don't have anything, Seth," Troy's mom said. "I

366

don't see how you can win. I just don't, and they've got school."

"We've got a shot," Seth said. "I just wish . . ."

"We all do." Troy's mom looked down at her plate. "But I've talked to everyone who'll listen and tried to get someone to say something. I've got nothing, and we can't *prove* anything."

Troy and Tate stayed up again that night. When Troy saw headlights flash on the street, he grabbed Tate's arm.

"It's him!"

"How do you know?" Tate asked.

"No one comes down here. It has to be him."

CHAPTER ONE HUNDRED AND FIVE

EXCITEMENT SWELLED INSIDE TROY until the car turned into their driveway. That puzzled him. When the car backed out and headed back down the street, Troy's fifty-fifty shrank to nothing.

Troy felt like throwing up, partly from nerves about court, but partly because his father had let him down, again.

"I'm so stupid."

Tate sat up and scratched her head. "Why?"

"My *father*." Troy spit the word like a nasty goober.

"It wasn't much time," Tate said. "We don't know what happened. It's not over. We still have a chance."

CHAPTER ONE HUNDRED AND SIX

THE NEXT MORNING TROY stomped into the bathroom, took a shower, and put on some church clothes.

Downstairs, Tate and his mom had already started breakfast. His mom wore a suit, Tate a dress.

"Like we're going to a funeral." Troy slouched down in his chair with no intention of eating. "My funeral."

"Why so glum?" his mom asked. "We have a chance."

Tate raised a hand. "That's what I said."

"See?" his mom said.

"And I texted Chuku. He's coming with his dad." Tate forced a smile. "Moral support."

Troy wasn't buying any of it. He had a bad feeling, but he wasn't going to say that to them. He rode to the courthouse in silence.

"I think that's it." Troy's mom pointed to a white

tower connected to what looked like a small Greek temple when they turned into the downtown area of Elizabeth, New Jersey. Troy and Tate hopped out of the car after his mom parked in a spot on the street.

Seth stood in front of the courthouse with Chuku and his dad, who looked somehow even more intimidating in a suit. They all shook hands.

Troy's mom used two hands to shake with Chuku's dad. "Thanks so much for coming."

"It's insulting." Chuku's dad spoke in a growl. "Why is it that they think my son can be bought? He's black, right? He'll jump through hoops for a football jersey or a pair of sneakers?"

"The whole thing is insulting." Troy's mom leveled a glare at the courthouse itself.

Troy wanted to throw up. He couldn't let go of the funeral thing and it didn't help that Chuku's gleaming smile was locked up behind a serious frown. What Troy needed from Chuku was a silly grin and a joke about how Troy's collar was too tight and to loosen up, dawg.

Troy looked at his friend, willing him to see what it was Troy needed, because surely he couldn't ask.

Instead, Chuku sighed and shook his head until his dad clapped a thick hand on his shoulder and they all walked up the steps together. At the top, several TV reporters waited with their cameras. Seth held up a hand and told them all, "No comment." Troy's mom did the same for him. They passed through the metal detectors together, leaving the cameras behind.

"That's why the judge is hearing the arguments in his chambers," Seth said. "He didn't want the media to turn this into a circus."

Ellen Eagen met them outside the judge's chambers and shook everyone's hands. She had dark hair, like her suit. Her big brown eyes swam with worry, even though she kept her wiry frame upright, like her chin. The judge had a long conference table in a room whose walls were packed with beige, musty-smelling bound books. Seth's team sat on one side of the table, two lawyers for the league along with the league president sat opposite them, and the judge sat at the head of the table wearing a suit beneath his robes.

The head of the league had a boiled lobster face with silver hair pushed straight back. His name was Rata-checz.

Chuku sat between Troy and Tate, with Ty on the other side of her. Tate leaned forward and whispered to Troy and Chuku, "Rat-a-checks, he looks like a *rat*."

Troy looked to see whether Chuku would crack a smile at that, but was only disappointed. He'd never seen Chuku so stiff.

When the door to the chambers opened suddenly everyone turned to see who it was.

Troy gasped.

He couldn't believe his eyes.

CHAPTER ONE HUNDRED AND SEVEN

THE TALL MAN WALKED in wearing the same dark suit he always wore and sat down beside the league director, the rat. The tall man towered over everyone, even in his seat.

The league director cleared his throat. "Your honor, this is Mr. Sommes. Mr. Sommes is the Summit school district's business manager. He has been instrumental in providing information to the league during this investigation, which we think adds even more credibility to our right to suspend the Summit football team."

Troy couldn't even speak. Everything started happening, and he felt as if there was no way he could stop it. Tate wasn't looking at him and he couldn't lean across Chuku to whisper to her about the tall man now that the hearing had begun. Troy boiled inside because he knew she'd be able to think of something. There he sat, useless as the league presented its information. Troy had trouble following the arguments as the lawyers cited different points of law and linked them to past cases they claimed were similar.

When they spoke about Chuku and the supposed "payoff," one of the lawyers cleared his throat and quoted the UPS man. "Your honor, we *know* a payment was made. If you read the statement of Mr. Bartleson, the UPS driver, which I've highlighted in our answer, and I quote, 'These belong to my man, Chuku Moore, payment in full,' end quote, you'll see it's irrefutable."

Troy's stomach sloshed like a barrel of acid, ready to burst. Chuku's dad looked like a stone monument titled *ANGER*. Chuku himself seemed to have lost all the color in his face. Troy swallowed down some sour bile and shook his head. Tate leaned forward and across Chuku's stony gaze she managed a look of kindness.

It didn't matter. This was all his fault, and he knew it.

Then it was Ellen Eagen's turn. She used many of the same twisted and puzzling terms and words the other lawyers had, and by the time she finished Troy had no idea where they stood.

Finally, the judge cleared his throat. "Before I close arguments, I have to ask you, Ms. Eagen, does your client, Mr. Halloway, have any evidence regarding the assertions of intentional malice?"

Ellen Eagen looked over at Seth and the rest of them and sighed. "Your honor, we would like to bring to the court's attention what we *think* is happening here."

"Because my son never took nothing to *play football*." Mr. Moore' voice cast an almost terrifying silence over the room.

Troy kept his eyes straight ahead.

The judge held up a hand. He spoke gently but firmly. "Mr. Moore, I know it doesn't always seem fair, but I have to follow the law. Now, Ms. Eagen, I asked for *evidence*, not speculation."

The room went quiet again.

Troy's mind spun and buzzed and then suddenly, everything began to float. It felt like a football play, complex and inexplicable, but to Troy . . . he just knew.

Troy stood up and pointed his finger at the tall man.

"*He's* our evidence."

CHAPTER ONE HUNDRED AND EIGHT

"WHY DON'T YOU ASK him?" Troy blurted out the question, continuing to point at the man.

Everyone looked at him with surprise.

"For . . . what?" Ellen Eagen asked.

"What are you talking about?" Seth asked.

"Malice," Troy said. "Intentional malice."

The tall man stood up and glowered. "That's enough from you. You're a kid."

Troy plowed on. "You're the one behind it all. *You* talked to the UPS man. *You* tricked the Dennaro kid into saying something stupid, just the same way you tricked Grant Reed by bringing him down to the office and making him feel that he had to talk."

"That's all easily explained." The tall man looked to

the judge. "I was helping the league. They asked me to help."

"Who asked who?" Troy raised his voice and pointed to the league director. "Did you ask *him*? No, the league didn't ask him to investigate Summit football; *he* came to *you*."

Troy saw the men on the other side of the table falter, but he didn't need it for confidence; he already *knew*. "But why? Why would he do that? Why would he report on his own football team?"

Troy let the question hang. He had them all. It was delicious. "Malice, that's why. Money. Greed. Malice. It's called Maple Creek. It's a development company that *he's* getting paid by. It's a payoff to ruin the football program so the school tears down the stadium and Maple Creek gets to build its shopping center. It's all there, in the town records, and when you look at Maple Creek's records, you'll see the payoff."

The league director's red face had gone purple, and he appealed to the judge. "That's not *evidence*. That's not *proof*."

The judge turned to Ellen, but he was talking to Troy. "You do need to show proof, Ms. Eagen."

Ellen looked at Troy.

Troy pointed again, this time right at the tall man's face. "There's your proof. Look at him. Look at his face."

The tall man had lost all color. Alarm bells rang in his eyes.

He scowled at Troy and marched toward the door. "I don't have to be here. If you have questions for me, talk to my lawyer."

The door banged behind him.

The judge stared at the door, blinking. "Oh, trust me. I will . . . I will."

Then the judge turned his attention to the league director and his lawyers. "Well, gentlemen? In light of that display, I'm inclined to allow Ms. Eagen and her client some time to look into these records. Or maybe you'd like to concede, given the scandal that seems likely to result and your undeniable connection to it?"

Ratachecz lost all his color and he leaned into a little huddle with his lawyers, whispering before clearing his throat. "I think we'll drop the suspension, your honor. Given the . . . unusual demeanor of Mr. Sommes."

"Excellent." The judge continued to scowl at the league's director. "I also think it would be appropriate, Mr. Ratachecz, for the league to apologize to Chuku Moore and his father. While Mr. Halloway is used to the rough-and-tumble ways of the media, Chuku is a young man who got dragged into this mess by *your* misplaced . . . enthusiasm, should I say?"

Ratachecz swallowed, then looked at Chuku and his dad. "The league apologizes to you, Mr. Moore, and to you, too, Chuku."

Chuku's smile returned and he nodded without ill

will, even though his dad couldn't seem to erase his own look of disgust.

"Well done." The judge smiled, raised his gavel, and banged it down. "Court rules in favor of the plaintiff."

The judge then turned to Seth. "Good luck with your perfect season. I hope you win Friday night."

CHAPTER ONE HUNDRED AND NINE

THEY STOOD, ALL OF them, in a little huddle outside the judge's chambers. Troy leaned close to Tate to whisper. "Did that all just happen?"

She smiled and pinched him. "It's no dream."

Even Chuku and his dad stood silent and dazed.

Seth suddenly laughed like a crazy man.

The rest of them looked at him with wonder.

He stopped. "I'm sorry. I just can't shake the feeling. I was on the kickoff-return team my rookie year. We were playing the Raiders and the kick went short. I scooped it up and started to run. They hit me so fast from so many different directions I had no idea what was happening. Thank God I was near the sideline because I got knocked out of bounds and the ball went flying out of my hands and my teammates helped me up and I had no idea where I even was."

Troy shook his head. "I don't get it."

"That's what I feel like right now," Seth said. "It's exactly the same. I don't even know what really just happened." He laughed again and said, "Well, not exactly. This time it feels great!"

Troy's mom put her arms around him and Seth. "Come on. Let's go home."

CHAPTER ONE HUNDRED AND TEN

IN THE LOCKER ROOM on Friday night little fits of nervous laughter erupted here and there, only to be swallowed up by the quiet rip and tear of tape being wrapped and torn, wrapped and torn, as players bound their joints against injury. Troy tied his cleats, then tied them again, only tighter. Nerves tangled his breath so that his lungs stuttered as they filled and emptied. He pulled shoulder pads over his head and laced them tight as well.

Chuku bounced and bobbed next to him, the music from his iPhone leaking into the stuffy, sweat-heavy air. He held out a fist for Troy to bump, then grinned ear to ear. Troy knew that's how Chuku rolled. He was back to himself. Bold. Bring the swagger. Killer Kombo.

Grant Reed looked over to Troy and gave him a thumbs-up.

Chance Bryant suddenly bellowed and smashed the meat of his fist into his own locker. "We're gonna *crush* these guys!"

The whole team followed their captain's cue. The noise grew and grew, until it was a steady roar that could be stopped only by Seth's whistle. Its shriek brought an eerie silence to the locker room again, and Troy became more aware of the sweaty leather stench of pads, gloves, and cleats.

Seth stood on the bench near the door. "All right. This is it. This is what we've been working for. Captains, lead them out."

Troy got up near the front of the line, a double column snaking across the parking lot, down the concrete steps, through the fence, and out around the field, where they waited beneath the goal posts.

Rain lashed the field so that tufts of moisture rose up from the turf like smoke beneath the white stadium lights. In the stands, the Summit fans braved the weather in bright-colored parkas, rain gear, and a smattering of umbrellas strong enough not to be flipped inside out by the wind.

Summit took the field with a war cry. Warm-ups were crisp, despite the rain. Troy felt a fire burning inside him. Chuku seemed to fly through the air. It was a thing of beauty, like Cirque du Soleil, part circus, part gymnastics, part Russian ballet, and all the while that brilliant smile flashing right out through the bars of his face mask. Troy's other receivers, Levi and Spencer, and his running back, Jentry, dropped only a few, but Troy knew the weather would wear on their hands and the ball as the game went on.

They assembled in the team room for Seth's pregame speech. It was brief.

"This is yours," Seth said. "It belongs to you . . . a perfect season, and the gateway to the state playoffs. Now . . . GO GET IT!"

CHAPTER ONE HUNDRED AND ELEVEN

TROY AND HIS TEAMMATES played their hearts out, but Montclair was undefeated as well, and they had a defense built on speed. That, and the conditions, took a big bite out of the Summit passing game. Troy had been right about the weather. By the time the fourth quarter rolled around, every other pass was being dropped, and Troy's team trailed by three, with only 1:22 remaining in the game. They had no time-outs left because they'd used them to stop the clock while Montclair still had the ball. Troy and the offense would take over on their own forty-seven-yard line. Seth gathered the offense in a huddle on the sideline.

"Fifty-three yards, guys." The rain had plastered Seth's hair to his head, but his eyes burned with a fire that couldn't be extinguished. "Fifty-three yards between you and a perfect season."

Seth looked around and bared his teeth like a wolf on the prowl. "Think about all the things against you guys. The other teams—heh—think about the people off the field, the lawyers, the judges, the politicians, and now this."

Seth raised his eyes and blinked at the pouring rain. "It couldn't get much tougher than this, but I know you guys. I've seen you work, and I've seen you keep going, no matter what falls in front of you. So this is it. Don't you quit! Don't you dare quit! You go get me a touchdown right here, right now, and it's a night you'll remember for the rest of your lives."

Seth put a dripping fist into the air. The team held up their own fists.

"Perfect season, on three," Seth shouted. "One, two, three . . ."

"PERFECT SEASON!"

Troy and the offense raced out onto the field, a battle cry tearing up their throats. Troy already knew the play from Coach Sindoni. He called it out and broke the huddle. Across the line, the Montclair defenders trembled like caged tigers aching to be let loose. Troy took the snap and dropped back. The offensive line bowed and broke, and Troy stood strong, waiting until the last instant before firing the ball and then being hammered into the turf.

The crowd cheered and Troy knew Chuku had caught

his pass. He struggled to his feet, and Jentry Hood ran down the field toward the place where Chuku had been tackled at the thirty-five. The chains were reset and the clock began to run: 1:14, 1:13, 1:12 . . .

Troy waved his hands at Coach Sindoni, who signaled another play. Troy got everyone set, shouting instructions through the rain and wind. He got under center, took the snap, and rolled to his right. The rush came fast and the cornerback blitzed off the edge. Troy dodged him and fired downfield to Spencer, but the ball—wet now and slick—flew wildly from Troy's hand and sailed too high over Spencer's head.

At least the incomplete pass stopped the clock at :56.

Coach Sindoni signaled another pass play. Troy gritted his teeth and called the play, knowing every pass would be a crapshoot. They went to the line. He took the snap, faked a run, and dropped straight back. The only receiver open was Levi on a twelve-yard crossing route. Troy fired. Levi caught it but was tackled immediately, so the clock kept running.

Troy scrambled to the line, took the snap, and fired the ball into the turf, stopping the clock at :39. His next pass was dropped. On third down, before Troy could even set his feet, the defensive tackle was on him, slinging him down. Troy popped up off the turf, knowing that the clock would now continue to run.

It was fourth down.

They had fifteen yards to go for a first down, and

twenty-three for the touchdown. The clock read :28 and it was running down. Troy waved his hand frantically and watched the flutter of Coach Sindoni's hands as he signaled the play, Alaska. Troy shouted at the top of his lungs and got everyone lined up. The clock read :17. All four receivers would run straight for the first down and stop. It was up to Troy to choose the uncovered man.

Troy looked out over the defense as they, too, scrambled into their positions. He knew what they were going to do without even thinking—man-to-man coverage with a single free safety. The two outside linebackers would come hard on a blitz. The clock read :11. He took the snap and dropped back. The blitzing linebackers streaked upfield and the right tackle missed his block.

The linebacker blazed straight for Troy.

CHAPTER ONE HUNDRED AND TWELVE

TIME SLOWED DOWN FOR Troy, as it sometimes did.

Maybe this time it had something to do with the game clock, running out of time, down to :00, so that time took on a new dimension.

While everything around him seemed to be moving in slow motion, his mind ran at a different, higher speed. He had a floating sensation, as if he got to watch things from above. He ducked under the linebacker and spun in the opposite direction, running clear of the pocket and buying some precious moments. Looking out over the defenders in coverage and his own receivers, he saw a pattern emerge. At the rate and direction of the bodies in front of him, he knew an opening would appear like the long hallway in a maze of rooms, not a passing lane, but one to run in.

Troy took off, straight up the middle of the field.

From the sideline, he actually heard the shouts of grief from the coaches on the sideline, and the collective gasp of the people in the stands.

It was all or nothing.

Troy would either score or the game would end. A smile broke onto his face as the first defender realized he was coming, spun, and fell in the tangle of his own legs. Troy hurdled him like a yard shrub. Shouts erupted from the defenders, alerting each other like a troop of baboons chasing down easy prey.

They reversed field and converged on Troy. He dodged one and ducked another. Chuku flashed past, taking out one defender with a bone-crunching block. The white flat band of the goal line gleamed up at him, just five yards away, when he pulled up short. The last defender flew through the air, launched like a deadly missile, grazing Troy's shoulder pads but flying past. Troy pumped his legs and dove, just as two more defenders caught him from behind. As he fell, he stretched out his arms with the ball clamped firmly in his hands.

He crashed to the turf. The air left his frame. Time jarred back into place and everything—the cheers, the boos, the hollering, and the torrential rain—all boiled around him, slamming back into place at full speed.

Gulping and gasping, he rolled over and looked up.

The ref stood above him, looking down, his face a puzzle.

Troy gulped.

The ref gathered himself and his hands shot up together toward the inky sky.

Touchdown.

Troy rose up and swallowed the storm of hugs and slaps and cheering. Chuku's bright grin lit up the night and his eyes sparkled as their metal face masks kissed. Chance roared with laughter and pounded Troy's back. Grant Reed howled like a wolf gone mad as he took Troy's hand in his own to shake and raise. Somehow Seth appeared in the middle of it all, roaring with delight. Everyone fell back so that Seth could wrap his arms around Troy's waist and raise him to the sky.

"Troy! Troy! Troy! We did it! We did it! We did it!" Seth spun Troy around, bellowing right in his face.

Troy laughed and cried and shook with joy.

It was . . . perfect.

PERFECT SEASON

The real story behind *Perfect Season*

A sneak peek at *First Team*

The real story behind *Perfect Season*

As I tour the country talking about reading as "Weight Lifting for Your Brain," one of the most common questions I get from students is: "How much of your story is based on your own real-life experiences?"

Much of what you read in all my stories comes from experiences I've personally had or ones I've watched others have (including my own kids or others who've played on the teams I've coached). However, some things are taken almost exactly from my own life. *Perfect Season* mirrors a true story more so than any of my other novels. Below are the five biggest real-life similarities between the book and my own perfect season.

1. Like the fictional Summit High School football team, the real-life 2011 Skaneateles High School football team I coached had a perfect season. With a 9–0 record, we were undefeated league champions, outscoring our opponents by an average of 38 points!

2. Like Seth Halloway, I was a former NFL player asked by others to coach a football team that had experienced nearly two decades of losing seasons and had gone its previous two years without a single league win.

3. Like Troy White in the story, Troy Green, my son in real life, was the star quarterback for our team, breaking multiple records on his way to first team All-State honors, earning the highest QB rating in NY State High School football and a full scholarship to the University of Central Florida.

4. Like Chuku Moore, an actual player (whose real name I won't mention for privacy reasons) moved into town to play football in order to be coached by a former NFL player. That player was African American, like Chuku, and like Chuku excited the disgraceful prejudices of a small group of mean-spirited

people in a mostly white town. He was offered nothing more from me than a chance to play football for a coach who doesn't care about the color of a person's skin.

5. Like the court case in *Perfect Season*, the Skaneateles team was suspended by league authorities for reasons based on anonymous, nameless, and unproven reports of lies. I then mounted a lawsuit against the league (which in a bizarre twist was later taken up by the same school officials who had submitted the bogus report to the league). Unlike the judge in the book, the real-life judge ruled that the league—as a private, non-governmental institution—had the right to suspend a team in its fold without having the burden of proof afforded in a court of law. In real life, the Skaneateles High School football team was banned from continuing its run through the state playoffs. My outrage at such an injustice is what prompted me to write *Perfect Season* as the sixth book in the Football Genius series where, as the author, I got to end the story as I thought it should have ended in real life.

FINAL NOTE:

Despite the strange and sad twist to the end of the real-life story, the experience I had as head coach of the Skaneateles football team is one of the best things I've ever done. I rank it right up there with being an NFL first-round draft pick and a bestselling author. It is a rare thing in *any* sport, during *any* season, to go undefeated. Think of it: never walking off the field as anything but a winner! I loved my assistant coaches (many of whom appear in this story), my countless friends and supporters in the town of Skaneateles, and most of all my players . . . I will *never* forget you guys, nor will I ever stop grinning ear to ear whenever I think about our truly perfect season.

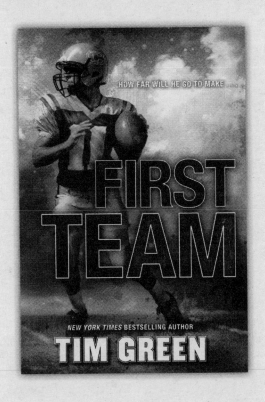

Brock was used to running. It's just what he and his dad did.

He could hear the thump of his own pounding heart. He looked out the window. The darkness outside their racing car was complete. Clouds covered the moon and a light drizzle rushed by in a mist. Up ahead, the headlights from another vehicle pulled out onto the road, blocking their path. Brock twisted around fast enough to make himself dizzy and saw headlights from the car chasing them. It sped at them like a burning rocket.

"Dad!" Brock cried as his father spun the wheel. Tires shrieked. The car slid sideways off the road. Everything scrambled. Brock's head boomed against the passenger window. He saw a flash of light, and the car shuddered to a stop.

"You okay?" Brock's father laid a strong hand on his shoulder, clenching it and turning Brock to look at his face.

Brock nodded and bit the inside of his lip, forcing back tears.

Brock's father flung open his door. "Let's go!"

He dragged Brock by the arm out into the wet night.

Brock's batting glove got left behind, but his baseball cleats helped him keep his footing as they sprinted across an open field toward a shadowy wall of trees. They were halfway to the woods when the vehicle that had been chasing them reached their car, pulled off the road, and shone its headlights on them. Shadows leaped from their feet, stretching like circus stilt walkers toward the woods. Brock heard a zip like an angry insect and then the nearly instant explosion of gunfire.

"Get down!" Brock's father screamed as he lowered his own head and Brock's by forcing his arm toward the dirt.

Brock stumbled and fell, but his father didn't slow down. Brock had to scramble to get his feet underneath him as his father dragged him toward the safety of the woods. Another bullet zipped by, and another gunshot echoed off the low hills like a fading song. When they hit the tree line, Brock's dad hauled him another twenty feet before stopping and crouching before him.

"Are you okay?"

Brock couldn't even answer, but he nodded his head and grunted.

"Come on." His father darted forward again, not running, but slipping through the trees slick as their own shadows, which were now lost in the inky web of branches. They stopped suddenly again.

"Shh." His father tilted his head like a dog hearing a silent whistle. From the direction of the shots came the faint barking of men's voices. Brock's dad cupped a hand around his phone to keep the light from bleeding into the woods and brought up a map application. He got his bearings, clicked off the phone, and whispered again.

"Let's go. This way."

Brock followed, straining his ears for a sound of the men following them. Above, the drizzling sky was only a bit brighter than the tar-colored twist of branches, a true midnight blue. They trudged for what felt like fifteen minutes through the trees before they came to an abrupt end of the woods. Before them, even in the darkness, Brock could see the very long straight opening with what looked like an abnormally wide road.

"What is that?" Brock whispered. "Where are we going?"

His father scanned up and down the long open space.

"It's a runway," he replied, keeping his voice low. "An airport. We have to get out of here."

"Can't we hide?" Brock looked back into the total night of the woods.

His father shook his head, still studying the runway. "They may have night vision. Heat detectors."

"Dad, who are *they*?"

"I think Russians."

"Russians?"

"Organized crime. But maybe the agency. It doesn't matter. Come on."

"Dad, what are you—" Brock's father dashed out of the woods, crossing the runway, then hugging the opposite tree line as they moved back in the direction of their abandoned car, which didn't make sense to Brock. He guessed the agency his father was talking about was the National Security Agency. He had learned only that night that both his mom and dad had worked for the government many years ago, before his mother had been killed.

The pale shape of a large metal building rose up before them. The curve of the rounded roof let Brock know it was an airplane hangar. His father circled the building until they came to a smaller building, with an office and a side door. Brock's dad picked up a rock and smashed the window. The crash of glass startled Brock, but the hissing rain seemed to swallow the sound. His father reached through the hole and opened the door from the inside so they could enter. They hurried through the office and into the enormous hangar. His father used the flashlight on his phone to locate a workbench, where he rattled through a toolbox before grabbing Brock's arm again.

"Come on."

Back outside they went. Brock had barely noticed the two planes crouching beside the hangar just beyond a fuel tank that looked like a huge, round vitamin pill. They stopped at the door of the bigger plane. Brock's dad let go of his arm. He pulled the triangular blocks out from under the landing wheels, then used the claw of the hammer he had to break open the airplane's door. Brock's dad climbed up inside, then turned and held out a hand for Brock. He took it and his father hauled him up and in.

"Hold this so I can see." His dad handed him the phone and lay down on the floor so he could look up under the instrument panel. "Move it down here."

Brock held the light down by his father's head, shining it underneath the panel. His father removed a pair of wire cutters from his pocket and snipped away, grunting as he worked. Brock jumped when the engine rumbled to life. His father wormed his way out from under the panel and into the pilot's seat.

"Dad, you know how to fly?"

Brock realized it was a silly question. His father didn't even look up from the control panel or the switches and levers he was flipping and adjusting. The engine's growl became a whine and they started to move. Brock's dad never slowed. They rolled right out onto the runway, gaining speed. They were halfway down the runway when a vehicle pulled onto the far end. The high beams of its headlights flicked up and down as it sped directly toward them.

"Dad!" Brock yelled. It was as if his father didn't see the oncoming car. They were headed straight for each other in an insane game of chicken.

The plane's engine screamed.

His father's face was grim as he gripped the controls with white fingers. His growl became an angry roar as they rocketed forward, right into the blinding headlights.

Brock shut his eyes and braced himself for the crash.

2

His stomach dropped to the seat of his pants. He was floating.

They were floating.

The plane skimmed just over the top of the speeding car and continued to rise. His father's angry roar morphed into a crazy belly laugh. Brock laughed too.

He and his father turned toward each other, their faces red, and lips peeled back from their teeth with relief and joy.

Brock turned away to look back toward the ground. The dark strip of the runway twinkled with little orange lights like fireflies.

"Wow. What is that?" Brock pointed down.

"What is what?" His father looked over Brock's shoulder out the window. "They're shooting!"

His father banked the plane, sharp. Brock's seat belt kept him from flying across his father's lap. They swerved back the other way, and he banged against the glass window just as he'd done in the car when they'd spun off the road.

"Dad!"

The plane lurched sideways and dipped. Brock screamed as the plane rattled and shook. His father fought with the controls.

BANG!

There was a flash outside Brock's window. Flames from the right-wing engine licked the night air.

"Dad! It's burning!" Brock shouted.

"Ahhh!" His father's arms shuddered, veins popping, muscles tightly cramped from the battle.

They were losing altitude. Beyond the airstrip, Brock saw the lake, dark as death, moving up at them fast. Suddenly, he felt calm. The roar of the engine and his father were like a soft ocean surf against the sand. He saw his mom from when he was just a toddler and she held out a square red block for him to hold. He saw Coach Hudgens and Bella. She smiled at him, so peacefully. Brock felt calm and relaxed and ready. He knew from stories he'd heard that this was what it was like when you were about to die.

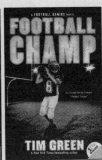

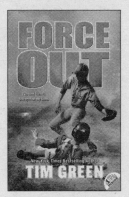